LOVING MY ANGEL

VIOLET HAZE

STOKED PUBLISHING HOUSE

Loving My Angel ©2015 by Violet Haze

Cover from Designs by Dana
Stoked Publishing House
ISBN-13: 978-0-9992261-4-8
First Edition: June 2015

*L*ife is bullshit.

Don't get me wrong. I know life isn't fair.

I've never expected anything to be handed to me.

I ran away from home at age fifteen. The place that was intended as a safe haven from the world, where a child is loved and cared for, didn't exist for me. I endured unimaginable torture and sadistic abuse in every form imaginable at the hands of those who were supposed to love me.

After a few traumatizing events, I went from place to place, looking for somewhere I could call home, getting involved in things I shouldn't have. For a while, I didn't know what time it was or where I slept. I would wake up in stranger's beds; sometimes dressed, sometimes not.

Five years in, a rude awakening in my world of despair had me seeking help.

I dragged myself out of the trenches with the help of a few friends and finished high school, went to college, got a good job, and finally found stability. For years, I've thrived.

Only to have it ripped away from me with one phone call.

Now, here I am, sitting in my living room a week later drowning my sorrows in alcohol.

So drunk I can't see straight, but what does it matter?

I didn't do everything right, I know that. I did shit backward and I paid for it.

Either way, I didn't deserve to still pay for it.

But it wasn't going away.

All my hard work down the drain.

Life is a bitch and if she were a person, I'd smack her so hard she hit the floor.

Then I'd kick her for good measure.

Instead, life is kicking me and laughing all the way out the door.

And now, I'm left wondering what the point was.

Why did I work so hard to turn shit around if life was just going to keep knocking me down? Am I missing something, and if I am, how the fuck am I supposed to know what the hell it is?

My chest feels as if it's going to burst as I sit here staring at the wall.

With a roar, I throw the glass bottle at the wall; half filled with alcohol, it shatters and I stare at it, mesmerized as the liquid rushes down the walls to the floor.

Then I rock back and forth as my chest aches with the tears I know won't flow.

With the knowledge that nobody is able to rescue me from my fate and I'm going to die alone.

So I figure what the hell, I may as well finish the job myself.

Grabbing my keys, I stumble out the door and into my car.

Tonight, my life as I know it will end.

And finally, I will have peace.

*G*od, she looks like shit.

Fifteen years have passed since I last laid eyes on Danita, but I'd recognize her anywhere.

It's a fucking miracle she showed up at my door. I don't believe in much, but seeing her standing at my door last night made me want to fall to my knees and thank who-the-fuck-ever for delivering her here safely.

Especially since she'd been so drunk, I don't know how the hell she hadn't hurt someone.

I don't know how she found me, and I don't fucking care.

Fifteen fucking years since she'd disappeared into the night.

And now, here she is, sleeping in my bed, looking as if she's had a real hard time.

Difficult times that never left.

Watching her is torture, yet I refuse to look away.

Her hair — pale and blonde — is fanned out on the pillow as she lies on her side. Her skin is dirty, her nails disgusting, her hygiene indescribable.

Even sitting here in a chair across the room, I smell her; a nasty mix of alcohol, stale cigarettes, and fuck knows what else permeates the goddamned room.

I'm going to need to sanitize my whole fucking bed, but since she passed out in my arms minutes after her arrival, I didn't want to chance waking her by dousing her in the bathtub.

And she doesn't just need a shower.

She would probably do well to have an hour soak in a tub filled with disinfectant followed by having every inch of her sickeningly skinny body scrubbed with soap until her skin is red.

I feel dirty looking at her.

I should shower since not even two hours earlier she clung to my body, refusing to let go to the point I had to call for assistance from my staff, but I won't even waste my time.

I've plans to drag her ass into the shower the moment she wakes up and I've a feeling I'm going to have to physically keep her in there.

Tossing a glance at the clock to discover it's nearly two a.m., I sigh while debating whether or not I want to lay next to her to sleep. My eyes travel down her body, covered by a sheet she's clenched in her hands — having pulled it up until her bare feet were uncovered —and eye the locked cuff around her ankle.

A cuff with a chain I've attached to the bed so she can't run off in the morning if she awakens before I do.

Knowing I'll need all my strength and wits about me to deal with her, I give in and head toward the bed. Deciding to keep my clothes on, I climb into bed.

She doesn't move, so I lean over enough to make sure she's still breathing, before lying back down on my side and closing my eyes.

AN EAR-SPLITTING SHRIEK WAKES ME UP.

The chain jingles, the bed jerking a little as she pulls at it. As she growls with frustration, I smile and slowly roll over.

Only for her body to land on mine, her aquamarine eyes wild and filled with confusion as she stares down at me, her nails digging into my biceps.

I don't move as she flicks her eyes down at my chest, then glances around the room before finding my eyes once more, glaring at me.

"Who are you? Where am I?" She rattles the chain with her foot, hissing into my face, "And why the fuck am I chained to your bed?"

"I'm glad to see you too, Danita," I mutter. "You fucking smell, by the way."

Her eyes widen and she scrambles away with a whimper, and then hugs her legs close to her body as she huddles at the end of the bed.

I keep my voice low and gentle as I sit up. "Don't be scared. You were pretty messed up when you arrived; I put the chain on you so you wouldn't hurt yourself by trying to escape while not in your right mind."

"I don't know you." Her lips quiver, tears welling in her eyes, her arms clutching her legs tighter. "How do you know my name?"

"Funny." I'm amused, yet not surprised, at her lack of memory. "You seemed to know who I was last night since you drove yourself here."

She doesn't respond, but I know she's studying my face. She pulls her bottom lip into her mouth, biting on it as her eyes flick from my eyes, to my hair, down to my mouth, and further south. And when her eyes find mine once more, they continue to lack recognition.

"Perhaps you're the messed up one," she remarks, her tone timid even though her words aren't. "You must be to chain up innocent women to your bed. A woman who doesn't know you!"

"You sure 'bout that, Angel?" I see the stuttering breath she takes more than I hear it at my use of her pet name. "Surely fifteen years has changed me, but not so much I'm unrecognizable I hope."

I could've just told her who I am. But I know she knows; her own damn subconscious led her here, so it will click eventually, if it hasn't already. It wouldn't shock me to discover she's faking ignorance.

I'm fairly sure she's buzzed; a quick glance at the clock shows the time as seven a.m. and with how plastered she was when she showed up, I've no doubt the alcohol has yet to leave her system completely.

Her face remains blank though, mouth turning down with displeasure. "People will be looking for me. Let me go."

"Nobody who cares." I give pointed looks to her hair, face, and dirty clothing. "When was the last fucking time you showered? You look like you've been rolling in a damn pig sty."

She shrugs, turning her face to gaze at the windows, shoulders hunched.

I stand up, walking over to where she sits and grab her foot, gripping it firmly to stop her instinctive kick from connecting with any part of me. When I lift a hand to pull the string holding the key over my head, her sudden cower pisses me the fuck off. Quickly unlocking the cuff, I toss it aside to deal with later.

Since Danita continues to refuse to acknowledge my existence, I make a decision. Keeping my grip on her ankle, I wrap my other arm around her waist and lift her.

Not that it requires much effort. She's always been a tiny thing, but now she's so light I'm afraid she'll break.

Of course, she's not pleased with me touching her. She thrashes in my arms, her hands going to my hair and pulling as hard as she can, but my grip is solid. She isn't breaking away, and too bad for her I like my hair yanked on almost as much as I like doing it to a woman.

"Put me down!" She yells this as I toss her over my shoulder, where she promptly starts pounding me with her fists on my back. "Right fucking now! You've got no right to touch me."

"Too fucking bad Angel," I respond with a chuckle as I head toward the bathroom. "You've no right to offend me with your odor, yet here you are, doing that very thing. Time for a scrub."

This only makes her wiggle harder.

Usually, a woman squirming in my arms would have me harder than a rock, but the only desire I have right now is to wash her and then burn her clothing.

She must be mentally ill, I think as I step into the bathroom and shut the door behind me using my foot. *Nobody in their right mind gets this dirty without washing themselves off.*

Reaching in with my free hand and turning on the shower, I set her down, holding onto her upper arms to make sure she doesn't run.

"You can undress yourself and get in, or I will do it for you." When she doesn't look at me, I cup her chin in my hand and make her, keeping my voice gentle and firm. "You've got three-seconds."

I hate to say the defiant look in her eyes pleases me, but anything is better than the deadness of them up until this moment. She doesn't move or even blink.

"One."

Nothing.

"Two."

When she doesn't react, that's when it dawns on me. She wants me to take her clothing off, so she can fight me. She likes it rough.

But, the instant I laid eyes on her, all I saw was how fragile she is. Any other time, I'm all for being rough, but no matter what she wants, she can't handle being mishandled at this point.

I won't tell her that though.

"Three."

She grins then, raising her brows as if to say, 'bring it' and I grin right back at her.

Then lift her into my arms and step into the shower with her, clothes and all.

And as the hot water pounds down on both of us, she screams, "Fuck you, Ryker! Fuck you, you son of a bitch!"

Yep.

Ryker, one. Danita, zero.

3 - DANITA

*H*ow the fuck did I end up here?

If there's one person I never expected to see again, it's Ryker.

Ryker fucking Redding.

Son of a bitch. How did a mission to die lead to his front door?

He's the last person I want to see and the last person I want to explain myself to.

As I stand in the shower with the hot water pelting down on me, all I can do is stare at him, cursing my own stupidity in my head. I don't even remember looking up his name and address. I've no idea where I am, but waking up in his bed had been a total shock.

I'm still not sure I can wrap my head around it.

Ryker.

My first love.

My *only* love.

We met when I was thirteen. At fifteen, he'd been new to town, and instantly took an interest in me, his next-door neighbor. For a year, he tried to get me to talk to him.

For a year, I resisted.

Until one day, he found me by the creek running a bit down from our backyards, and sat beside me in silence.

And waited.

When I'd started to cry, he hadn't even asked why. He didn't question me. He'd simply taken me in his arms and hugged me.

He isn't holding me now, but his arms are loose around my upper body. I bring mine up and push on his chest.

I'm glad when he accepts my silent demand to release me and drops his hold, because he has to quit touching me.

I can't handle it.

I don't deserve his kindness.

He has no idea how much I warrant nothing but his disgust.

Hopefully, I die before he finds out, since I'm sure I couldn't handle his hatred.

It would ruin the only happy memories I have, of which there aren't many.

I drag my eyes to meet his.

I'm not sure what to make of him. He was right about one thing though — even in the fifteen intervening years, he hasn't changed much. His hair is the same medium blond I remember, his eyes green-gold, and his muscular five-eleven height dwarfs my five-three frame.

"Angel."

His beautiful mouth moves and instantly I'm pissed. "Stop calling me that. I'm not a fucking angel."

Narrowing his eyes, his lips twist. "No. You'll always be my Angel. Get used to it."

"Not." Crossing my arms over my chest, I glare at him. "I'm not your anything. I'm not anybody's anything."

Except their nightmare perhaps, that is.

"Are you going to take your clothes off or do I need to take them off for you?"

My clothes are drenched now, as are his. It's stupid for us both to continue standing here in them, and I know the sooner I'm clean, the better the chance I have of getting out of here before he convinces himself us meeting again is divine intervention or some shit.

"If I shower and make myself smell nice, will that shut you up?"

"It's a start." His disapproving gaze flicks down my body and back up quickly. "After that, breakfast. You're too skinny. How much do you weigh, or do I not wanna know?"

I grab the hem of my t-shirt and pull it over my head, dropping it to the shower floor as I unbutton my way too big pants, taking them and my underwear off without answering him. When I stand up straight again, he's taken off his shirt, but I know the moment he looks at my body because the sharp intake of his breath is unmistakable.

"What the fuck, Danita?" He wraps his hand around my upper arm. "You're covered in bruises!"

I know what he sees.

Or rather, what he thinks he sees.

Somebody abusing me. Somebody treating me badly.

But I asked for those bruises, every single one of them.

Confusion is written all over his face as I grin at him, lifting my chin as I declare, "It's not what you think."

"I see," he says, mouth flattening out in a grim line, dropping his hand from my arm as if he's been burned. "So not only do you like to fight, but you're a masochist as well."

"High pain tolerance. They have to hit me pretty hard to make me feel it, which is exactly what I ask them to do. Looks bad, but I don't really feel it."

He nods, hands going to the button on his pants, and I look away as he strips off the rest of his clothing. He picks up mine and tosses the pile out of the shower, then gently guides me under the water with a shake of his head.

Before I can say anything, he's tilting my head back under the water, gliding his hands over my hair. His eyes burn into mine, and unable to handle him looking at me, I close them. He removes his hands from my hair after it's wet enough, and after the snap of a shampoo bottle top, they're back in my hair.

"Turn around."

He's standing so close I feel his breath on my ear as he speaks. Not opening my eyes, not saying a word, I turn so my back faces him. His hands glide through my hair in an instant, soaping the bottom before returning to my scalp, massaging it.

It's been so long since someone has touched me this

way; I'm not sure what I feel, especially as the scent of the shampoo reaches my nose. I can't help it; I giggle.

"Green apple? That's a bit of a girly scent, isn't it?"

His hands slide out of my hair, resting on my shoulders, his mouth near my ear once more as he says, "Well, you're a female aren't you? I sent someone out while you were sleeping last night to get some items for your use."

"Thank you," is all I say, the touch of his hands distracting me from anything else, but making me want to clarify my current state. "I'm usually not this dirty."

And I'm not. It's been a rough few days, and I've been depressed. But I won't share that with him; he doesn't need my burdens. And even if I could, I'm not sure I'm ready to say any of it out loud.

He stays silent, reaching past me to pull a loofa off the wall and making it soapy with body wash, then proceeding to clean every inch of my body. When he's done with my backside, he indicates I should turn around without saying a word. I notice him pause as he squats, wrapping a hand around my smooth leg, before sliding it up and down.

I know what he's thinking, confirming it moments later with his question, "Laser treatment?"

"Oh yeah. Everywhere. Well, except my head of course."

He keeps his eyes on my legs, surprising me by not looking elsewhere to confirm what I've said, and resumes his ministrations.

I don't know why I'm letting him continue to touch me. Every stroke of the loofa and every touch of his fingers has me wishing he would just fuck me right in this shower. Which can't and shouldn't happen, no matter how much I want it to.

And when he stands up and holds out the loofa to me, I'm disappointed and relieved at the same time.

"I'm sure you can finish while I wash up."

I take it and move out of the way, holding the loofa clasped between my hands, arms against my chest as I watch him step under the water. He turns the dial, making it so hot the steam thickens between us, then tosses his head back and runs his hands through his hair.

I'm mesmerized. Taking this chance to examine him, I finish washing myself as I take his delicious form in. He's got a bit of stubble I want to touch, and his exposed neck has me wanting to lick and nibble on it. I know he's strong after the way he lifted me and held me, but it's much more obvious underneath his clothing. He's not insanely ripped, but he certainly takes care of himself and works out.

As my eyes go lower, I wonder if he doesn't find me attractive. He hasn't reacted at all to my nakedness.

Sure, I was dirty when we got in, but I'm not dirty now.

Deciding to see where I stand in a moment of curiosity, I step forward as he finishes washing out the shampoo and then give in to my impulse. Stepping on tiptoes and placing my hands on his shoulders, I press my lips to his neck before he can react to my sudden movement.

"What are you doing?" He questions me, his arms wrapping around my waist and pulling me close, even as the words fly from his lips. "Angel…where've you been? Why did you leave?"

"Nowhere. Everywhere." Unable to look at him, I speak into his shoulders while my fingers dig into his shoulders as I continue to press kisses on his neck, tears filling my eyes. "I can't explain. I'm so sorry…"

One hand slides up my neck and into my hair. Tugging gently, I let my head fall back, my eyes closing in reaction. His lips hover above mine as he says, "I've never been happier than the moment you showed up on my doorstep. You take all the time you need to explain; I've got all the time in the world."

He doesn't kiss me. He tucks my head back in the crook of his shoulder, and as I press one more kiss, I close my eyes while another tear falls.

Because the hardest part of all this is having to tell him I've not got all the time in the world.

That I'm dying.

And there's nothing anyone can do to stop it.

*a*fter leaving her alone to finish her grooming, I ordered breakfast made.

Now, as we sit eating, her head is bowed while she picks at her food and I try to hide the fact I'm watching her. She occasionally takes a bite, chewing slow and grimacing each time, as if she has to force herself to swallow it.

No wonder she's so fucking skinny.

But now that she's clean, there's no denying how gorgeous she is. Her hair is hanging down her back; so thin it's drying quick. I gave her some clothing I had picked up for her, and even though the clothes hang a little on her frame, the pieces are much better than the nasty shit she was wearing before.

It took every ounce of control I had not to respond to her in the shower.

I knew precisely what she wanted as she kissed my neck. She wasn't sure where she stood and whether or not I found her attractive, but I had to give it to her — it'd been brave to just go for it after all this time.

And I know my reaction left her even more confused.

However, it's helped me make a decision.

She is going to stay with me, whether she likes it or not. Because something is wrong, and I'm going to get to the bottom of it.

"Do you have a job?"

She lifts her eyes from her plate in almost slow motion, placing her fork on the edge of the plate with deliberate gentleness, tilting her head to the side while asking, "No. Do you?"

I raise a brow and lift a hand, gesturing to the house around me as if to ask, 'what do you think?' and she blushes as I say, "I own several businesses, yes. Now, if you don't have a job, how do you live?"

Her eyes go back to her plate and she shrugs. "I live with whoever will take me in."

"And where would that be most recently…?"

"Friends." She stabs some eggs with her fork and shoves them in her mouth, glaring at me. "I have quite a few."

"Is that right?" Something in the tone of my voice makes her look up as my eyes drop from her head, to her body, and back again. "What type of friends? Drug addicts? Alcoholics? Morons who can't see you're starving? People who let you get behind the wheel of a car while totally smashed? Nice friends."

Her fork clatters to her plate as she pushes away from the table and stands up, her offense at my words clear in the stiffness of her body. "No, jackass. They weren't home when I drank." She holds out her hand. "Like I said, they will be looking for me. Give me my phone and my keys so I can get the fuck out of here."

"I don't think so." I hold up a hand as she opens her mouth to protest. "I've checked your phone; nobody has sent you a single message, so obviously they aren't too worried. And you're not getting your keys. Your car is safe and locked up in my garage."

"You—!" She stalks over to my seat and pokes me in the chest with an angry stab of her finger. "You can't keep me here! I'll call the police."

Capturing her hand with mine, I bring her fingers up to my lips and kiss them. "Go ahead, Angel. I'm sure they'd love to see the video of you nearly crashing into the tree in front of my house and stumbling as you walk toward my front door."

The moment she realizes she's trapped, she yanks her hand from mine and like a caged animal, releases her anger. She swipes her arm across the table top before I can even fathom her intentions, sending our plates and cups to the floor in a loud crash.

In a flash, I pin her against the wall, my hands wrapped around her wrists as I hold her arms immobile between our bodies. She's like a fucking feral cat, hissing and thrashing as much as possible to get loose, even going so far as to lower her head and try to bite my hands.

I don't budge as I hold her in place, restraining her completely. There isn't a spot we aren't touching and my cock jumps to life, the response instinctive, especially since I love a little fight.

I watch her eyes widen, flying to meet my gaze when she feels me against her, and she sucks in a breath. The look on her face is quickly replaced with one of desire and knowing. Her tiny frame softens beneath mine, her lower body moving into mine, rubbing against me in a blatant attempt to get what she wanted in the shower and failed to obtain.

"I knew you found me attractive. You always did." She pulls her lip in, biting it for a moment, and then releases it slowly and smiles as she demands, "Kiss me. You know you want to."

I won't lie. I want to take her up on her offer, but all I can focus on is how fragile she feels in my arms, along with the bruising all over her body. And the scars.

She probably thinks I didn't look at her in the shower, but I absolutely fucking did.

I thought I'd seen it all with the bruising, but then there were the tiny sliver of scars on her legs, her thighs, and her arms — especially her wrists. None looked recent, yet those marks told me one thing — at some point in her life since she'd left, Danita had been a cutter.

I'd also seen a scar on her stomach. Again, barely noticeable, and along her lower stomach, making wonder what she'd needed surgery for.

"Touch me." She wiggles her lower half while tugging her arms toward her chest. "Let my arms go and touch me."

"No."

Her eyes narrow. "Why not?"

"Because you don't want me." I release my grip and step back, freeing her. "You wouldn't care who was touching you, as long as they did."

Her mouth drops open, but she doesn't respond. Instead, after a moment, she crosses her arms over her chest and lifts her chin in defiance. "If you're going to keep me here, I'll need my things."

I look down at the mess on the floor, and then back at her. "I'm not keeping you here. You have a choice. It just so happens the choice you'd rather take has consequences." Turning, I head to the door and open it. "My driver, Kevin, will take you to get anything you need. You will find him outside waiting for you. If you fail to return this evening, you know the consequences."

Then, without another word, I exit the room feeling like a gigantic fucking asshole even though I know she'll be treated better here than she has in her whole life.

Kevin pulls the car up in front of the apartment, asking, "Do you need my assistance ma'am?"

"No, thank you." I open the door and stare at my apartment building. "I'll be right back."

He nods at me as I exit the vehicle and shut the door behind me.

For a few moments, I stand there, taking in everything that has happened.

I know when I head inside my friends won't even question where I've been. They'll hug me, they'll ask how I am, and that will be that. It wouldn't be the first time I've gone somewhere overnight without saying anything.

Ryker didn't know that though.

My friends were used to me. They understood.

He would understand if I told him, I'm sure. He seems like a decent man.

Well, except for the whole blackmailing me to stay thing. I even asked Kevin on the way out if there were really cameras outside and he'd pointed them out.

Kevin had my purse in the car, handing it to me when we got in, and informed me about the location of my vehicle and why I wasn't going to be able to drive it.

Apparently, it was being repaired due to some small damages obtained the prior evening.

The look of chastisement on his face said it all, but nobody can be angrier at me than I am at myself. I don't remember driving, but damned if I don't know how bad what I did was. I'm an idiot. I could've killed someone beside myself and wouldn't that just be fucking grand?

I told him to keep the keys. I shouldn't be driving if I can't keep it together, and after last night, I have no right to do so.

Destroying other people isn't something I want — especially now.

Which is exactly why Ryker is no doubt punishment for my sins.

I wanted to die without facing him. I don't want him to see me like this, or how I'll be, or know where I've been and what I've done.

But as always, the world has proven it doesn't care what I want.

It wants me on my knees, left with no dignity, no pride, and no wound left unopened.

Fucking grand.

With one more glance at the car where Kevin awaits my return, I head inside the building to say goodbye.

"DANI," VANESSA GREETS ME WITH A HUG AS I WALK INTO the living room. "You doing all right?"

"Yeah." I pull back and sit on the couch, patting the seat beside me. "Sit for a moment, will you?"

"You gonna apologize for the mess you left?"

Tears prick my eyes, as she looks at me with sympathy in her own kind green eyes. "You know I'm sorry. I'm way more sorry than you could possibly know."

"Hey." She pulls me into her side with an arm about my shoulder, hugging me. "I'm just kidding. I can't even imagine how you feel, truly. But you look all serious, so what's going on? More bad news?"

With a self-deprecating laugh, I snuggle into her side. "You could say that."

She's silent, waiting for me to explain, and I try to find the words to tell my best friend my situation without her hauling ass to head to Ryker's place and threaten him with bodily injury.

Not that she would win.

Vanessa is a lovely woman, and a bigger woman, but she's more cuddly than ferocious, even if she thinks differently. However, she's the kind of friend anyone would want on their side: she's loyal, sweet, and honest, yet fair. Over the years, she told me over and over how stupid I was being, but understood she couldn't save me if I didn't want to be saved. She let me make mistakes, but made sure she was there when I came crying.

And even though we were similar in age, she became my mother figure, and everything I aspired to be.

Aspirations that now don't matter.

Sighing, I say, "You remember *him*, don't you?"

"I remember lots of 'him's' but I think I know who you're talking about. Run in to him, did you? How'd you manage that?"

I pull away, hugging my knees to my chest as I retreat to a corner of the couch, looking at her as I frown. "Apparently, in my drunken stupor, I showed up on his doorstep last night."

"Danita Natalie Barlow, I should whoop your fucking ass. You left here *drunk* and drove all that way?"

Her rising voice makes me wince. "It was stupid. There is no excuse, and he confiscated my keys and my car. His driver brought me here to get my things."

"Whoa, whoa, whoa!" She holds up a hand, face filled with a mix of confusion and interest. "First off, yes, it was stupid, and thank fuck you didn't hurt anyone. You didn't hurt anyone did you? Second, what? A driver? Your things? Why? Are you going there to stay? What in the world…?"

"No, I didn't hurt anyone. And yes. He says after fifteen years, we should catch up, and he has lots of space."

God, I hated lying to her, but like I said, her going there and perhaps finding out he would have me arrested wouldn't help anything.

"Does he know?"

"No, and I don't really know how to tell him, either."

She leans in and takes my hand in hers. "Dani, look at me." When I do, she smiles even as her eyes shine with her usual warmth and concern. "He should know everything. *Everything*," she emphasizes when I open my mouth to object. "You've got nothing to lose, darling, and if he loved you like you said he did, then he deserves your honesty."

"I'm afraid." I close my eyes as a wave of pain hits me, emotionally and physically, causing me to grit out between clenched teeth, "I'm afraid he won't understand. And pills. I need my pills."

She gets up and rushes off immediately, coming back seconds later with my pills in hand and a bottle of water, watching as I gulp them down before saying, "This is one example of why he needs to know. And you don't need to be afraid he won't understand if you tell him everything. It will make sense then."

"I'm not sure. I woke up chained to his bed, after all."

"What?"

The shocked look on her face is so comical a little laugh escapes me. "He said I was so out of it, he didn't want me trying to leave and hurting myself."

"Okay, so he's thoughtful, at least?"

I shake my head and fill her in on the rest of the morning, including the way he thrust me into the shower, and she clucks her tongue. "Sounds like he won't take your bullshit. Good for him. And you did smell, to be honest."

Yes, I did.

"Aren't you supposed to be on my side?"

"I am when it counts," she says, chuckling. "Is there anything I need to know that would change my opinion right now?"

I think about telling her, but then decide against it.

After all, I guess I need to face the music at some point.

It's now or never.

Ah, the irony.

I shake my head. "Help me pack, please?"

Just then, the horn honks, and I realize I've been up here for thirty minutes, keeping Kevin waiting.

Great, I think. *He probably thinks I'm so fucking inconsiderate.*

And in some ways, I have been in the last twenty-four hours, so Vanessa helps me get everything together, and after making me promise to contact her every day with how I am, she helps me take my stuff outside.

Minutes later, along with one huge apology to Kevin, I'm physically on my way back to Ryker's.

Mentally, a memory from the past catches up to me.

Sixteen years ago

"RYKER," I WHISPER AFTER I LIFT HIS WINDOW AS QUIETLY as possible. "Are you awake?"

It's three a.m. but I can't sleep and he told me I could come over any time. I'm guessing he didn't mean middle of the night, but I need him. I can't breathe without him.

"Angel?" His voice drifts from the bed to the window, nearly as quiet as my own. "What're you doin'? Come inside before you get us both in trouble."

He sits up as I climb inside, and as I close the window I say, "Don't get up. I just don't wanna be alone. Will you hold me?"

"Sure," he mumbles, sliding back under the blankets and holding them open for me. "Just can't stay for long."

Unlike what my mother and stepdad think, Ryker and I aren't boyfriend and girlfriend. I don't even think he likes me like that; pretty sure he's interested in this cheerleading chick, Fay. She's always making googly eyes at him, and he seems to enjoy it. I also know she's jealous that Ryker hangs out with me and hasn't asked her out yet.

Not to mention, at fourteen, I'm not allowed to have a boyfriend. My parents forbid it.

Although I shouldn't care what they think, but I'm too afraid to disobey them.

Well, kind of. I think if Ryker asked me out, I'd say yes but I wouldn't tell them. I wouldn't tell anyone.

I slip into the bed, his arm coming around and resting on my waist as I snuggle up to him, his breath on my neck.

I keep my voice low as I cover his hand with my own, and his arm tightens as he pulls me as close he can get me. "You're the best, Ry."

"I know."

It's silent for a while after that, but I know he's awake. He shifts behind me, alternating between slightly pulling away and snuggling me, and my eyes widen when I realize why.

I'm only fourteen, but I'm not stupid. I'm a girl, he's a boy, and even if he doesn't like me like that, his body does.

I'm not afraid he'll do anything. He's trying really hard to move and hide it.

I giggle as he shifts again, and he says, "Shh. Why're you laughin'?"

"Do you think I'm pretty Ry?"

He stiffens, his arm loosening for a moment, before pulling it away. "You know I do. You and that hair…you're like an angel."

"Yeah, I know you think I'm an angel." I roll over to face him, although it's almost too dark to see anything except his outline. "How 'bout Fay? You think she's pretty, right?"

I hear him swallow before answering, "Yeah, but she's not as pretty as you. Or as nice."

"You're just sayin' that 'cuz you're my best friend. My *only* friend."

"No." He puts his hand on my face, cupping my cheek, and I can't breathe now for a different reason. "I'm saying it because it's true. Some people are good to look at, but ugly on the inside. You're not. You're pretty inside and out."

"Is that why you let me climb in your window and lay in bed with you?"

"I'll do anything to make you smile, Angel, even if it means risking my own ass with my parents." I don't know what to say, but he doesn't give me time to say anything. "You don't smile enough. Only with me."

His thumb moves, stroking my cheek, and I wish for things I shouldn't as I whisper, "You're the only thing that makes me happy enough to smile."

I wish he knew. I wish I could tell him why I always seem sad. But I can't. In my fear, I keep it locked on the inside because I'm afraid if I let it out, nobody will listen. Nobody would protect me, that's what I've learned.

Not even Ryker, my best friend, could save me.

"Angel…"

"Yeah?"

My response comes out squeaky, and he laughs softly. "I've been wanting to ask you somethin' but I don't wanna freak you out."

"You won't."

He moves closer to me in the dark, hand sliding off my face, down my neck, and onto my shoulder before he stops. His lips brush against my cheek as he asks, "Will you…be my girlfriend?"

"I'm not allowed to have a boyfriend."

"You don't gotta call me your boyfriend. Just let me call you my girlfriend. You can deny it if you want; we'll know the truth."

It's probably 'cuz I want to be his girlfriend that his idea seems fine with me. "Okay, I guess I can do that."

His lips slide my cheek and to the corner of my mouth where I feel his mouth curve into a smile. "I want to kiss you. Can I kiss you, Angel?"

"Ain't that what a girlfriend is for? Kissing?"

"Only if she says so."

I don't respond with words. I should be nervous but he's done asked me to be his girlfriend which means he wants me to kiss him, so I put my hands on his face, and slide my lips to meet his. I think he stops breathing as much as I do, and I don't know why he does, but for me it's 'cuz something like a thrill shoots through me. I've never kissed before, but I do what I've seen on TV and part my lips a little.

He overtakes me, but not in a bad way. He moves so he can roll me on to my back, his tongue sweeping inside my mouth as he has our bodies touching all over, resting on his elbows over me as he uses one hand to angle my head and I dunno, kiss me better.

Whatever he's doing, it feels nice, and he doesn't touch me anywhere else.

We kiss and kiss for ages, but nothing more happens.

And soon, soon he's telling me goodbye.

For once making me look forward to tomorrow and loving him more in the only way a fourteen-year-old girl can.

6 - RYKER

She doesn't speak to me when she returns except to ask where her room is located.

Kevin carries her stuff up to her room, and several hours later, I head up to let her know dinner is ready.

I could send someone to do it for me — after all, that's what I employ them for — but I want her to know I'm around, and I'm here for her.

I know she's pissed at me.

But I'm glad she made the right choice.

She doesn't know I wouldn't really turn her in to the cops, but since she hasn't seen me in fifteen years, she wouldn't know that about me.

We were nothing more than kids when she knew me before, which in the real world, after this long means fucking nothing. Neither of us are the same. I don't know her and she doesn't know me.

Something I plan on changing a-s-a-fucking-p.

It's hard to see when I go to enter her room, as she hadn't bothered to open the drapes, leaving me to pause at the door to let my eyes adjust. A quick glance around inside tells me she'd put her things away, and although snooping while she's sleeping might tell me what I want to know, I've no intention of invading her privacy.

I approach the bed, grateful for the thick carpet that silences my steps, and sit on the edge beside her sleeping body.

The sheet is drawn up under her arms, and she rests with her hands under her cheek, her mouth slightly open, her hair fanned out behind her on the pillow. Looking like the angel I nicknamed her, as always.

Even now, I can't get over how thin her wrists are, but she does look healthy. Her hair is shiny, her nails aren't brittle, and her skin is flawless. Her layer of dirt had been deceptive, but I've not figured out why she ended up that way.

I hover between wanting to wake her up to eat and leaving her sleep because she obviously needs it, but before I can make up my mind, her eyes flutter open.

"Now who's sneaking into whose room?" Her tongue darts out to lick her lips as her mouth curves up, her words mumbled.

Reining in my intense desire to use my mouth and tongue on her, I shrug, trying to seem nonchalant at the mention of her long ago visits to my room even though I'm pleased she remembers. "It's dinner time. I came to wake you up."

Clutching the blanket to her chest, she uses her other hand to sit up, then shoves it through her hair. "So late? I only meant to nap…"

"Guess you needed it."

"Guess so."

What follows is one of those silences where you both say nothing, yet something is being said even if you don't know what. She's staring at me, and I'm staring at her, and it's fucking maddening.

I want so many things as I imagine her naked beneath the covers, even as I want to protect her and her obvious frailty, which makes my build work against me because next to her, I'm a giant.

But then I remember those bruises, and the look of absolute pleasure on her face when she talked about how she liked to be hurt deliberately, and on the one hand I want to be the one to do it, while on the other I wanna beat the last fucker who gave her what she wanted to a bloody pulp.

I can't touch her though, not yet. So with a cough, I stand up and walk away, tossing her a look over my shoulders. "I'll see you downstairs."

"Okay. I'll be down in a few minutes."

Her voice is filled with disappointment as I leave the room.

Or maybe it's just my imagination.

Either way, something in her voice reminds me of a day so many years ago when she revealed something I'll never forget.

Sixteen Years Ago

I'm closing my locker when Angel approaches.

I don't even think of her as Danita, and I think she likes it that I don't call her by name.

We've been dating a month now.

She seems to have given up on pretending I'm not her boyfriend, as she closes in on me and jumps up, wrapping her arms around my neck.

"Ry," she says with a kiss on my neck as I embrace her. "Let's skip today. I wanna be alone with you."

I love when she has her lips on me and when I can put mine on her. Ever since I asked her out, it's what we spend the majority of our time together doing. She doesn't ask for anything more, and I don't dare ask.

After all, I'm sixteen and she's fourteen. We've got a lot of time to do that, but it doesn't mean I don't think about it.

A lot.

"We shouldn't, Angel. I've got a test coming up, and they'll call my parents if they notice—"

"Please?"

It's hard to ignore a plea like that, because she never asks me for anything. I think it's hard for her to ask anyone for something, and there's something in her voice that begs me to give in to her. So, I do.

Within minutes we're sneaking out of the school to my

car, then driving to this little place we found in the woods by our houses. We'd discovered it when we crossed over the creek one night as I chased her in a bit of fun shortly after we began dating. Now, instead of her sneaking in my window, we met there when both our parents went to sleep, and so far, nobody seemed the wiser.

It's accessible from an entrance on the other side, so I safely park my car where it won't be noticed.

When we step inside, that's when I notice it's been cleaned, and Angel is smiling from ear to ear.

"I cleaned it last night." She takes my hand and drags me to the area with the small bed we lay on. "I couldn't sleep and I couldn't get you up."

"I'm sorry. I was tired." I don't even remember her trying to wake me, so I must've been out cold. "You know I'd never ignore you Angel."

"I know, but I can't sleep without you."

"Is that what you wanna do right now?" I sit on the bed and pull her on to my lap. "You want to sleep?"

"Kinda." She moves off my lap and pushes me on the shoulder until I lay back, then straddles my lap and bites her lip. "Have you…you ever been with a girl, Ry?"

Her question makes me nervous and horny all at once, because I think I know where she's going with this, so I answer honestly. "No. Have you?"

She giggles. "I don't like girls."

I laugh because we both know that's not what I meant, but before I can say anything else, she's leaning forward, which puts her boobs right on my chest. Her lips are on mine, her hands gripping my shoulders, and all intentions of questioning her go out the window.

"Do you want to touch me Ry?" She moves her hands up my neck and into my hair, keeping her lips real close to mine. "I want you to."

"Yeah, but…" Even as I pause while talking, my hands are finding the hem of her shirt, and I'm slipping my hands underneath it, one heading to her back as the other slides up the front of her body she's lifted just enough to give me access. "Are you sure? We don't have to; we can wait."

She's moved her head to rest in my shoulder, and I feel her shake her head. "I don't want to wait, Ry. I love you."

"I love you, too, Angel, but—"

All of a sudden, she sits up and pulls her top over her head, only to have her bravado fail her as she covers her boobs with her hands. They are in a bra, and I register the rattiness of it for only a moment before I look up into her eyes. This is the first time I've seen her without her shirt, but I don't want to disrespect her and she's obviously embarrassed since she's covering herself.

There are tears in her eyes, though, and I put my hands on her waist because I'm not sure where else to put them. "What's wrong?"

"Promise me you won't be mad."

"Mad about what?" She holds my gaze, and I'm afraid to look away, so I tell her, "I'd never be mad at you Angel. Ain't nothing you could do right now that would make me mad at you."

She reaches behind her back, pulling the straps around

after a few seconds, then stops, holding the bra against her body. "Promise me you won't say anything, Ry, no matter what it is. You're the only person I trust."

That's when I realize this is about so much more than sex with me, and feeling sick to my stomach, I make a promise I know I shouldn't. "I swear, Angel."

She nods, sliding the straps down her arms and off: first the left, then the right, then drops her arms straight, the bra falling on to my body, but I don't notice. Instead, I suck in a breath at the bruises.

They're on the underside of her boobs, just under the nipples and around the edges, where they can't be seen when covered by her bra. Varying shades of them, which I know means some are newer than others, and by the fact she has looked off to the side once her bra dropped indicates her shame — and instantly, I'm pissed, even though I told her I wouldn't be mad.

"Who?" I spit the words out between clenched teeth. "Who did this?"

"It doesn't matter."

It mostly certainly fucking does matter, but I won't press her. I can't imagine how much it took for her to show me this.

I move my gaze from her chest to her face, watching her lip wobble following her whispered words, slamming my eyes shut as I ask a question I don't want to, but need to. "Is there anything else you wanna tell me?"

"Nobody else would believe me if I told them," is what she says next. "I can't...I don't dare say anything." She chokes up and I open my eyes to find her staring into mine. "If they didn't believe me, I'm afraid of what might happen."

I see the fear in her eyes and on her face, but she didn't answer my question, and I have a sick feeling I know exactly who is abusing her. "I'll kill him."

She leans in, a hand on my chest, and shakes her head. "No. You promised."

"Angel, this is different, he's hurting you—"

"No, please." She kisses my lips. "Just make me forget. I know you love me. I want someone who loves me to touch me. Please?"

"I can't touch you there. Look at you; doesn't it hurt?"

"A little. I—once I met you, I try to think about how happy you make me and I barely notice he's there. I...I need you to give me the real thing, Ry, please."

I must hesitate a moment too long, because she hops off me and grabs her bra, tears streaming down her face as she puts it on. "It's okay, you don't have to, I know I'm ugly, I know—"

"Angel!" I raise my voice, interrupting her self-loathing speech, and her wide eyes jump to mine as she freezes in place. "Tell me one thing." I swallow past the lump in my throat, tamping down my disgust at knowing she imagines me as her boobs are being mauled by an asshole, and ask the most important thing. "Has he...?"

She shakes her head, face flaming as she glances away from me, holding the cups of her bra against her chest. "He...he touches m-me, though, down th-there...and h-himself. He m-makes me hold a p-pillow over m-my f-face and—"

"Oh god, baby, stop. Please stop."

In that moment, I want to touch her and give her exactly what she wants because I love her. I can't stand the pain on her face, knowing that even if I explain why I don't want to touch her when someone else is violating her body against her will, she won't understand. She already thinks I'm rejecting her because of the bruises, and I can't let her go home thinking I don't love her enough to do what she asks me to.

I stand up and pull my shirt over my head, then step close and tug the bra out of her hands.

And as I tug her against me, she wraps her arms around my neck, and whispers, "Thank you."

Then I give her exactly what she wants, vowing in my own head to find a way to do something about what's going on without her knowing.

*H*e's staring at me.

We've already eaten dinner, and afterward, he asks me to join him in the living room to watch a movie.

Since I slept, I'm not really sleepy, and even though I'm tired, I accept his invitation.

When I choose a comfy chair to sit in, he doesn't say a word. He takes the couch nearby, and stretches out on it so he is able to glance between the television and me.

But apparently he's decided I'm more interesting than what's on.

I bring my legs up, hugging my knees to my chest as I make sure my maxi skirt is covering every inch of me, then cross my arms on top and rest my chin on my hands as I glare at him. "What?"

"Can't believe you're here is all."

"So you're going to stare at me constantly?"

"Does it bother you?"

I hug my knees tighter and look away. "I'm nothing special to look at."

"I disagree."

"Shocking."

He's silent for a moment, until I look over at him, and he smiles. "You should come lay here with me."

"No."

"Why not? Afraid I won't be able to control myself?"

He's not even got one eye on the TV now, as all his focus is on me as he rests with his hands behind his head, lips curved in amusement.

I hadn't even studied him at dinner. I ate my food — well picked at it really since I had nearly no appetite — and ignored his disapproving looks the whole time. He's wearing a white button down, but it's unfastened 'til halfway down, and his sleeves are rolled up. His jean-clad left leg is closest to the back of the couch and is bent while the other leg is straight, and I know if I walk over there and place my body atop his, the bent one would come around to trap me against his body.

If only he knew how badly I wanted to let him do just that.

When I don't answer, he asks, "Where'd you go when you first left here?"

This is it.

The beginning of the end.

I wish I were kidding, but I'm not. I know what's coming.

I take a deep shuddering breath, and then release it slowly.

"You remember me telling you I never met my father?"

"Yes."

"Well, turns out he lived about two hours from here all those years. I found a picture of a strange man in a weird spot on the bookcase, and when I asked my mother who it was, she was drunk and got all sappy, telling me it was my father. Gave me his name and all." I toss Ryker a half-sad, half amused smile. "All those years and all I should've done years before was get her drunk and ask her questions. A few days later, I left and showed up on his doorstep."

"Oh, I bet he took that well."

"Yeah. He didn't know I existed and if it weren't for his wife insisting I could come inside, I'm sure he would've shut the door in my face." I brush my hair away from my face, and slide my feet off the chair until they hit the floor, then stand up. "Turns out, I have a sister a year older than me. Him and his wife were separated at the time, and he told her he'd slept with someone else, but maintained he knew nothing of me."

"Did you believe him?"

I shrug in response as I stare at the floor. "It didn't matter. I needed a place to stay, and his wife made him let me."

"Why are you standing?"

Glancing over at him, my face heats. "Oh. I think I'm going to bed now."

"You think? You aren't sure?" In one swift motion, he

swings his feet to floor and stands up, walking over to me and staring down at me with our bodies inches apart. "Need some company?"

"I don't think so." He's so close I can smell the spiciness of his cologne, the freshness of his detergent, and the sweetness of his shampoo. I swallow, wanting to step back at the same time I want to lean in, yet I'm frozen in place.

"Again with the thinking." He lifts a hand and with two fingers, tilts my chin up until our eyes collide. "There was a time you couldn't sleep without me next to you."

If a touch from him hadn't stolen my breath, the look in his eyes would've. It's a look that says I'm his and he's mine; even though it's no longer true, I wish it were. His two fingers under my chin slide to the left side of my jaw, his thumb skims across my cheek, and before I know what he's doing, his hand is fisting my hair and tugging my head back until my neck is bared.

His other hand comes up to my waist, and brings my body against his, where I can feel every inch of him. A whimper escapes through my parted lips as he nips at my neck with his teeth, and then flicks his tongue over the same spot in an attempt to ease the pain.

If only he could ease all of my pains.

"Ryker...please." I'm pleading, but I'm not sure for what, and he laughs.

"Please what?" The hand at my waist slides down and cups my ass through the skirt, grinding our lower bodies together in a clear attempt to make the hardness of his cock apparent. "Please let you go? Please fuck you? Please don't begin to make you pay for the way you left me without a word?" I let out a small sob at the agony in his words, which in some ways, seems bigger than the throbbing in my heart. "Plead for it, Angel. Beg me for whatever it is you want, because for the foreseeable future, you're at my mercy."

Tears prick my eyes, never wavering from his even as my lips wobble with my efforts to keep inside the cries yearning to break free, something I can't allow to happen. I haven't made it this far to break down now, but even with this thought, I feel my defenses weaken just a little as his gaze burns into mine.

"What do you want, Ry?" My tongue feels heavy in my mouth, his cock jumping against me at my question, and I long to squeeze my legs together to ease the ache between them. "I won't plead for anything until you tell me what you want."

"We're going to play a game."

I feel his hand slide from my ass to my thigh, opening and closing it, only to realize he's slowly scrunching the skirt up so he can stick his hand under it. With my hair still caught in the trap of his other hand, I'm defenseless against him and his touch, and suddenly I'm not sure what the problem is with that.

"You've got two choices, Angel." He brings his lips to brush against mine, followed up by trail of kisses down my neck, and back again. "You can tell me why you left and didn't tell me first. Or," he says, his cheek touching mine as he smiles so I can feel it, only I know it's not a sweet one, "you can fuck me. Which one do you choose?"

When I don't answer right away, he slides the hand now under my skirt in between my legs, cupping me through my panties. He rubs back and forth with his fingers, slow and steady with the purpose of torturing me with no relief in sight, using his mouth to nip and suck on my jaw and neck.

"What if I don't want either?"

He moves his hand up in answer, gliding it inside the top, using his hand to lower the panties down enough to bare me. "I'll bet my whole fortune that you're lying about wanting to do at least one of those." His hand, which he rested on the center of my ass to keep me snug against him, dips lower and lower until he's slipping the tip of two fingers into my pussy from behind. As a low moan of pleasure is wrenched from my throat, he chuckles and moves his mouth to mine, stilling his hand in place as the other grips my hair more firmly. "That's what I thought. So, what'll it be, Angel? Confession or submission?"

The way he's holding me would leave me in a precarious position should he choose to let go. With his hold on my hair, and his hand between my legs along with our height difference, I'm on my tiptoes with my back slightly bent. It's a position which has an effect on my mind I can't really explain but wish I could, even to myself. It's one that makes me want to give in.

I continue refusing to answer, and his fingers plunge a little deeper, making it so my automatic response is to bring my arms up to his sides and clutch his shirt in my fists. I didn't want to touch him, but his movements have me wobbling, and I need an anchor.

It's not that I don't want his hands on me; in fact, I'm immensely enjoying it. But it's a power struggle, and I want to win. I don't want to be the one to give in, because once I do, I know every single wall I have built against him will no longer protect me. I would rather be unresponsive than have him hate me, which I've no doubt he will. No doubt at all.

"Please." His fingers slip in and out of me again, and even though my body begs to let him give it what it wants, I force myself to say, "Please. I'm tired. Let me go."

Instead of doing what I ask, he releases my hair, removes his hand, and in one smooth motion I'm pretty sure I'd find impressive if I weren't so tired, picks me up and carries me out of the room and up the steps.

Even though it's dark, I know we're not in my room when he enters a door close to the stairwell, a sliver of moonlight showcasing the large bed against the wall. He places me in the center of it, then starts stripping.

"You can take your clothes off, or I can rip them off you," he declares, his words harsh as he unbuttons his cuffs, followed by the ones down the center before shrugging out of his shirt. "You've got until I'm done."

I stare at him, mesmerized and thrown for a loop, because this is and isn't the same Ryker I used to love. He took care of me after my drunken arrival as he would've when we were younger, when I needed him to be there for me when I couldn't even be there for myself, but now…now he's a grown man, one I've hurt in the past, and one who is obviously used to getting what he wants.

His hands move to the snap of his jeans, staring at me all the while, and I move to obey his command even as I admonish myself in my head for giving in even a little. I get up on my knees and reach for the hem of my shirt, crossing my arms to bring it up and over my head, not bothering to look at him as I drop the shirt over the side of the bed and slip two fingers on each side of the band of my skirt. Wiggling it along with my panties down my legs, I fall back on my ass and pull the items off the rest of the way, tossing them over the side as well.

Then, I refuse to meet his eyes, crawling to hide my naked body under the covers, and pull them up to my chin as I face away from him, waiting for the moment he hugs his body to mine from behind.

*I*t's hard not to chuckle as Danita huddles under the covers, facing away from me, blankets to her chin as if it will stop me from touching her.

Just as I said we were going to play a game, I know she's playing a game with me. If she truly didn't want to do anything she'd tell me to stop, make it very clear my attentions aren't welcome, but she hasn't.

She merely wants to win in a battle of wills, and she won't.

So, after I've stripped naked, I climb into bed and settle against her back, skimming a hand up her thigh, over her hip, then down her stomach. My other hand slips under her body, my arm closing around her torso to tug her against me, as I move the hand on her stomach down between her legs.

Stroking with one finger, then two, her wetness makes it easy for me to slide both digits between her pussy lips, then inside. Using my thumb, I circle her clit, smiling when she gasps in delight and opens her legs wider. I lift one leg, bringing it around to trap hers, making it impossible for her to deny me access.

"What do you want right now, Angel? More than anything in the world…if you could have it, what would it be?"

I know I'm torturing her.

That's the whole fucking plan.

I want her to want me, and she does. But she doesn't want me bad enough to let go of her secrets; that's all right, though, because I've got a few secrets of my own. And her game playing is feeding her right into my plans.

She doesn't answer me, so I curl my fingers up, caressing her g-spot with enough pressure to make her feel it, but not enough to get her off. Her instant reaction is to move against my hand, trying to get what she wants, and I pause the strokes as she whimpers in frustration.

"Tell me what you want."

"I want to leave."

Bingo.

Dropping deceptive, sweet kisses on her neck, I make my way up to her ear, then take the lobe between my teeth and increase the pressure until she wiggles in protest, removing my teeth and sucking on it in apology. "What if," I whisper into her ear, "we make a deal we can both live with?"

Her form goes motionless at this, giving me the opportunity to fuck her with my finger once more to keep her distracted enough to listen without interrupting, and I grin as she says, "W-what kind of deal?"

I withdraw my hand, then arrange us both until I'm hovering over her, our bodies so close my cock rests against her stomach although I'm careful to keep my weight off her.

"The kind of deal in which, in thirty days, you would be set free no matter what."

"And it would include...?"

I like the fact she gives nothing away. Her voice is neutral, almost flat, and tired.

She doesn't know after she's agreed that I will let her sleep. I'm sure the fact my cock — hard as a rock for *her* — which is resting against her, reminds her of my desire for her, and of the way her traitorous body responds to me even as she implies she's not interested. But all I want right now is her capitulation, for her to play right in my hands without being aware of what she's done.

I lower my head, using nothing but my mouth as I capture her lips, running my tongue along them, seeking admittance into her in a simple yet primal way. I don't coax; I increase the pressure until she gives me what I want, what belongs to me.

Once in, devouring her is the simplest way to describe what I'm doing. I give her no rest, no quarter, as I use my tongue and lips and teeth to show her I'm in charge. I angle my head to the left, then the right, sweeping my tongue around her mouth, to the back, along her teeth, tangling with hers only to begin again, on repeat.

When I pull away, she gasps for air, and I shove forward with my plans. "You will do whatever I want, whenever I want, how I want it. And in return, you get the same courtesy from me."

"Whatever…?" She's still panting hard and I know even saying that one word has stolen what little breath she's gained back.

I smile even though I know she can barely see me in the darkened room. "Yes. If you share anything other than your body, it will be because you want to, because I've earned it. And the same goes for me. Our secrets are our own. You can share all, or you can share none, but you will be mine physically if nothing else. Agreed?"

I pause and wait for her response to my offer, which I know may take her a bit to process.

I'm taking a bit of a gamble here, but I've every confidence in my ability to get her to open up to me in thirty days time.

She opened up to me long ago before we ever had sex, and I know she's built up protections in the intervening years, but I'm not worried.

Her reply, when it comes, is not what I expect. "I don't think you can do the things I would request."

All right, I'm intrigued, so I ask, "And what would that be?"

"Hit me."

I'm only taken aback a little, aware from the bruises fading on her skin that she likes to be hit, but I don't let it show. "Where?"

"In the face." She shocks me with that one. I suck in a breath, and she laughs. "Like I said, you wouldn't do it, which means you'd break the rules."

Ah. She's counting on me turning her down.

I ask the obvious question. "Have you ever had it done? Or does every man deny you?"

"They all deny me. They are too afraid."

I lift a hand and run it down from her hair to her cheek before gripping her chin between two fingers. "And if I hit you…if I give you what you want right now, you agree to the terms?"

"Y-yes."

Her stutter gives away the fact she thought I'd turn her down. She's shocked I'm not pulling away and saying, "Fuck no," which makes me grin. And, kinky fucker that I am, my cock jumps at the very idea of pleasing her this way.

I lean in and with my mouth against her ear, whisper, "How hard?"

I'm so close I hear her swallow, her body tensing for a moment beneath mine, then relaxing as she says, "Like I've smarted off. Enough to sting, but not cause true pain."

God, I love that she knows what she fucking wants. But, as always, I take it a step further. "Smart off to me then."

"Jerk."

It's a lame attempt, so I give her a lame response, tapping her cheek lightly with the tips of my fingers and no force.

"Try again, Angel."

"Don't fucking call me that."

Hmm, better, but not quite.

I switch to the other side and tap her a little harder, enough to get a small 'pop!' and she growls at me, "You hit like a girl. I could hit myself harder than that."

Since I'm unable to prevent my mouth from curving up at that, I pull my hand back to give her exactly what she asked for. When my hand connects with her face, it makes a nice slapping sound, her head turning the merest fractions, the mark of my hand on her cheek blooming in an instant, and her body bucks against mine in reaction as she gasps.

When she turns her face to me once more, she brings her arms up and wraps them around my neck, and demands, "Again."

The best slap is one she doesn't know is coming, at least, it is in my opinion. Cradling her cheek in my head, I caress it with the pad of my thumb, holding myself up on the elbow of that arm, as I use the other to reach between us and take my cock in hand. "Open your legs, then wrap them around me."

She hesitates for a moment, but does as bid once I tap her on the cheek with my thumb in reminder, and once I'm settled in between her legs, I place the tip of my cock at the entrance to her pussy and run it up and down, teasing her and myself. "I was going to get you to agree, then let you sleep as you wanted, but now…I've changed my mind." She says nothing, leading me to lean in and take her lower lip between my teeth, where I nip to get her attention. "Do you want me to fuck you, Angel? I need you to say you agree, for clarification purposes, and after that, it's game on. You will get exactly what you need."

My mouth is so close I feel her tongue dart out and wet her lips, then she murmurs, "I agree."

Even thought I want to plunge into her, I don't, choosing to stick the tip in and then pull back out. "Louder."

"I agree!"

Once again, better, but not quite. Against her mouth, I smile and tell her exactly what I want. "Scream it like you'll be screaming my name by the end." When she sucks in a breath, I clarify, "Don't worry. My room is soundproof."

"I agree," she screams, throwing her head back. "Now fuck me, damn you!"

With a swift thrust, my cock is deep inside her, and at the same time, I slap her across the face, harder than before, yet sufficient for her needs. Her arms tighten around my neck, along with her legs around my waist, as she moans with pleasure at getting what she wants.

Controlling my desire to fuck her hard and fast, I follow up the slap with kisses meant to soothe the sting. She keeps her head turned to the side, eyes closed, her breath hitching with each touch of my lips to her cheek. I glide my lips along my jawline until I reach her ear, taking the lobe in my mouth, teasing it between my teeth.

Her hands slide up my neck and into my hair, tugging on it. In response, I slip my fingers into her hair, grabbing a fistful as I move my mouth over her ear, whispering into it,

"I will match you tug for tug, so be careful what you wish for."

I drag my head away from hers as she turns to face me, her hands tightening in my hair but no longer tugging, and before she can speak, I cover her lips with mine, ravaging her mouth as a man who has gone too long without a taste of her. I move inside her, withdrawing my cock to the edge, then thrusting deep and fast. Her whimpers are swallowed by my domination of her mouth, her hands release my hair at each withdrawal only to clutch it once more with every plunge of my cock, and she moves her hips to meet me every time.

Suddenly, she's yanking her mouth away from mine, and wails, "Why does it have to be you who gives me what I want?"

I pull back, then slam into her in answer, her back bowing as she cries out. She hasn't let go of my hair though and when her reaction means she's tugging on my hair until it hurts, I jerk her head back, leaving her neck exposed as she lets out a sob.

My assault — on her senses and her body — is relentless as I respond to her question while continuing to fuck her fast and deep, my grip on her hair steady, feeling her body tighten around me as she gets closer and closer to coming. "When haven't I given you what you wanted, Angel?" I take small nips at her neck, each hiss out of her in reaction pleasing me. "The answer is never. I've *always* done whatever you've needed, in more ways than you could know."

"Ry...please..."

"Please what?" I know what she wants, but I'm going to make her ask. "You can't until you beg."

"I—" A tear slides down her cheek, her lower lip quivering as she swallows, then whispers, "I need to come. Please, I need you to hit me and let me come."

"No."

"Oh, god." The tears come faster now as she removes one hand from my hair and puts it on my shoulder, nails digging into my skin, which only makes me fuck her harder as I enjoy her cries for relief. "Please. Fuck, Ryker, please."

"You don't need it," I murmur, sliding my tongue along her neck until I reach her ear. "Come without the hit, sweetheart. You can do it."

"N-no, I c-can't!"

"Yes," I say with a hard thrust, "you can. Now, Angel. Come *now*."

She takes her other hand out of my hair and starts beating at my shoulders, bucking against me before dropping her legs from around my waist. I release her hair and grab one leg, gripping tightly as I refuse to quit fucking her, my own desire to come harder and harder to ignore, my control slipping.

"You said you'd do whatever I want." She smacks me, over and over, making me chuckle at her anger. "Stop laughing and hit me, you fucking bastard!"

Leaning away completely, which takes my upper body out of her area of attack, I get up on my knees and slip my free hand between us, manipulating her clit with my hands, holding her other leg in such a way she won't be able to sit up.

She writhes against the bed, against me, which only inflames me further, and she glares at me, face flushed. I remove my hand and lift it, watching her eyes widen moments before I bring it back down, hitting her harder than before right on her clit.

Her moan is priceless as she orgasms, mouth dropping open on a wail of, "Oh god, Ryker, oh my god!"

Her own release is the catalyst for my own, and I grip both her hips as I come, filling her with a groan of my own.

Then, I collapse on top of her, and in the sweet way she always did in the past, she wraps her arms around my neck and pulls me in for a kiss.

9 - DANITA

*W*hen *haven't I given you what you wanted, Angel?*

Ending our kiss, Ryker rolls off me, and the bed, but I don't turn to watch where he's going.

Still reeling from the way he played my body and mind, I replay his question over and over in my mind, because the answer is obvious.

Never.

He always gave me what I wanted and what I needed without fail.

He doesn't get it though.

He's not the problem. He was everything a girl could want in a boyfriend when we were together, and now, he appears to fall into the same category.

It's me who is the problem, only he doesn't wish to see it.

His blackmail to keep me here despite my disappearing act fifteen years ago is proof of that.

When the bed dips, I turn my head to find him with a washcloth in hand, and before I can protest, he's sliding it between my legs. It's lukewarm, making me sigh and open my legs a little wider to give him better access.

"Tell me about this," he says while using two fingers to open my labia, stroking each side in a gentle and firm manner. "How long has it been since you had the laser treatment?"

"Um…" I close my eyes, clutching the sheet with my hands as he replaces the cloth with his mouth, and licks my clit. "I was nineteen."

"Why'd you do it?" At the insertion of his fingers, accompanied by another lick, I'm convinced his plan is to drive me crazy — with his cock, his tongue, his hands, and his sheer determined will. As pleasure spirals through me, fogging my brain, his voice breaks it, stern as he commands, "Answer the question."

"A man I dated…" My breath catches followed by a whimper as he sucks my clit into his mouth, flicking it with tongue over and over. "He…he liked it. I did it…to please him."

My hands find their way into his hair, moaning while he alternates between sucking, licking, and flicking with his tongue, and curling his fingers into my pussy. Together, the sensations are enough to drive me mad, and get the response he wanted out of me while we were having sex: me coming without being hit.

Something I don't want to happen.

Or do I?

"Oh god!" He starts humming, which imitates vibrations, and I yank on his hair as my body hovers on the precipice of an even bigger orgasm than earlier. "Fuck you, Ryker, don't—ahhh, please!"

I want him to stop.

I don't want him to stop.

I can't fucking decide but it no longer matters. "I—I can't! Hit me, please!"

His eyes open, lifting to meet mine, and he holds up his other hand, with one finger in the air.

His middle one.

Before I can even register my disbelief at him flipping me off, he takes my clit between his teeth and nips it enough to send me over the edge.

And lets go, withdrawing his touch as sweet pleasure ripples through every inch of me, and I break out in sobs.

Leaving me unsure how I'll survive a week of this, let alone a month, because it doesn't just affect my body.

It impacts my heart and I've never been able to protect that, especially from him.

It's always been his, which is the last thing he needs to figure out.

With no further thought, I slide out of the bed and run out of the room until I reach mine, shutting the door as I lock it behind me.

Then, climbing into bed, I curl into a ball as the torrent of tears persist, and remind myself why loving Ryker over again is a bad idea.

Fifteen Years and One Month ago

I CREEP FROM MY ROOM, ALTHOUGH THIS TIME IT ISN'T through my window, but through my own door.

I inch toward the bathroom, walking as quietly as possible, doing my best to avoid the places I know creak, but I hit a spot and like a flash, my stepdad opens his door.

"What are you doing, Nita?"

I flash him a non-threatening smile even though my stomach wants to revolt at the sight of him. "I'm just going to the bathroom, daddy. I'm sorry. I have to pee and I can't wait."

"Right." He looks me up and down, smiling *his* creepy smile as a reminder of him having his filthy hands on me just thirty minutes ago, and nods. "Go on, then get back to bed. I don't wanna hear you again."

"Thank you, daddy."

I walk faster and close the bathroom door, then wait until I hear his door shut before pulling the item I hid in my pocket.

Tugging my shorts down, I take a deep breath as tears threaten to spill over.

I'm in so much trouble and I know it as I stick the pregnancy test — I took it out of the package in my room before hiding it in my pocket so I wouldn't make noise while so close to his door — between my legs and do as instructed.

68

Laying the test on the counter, I shut my eyes and count to ten as I finish going to the bathroom, even though I know what the results will be.

Standing up, I look down, my hands automatically coming up to grip the edge of the counter at the two lines, one nice and dark, staring back up at me.

I shove a fist against my mouth to stifle a sob of elation and despair and fear. I'm not shocked, though, because once I realized I'd missed my last three periods, following the last few weeks with my head in the toilet at school, I knew I was pregnant.

Pregnant with Ryker's baby.

Our baby.

I've no idea what to do, but I know I have to get away from here, especially since I'm sure I'll start showing soon.

I know if my stepdad finds out, he will hit me even more.

And I can't let him hurt my baby.

Quickly, I dry off the end of the test, and hide it as I did to get it in here, then turn on the water and wash my hands.

Then, I head back to my room, sighing with relief as I hear him snoring all the way out in the hallway.

Once inside, I shut my door as quietly as possible and begin packing a bag.

I've got my real father's info and I already got a bus ticket with money I'd hidden from my parents the last few months.

I open my window as I do every night, only this time I

jump out with my bag, and head in the opposite direction of Ryker's window with plans to call him the next day to tell him what's happened.

Only I never make that phone call.

And soon after, Danita Ruthanne Carson disappears into thin air.

It's nearly six a.m. when my door is unlocked from the outside and Ryker enters the room, closing the door before striding over to the bed. I hear him drop whatever he's wearing on the floor, then he climbs into the bed and snuggles up to me from behind.

"Get out," I mutter, shoving my elbow back into his stomach, smiling at the satisfying 'oomph' sound he makes. "I don't want you in my bed."

No verbal response is forthcoming, but he tosses his leg over mine and slides one hand to rest on my stomach, the other gliding under my neck and his head resting on the pillow behind me. I feel his breath on my ear and the heat emanating off his body is comforting.

I haven't been able to sleep, and about twenty minutes ago, finally had to give in and take a pain pill. It would kick in soon and I'm glad he hadn't come in before then.

I'm not ready to explain that yet, and honestly, if I can make it the whole month without telling him, I won't.

"Angel?" He kisses my shoulder and pauses, then asks, "May I ask you something?"

"Didn't you just do that?"

He sighs. "Yes."

He goes quiet and I roll my eyes even though he can't see me. "Go ahead."

"Why couldn't my parents or I find you after you left?"

I stiffen, not expecting that question. "I didn't know you looked for me."

"I did." His hold tightens on me, pulling me as close as humanly possible, and kisses my neck. "As much as possible, but it was like you ceased to exist."

"You didn't look through my purse when I got here? Check out my ID, etcetera?"

"No. Why would I?"

I want to make a smartass remark, but since I'm too tired, I answer his question. "A few days after I went to my father's house, I told him and his wife what had happened. At first, they gained emergency custody, and one day they were taking me to court to make me change my name. To protect me, they said. I got a new middle and last name, and due to the circumstances, it was kept private."

"Did they call the police?"

"Yeah, but I guess they didn't check on my allegations until a week or so later, and apparently, my stepdad had died by then. They told my father that my mother killed him in self-defense."

"That's what they say, yep."

Something in his words and the way he said them makes me want to ask him if it's not true, but I'm too tired.

My eyes start to drift shut, and I cover his hand on my

stomach with my own, as I say while yawning through the words, "Ry…I want you to know, I was going to call you. I never meant to leave you wondering."

I don't even know if he heard me or responded and when I wake up later in the day, he is gone.

Fifteen Years and Three Weeks ago

She's gone and she didn't even tell me she was leaving.

I worried for three days when she didn't come over to my house, didn't show up for school, and didn't answer my knocks at her window. I wanted to call the police, or tell my parents, but because I promised her I wouldn't say anything, I didn't say anything like an idiot.

Finally, on day four, I went to her house when I knew her stepdad wasn't home and her mother answered the door.

"She ran away," is all she said, following it up by slamming the door in my face, which only made my anger and hopelessness rise.

I pounded on the door until she opened it once more, where I proceeded to curse her out and tell her exactly

73

what the man she was married to had been doing to her daughter, until her face turned white and she told me I was a fucking liar, and closed the door once more with a bang.

And now, one week after Angel disappeared, I'm walking past her house.

I almost don't stop, but at the sound of glass breaking and raised voices, I run to the door with the silly notion that Angel has returned and needs my help running through my mind.

Only she hasn't come back.

Instead, her stepdad has her mother up against a wall in the living room, choking her. "Where did you hear such things?" He's shouting as she claws at his hands with her own, feet kicking uselessly at his as she struggles to free herself. "Tell me you stupid fucking bitch!"

I can smell the alcohol from here as I cough to get his attention.

He drops her and she scrambles away, his attention all on me as I say, "It was me. I told her."

"Oh, is that what the little whore told you?" He sneers at me, laughing as his wife exits the room, then advances on me until his smelly, ugly face is in mine. "I know you were fucking her. She thought she was so sly, but I knew."

"I saw the bruises," I said, my voice rising, unafraid because he's so drunk one punch from me would probably put him out. "She told me what you were doing to her, you sick bastard."

"That didn't stop you from fucking her, did it?" He laughs again. "Tell me. Did she enjoy it? God, I imagined sticking my dick in her, but I knew that was the easiest way to get busted. But god, did I enjoy sticking my fingers in her. Did she tell you I used my ton—?"

He doesn't even finish his sentence as I let my fist fly, punching him straight in the face, and he stumbles back.

I'll give it to him, he's quick to recover, coming at me and landing a few punches here and there.

But it's the sound of the gun clicking that has him pausing and turning to face his wife after hitting me in the face hard enough to make me fall down. I watch from my position on the floor, unable to look away.

"Now baby, put the gun down." He takes a step toward her. "Ain't no reason for anyone to get shot here."

"Don't come near me! How dare you touch my baby girl. If I had any fucking idea, I'da killed you before now!"

He pauses and puts his hands up. "Don't listen to this stupid kid. I don't want anyone but you baby. I never touched her, I swear."

"Liar!" She keeps the gun aimed on him, swinging her eyes to me, and then back at him. "I heard you tell him what you done to her."

"I didn't mean it. Come on now, baby, give me the gun."

Like the dumb fuck idiot he is, he takes a step toward her, and she shoots him once. Twice.

After he falls to the floor, she lowers the gun, and gazes right at me with her battered face and torn clothing, pointing at the kitchen with her free hand. "Go on, you get on out of here. No reason for the cops to find you here and

I'm sure someone's called them by now. Go out the back door."

I scramble to my feet and walk around his body. Just as I'm about to leave the room she says, "Just so you know, she's okay. I can't say no more than that, but she's all right."

I don't look back. I don't nod or even acknowledge her statement.

Once outside, I take off at a run, making it to our little place in the woods before I stick my head in my hands and break down.

IT'S NEARLY ONE P.M. AND I'M EATING LUNCH WHEN SHE walks in and sits down at the table to the right of me.

After she'd fallen asleep, I'd lain there, enjoying the simple fact she was in my house, in one of my bedrooms.

I also wondered, after my mind drifted back to the day her mother killed her stepfather, if giving Angel such information was necessary. So this morning, my goal is to decide if I tell her or not.

She's dressed in light blue tank and loose grey yoga pants, her feet bare, hair hanging down her back. She seems relaxed for the first time since her arrival, as if she's at peace with the fact I've trapped her here.

I still won't apologize for that since I always do what I need to do.

And right now, I need her here with me.

Last night merely solidified my decision.

"Morning," she says with a bright smile.

Unable to resist wanting to share in her cheerfulness, I lean in and press my lips to hers, murmuring against them, "Morning to you," before sitting back and returning to my food.

As a plate is set in front of her, she waits until we are alone to ask, "Why do you have so many people here doing things you could do for yourself?"

"Because I pay them to do it instead?"

She takes a few bites of food, then starts playing around with it as usual, muttering, "Yeah, I get that."

"I'm not understanding the problem."

"You're the only person who lives here." She shrugs as she stares down at the plate. "I just wonder why you need such a huge staff."

Finishing up, I put the napkin on top of my plate, and laugh. "Honestly, this is a big place. It needs a huge staff, and, for the record, most of them came with the house when I purchased it."

At that she lifts her head, pushing her plate away. "I'm done."

"You barely touched it."

Her posture stiffens at my hidden reprimand. "Well, that's because I ate all I need."

"Please eat, Angel. You are so skinny it's scary."

She smacks a hand flat on the table, glaring at me. "You think I don't know that? Just leave me and my eating habits alone. I'm not that hungry, *okay*?"

As we stare at each other, she frowns at me, which

deepens the more I grin. "I like you more when you've got that fire in your eyes."

I worry about her weight, but it doesn't stop my cock from growing hard at the thought of fucking her the night before, or having my head between her legs, and it doesn't stop me from wanting her now.

I'm pretty sure I'll never stop wanting her, desiring her, or fucking her.

And although her mood swings might give me whiplash, it doesn't lessen her appeal.

If anything, I want to know why she's so prickly, and if I have to, I'll fuck the reasons for it out of her.

I grab her hand with mine and tug on it. "C'mere."

She opens her mouth, only to close it again, no doubt recalling the rules of doing whatever I say. I push the plates to the center of the table, scoot my chair back, and once she's standing in front of me, I begin to undo my belt.

"On your knees." Her instant compliance pleases me, my cock rock hard at the idea of having her lips wrapped around it, and when she shoves my hands aside to finish unbuckling my belt, followed by my pants as she places herself in between my legs, I oblige her desires by fisting her hair in my hands. "I thought you said you weren't that hungry?"

Freeing my cock, she responds by squeezing my cock with her hand, then covering the tip of it with her hot mouth, eyes wide as she gazes up at me. Gliding her hand up, she gives the tip a quick lick, then runs it down and around, before removing her lips and licking under the edge. My hands grasp her hair in reflex as she puts it back in her mouth, slowly working my cock further and further in as the hand wrapped around my shaft moves up and down with just the right amount of pressure.

I relax in the chair, letting her pleasure me with nothing more than encouragement from me in the form of moans, the hands in her hair merely an anchor. I shut my eyes and with a groan, lean my head against the back of the chair, murmuring, "Damn Angel, I love your mouth. I knew it would be put to good use this way."

It's crazy, but I've been waiting my whole life for this moment. When we were younger, she never did this, and I never asked.

She hums, mimicking my actions from last night, and I let her blow me for another minute. I'd love nothing more than to get off in her mouth, but I have different plans for today.

I tighten my hands and tug, making her gasp and freeing my cock from her mouth, before demanding, "Stand up, take off your clothing, and bend over the table."

I release her and she stands there, messing with the hem of her shirt and staring at the floor. "H-here in the dining room?"

"Yes." When she doesn't move, I sigh. "You just had my cock down your throat while on your knees and now you're worried about doing something in here?" She nods, still staring at the floor, so I use two fingers to bring her eyes to me. "Don't worry about it. Do what I say."

My words are accompanied by the sound of my belt

sliding out of the loops, matching the ends before holding it up in front of her widening gaze. I lower it and tap my leg, giving her a stern look. I don't even need to repeat myself as she scrambles to obey.

When she's nude and bent over, I push her head down until her cheek is resting on the cool surface, and she whimpers.

Sliding a hand between her legs, I discover her wet; so wet her own excitement is evident on the inside of her thighs, and I want nothing more than to shove my cock deep inside her and make her scream.

But first, a treat for her.

"Tell me," I whisper into her as I lean close, knowing my cock rubs against her ass I do so, "do you like to be hit with things other than a hand? Say…like a belt?"

"Yes."

I smack her ass with my hand. "Yes, what?"

"Yes, Ryker?"

Her unsure reply is accompanied by the rise of her ass against my cock, giving away her desire to have me inside her, and I chuckle before grabbing her lobe between my teeth and biting down until she gasps. "Good girl. I want you screaming that by the end."

She whimpers as I stand up, taking my warmth with me, and she shivers in what I hope is anticipation for what it is to come.

"Angel, how hard do I have to hit you to make you scream with this?"

"Uhm…"

Her answer doesn't come fast enough, even though I haven't given her the rules, and I bring the belt down on her ass. She doesn't make a noise, but her feet rise on tiptoe for an instant before hitting the floor once more.

Interesting.

"How hard, Angel?"

"Hard. Really hard."

The reply comes with such speed I laugh. "And where can I hit you with this, sweetheart?"

"Eh-everywhere!"

I bring the belt down once more, the whooshing in the air the only warning as it lands on the underside of her ass and the upper part of her legs. Her only reaction is a small gasp. "Indeed?"

"Yes, Ryker."

Opening the belt to its full length, I step back and analyze for a moment, then lift the belt and swing. The tip of the belt snaps against the heels of her feet and she howls.

"Guess you didn't think to test your theory there," I comment as she lifts her feet, supporting herself with the table as she shakes her feet, then slowly puts them back on the floor. "Don't lift them off it again."

She mutters something, and I repeat my action, making her howl even as she obeys my command not to lift her feet; instead she raises herself up on her tiptoes, going really fast up and down as she tries to soothe the sting.

"What did you say? I didn't hear you."

She sniffles, pausing a moment too long, so I bring the belt down on her ass, although it's much harder this time.

And again.

"I said," she screams, "that only you could find my fucking weak spot you asshole."

"Are you not enjoying this?" I smack her ass once more, slipping a hand between her legs to find her more wet than before. "That's what I thought. And damn right it would be me who finds your weak spot; I know you better than anybody else."

I work her up, slowly hitting harder and harder until color blooms on her back, ass, and legs, her whimpers and groans getting louder and more pronounced. With a second to last lash, I kneel between her legs, a hand on each thigh as I push them apart.

"Open them wide." She moves, but not enough. "More, now. Wider. As wide as you can go."

Licking up her arousal, I work my way up to her pussy, massaging her hot legs with my hands until my face is buried in between them. I shove two fingers inside her, stroking and massaging as I suck her clit into my mouth, working it up into a frenzy. As her muscles tighten, and her orgasm is imminent, I move away fast, standing behind her as she cries out.

"Keep those legs spread."

The swoosh of the belt is only her warning before it catches her between the legs, and her scream is everything I hoped for.

"Oh yes, Ryker! Fuck, fuck!" Her whole body shakes, her legs quivering as her fingers search for something to anchor to as her back bows as she comes hard and strong. "Ohhhhhh!"

Good thing I'm there to catch her when she starts to slip off the table, too weak to hold herself there.

I place her gently on the floor on her stomach, running a palm down her back in an attempt to soothe her, until she murmurs, "Aren't you going to fuck me?" She lifts her ass up in the air a little and wiggles it. "You didn't get me worked up for nothing, did you?"

She gets up on her elbows and tosses me a grin over her shoulder, before stretching out like a cat, her back bowing as her ass rises higher. I take in the welts on her back, ass and legs, gazing at it like a piece of artwork I can't tear my eyes away from because of its beauty, and say, "I wasn't planning on fucking you, no. I'm sure you're sore."

Turning to face me, she gets up on her knees and with a poke on my shoulder, indicates I should lie down. I fall back and she straddles me, fisting my cock before placing it at her entrance. "Here's the thing Ry. The moment I slide down on your cock, I'm going to come again. *That's* what being hit does for me, which is exactly why I enjoy it. So be prepared to roll on top and take over."

I open my mouth to suggest I take my pants off first, but I'm too late. I have just enough time to grab her hips as she sheaths my cock in her with one hard thrust, her head instantly falling back as she screams, her body shaking and her pussy clenching around me.

She doesn't even flinch as I sit up and flip her onto her back, fucking her hard and fast once her legs are wrapped around my waist, and her arms around my neck. I take her mouth in the same way I take her body and as I inch closer and closer to coming, I rip my mouth away from hers, wrapping my hand in her hair and murmuring harshly against her mouth, "Do you want me to come for you?"

"Yes."

"Beg. Make me believe you want it more than anything in the world."

She slides her hands up in my hair, mimicking my hold and I grin against her lips as she pleads, "Please, come for me. I want you to come for me. I *need* it."

"Where, Angel?"

"In my pussy. Please, please." She thrusts up as I thrust in, fusing our mouths together once more, tightening her hold on me as I fill her, and she sobs into my shoulder as she comes one last time. "Oh god!"

Rolling off so as to not crush her, we both lie there trying to catch our breaths, and as I look over at her, I realize one thing:

If I didn't already love her, I would've in this moment when her hand finds mine and she interlaces our fingers, holding me tight.

I also know I'm definitely going to have to tell her because she deserves to know her mother stood up for her, even if it had been too little, too late.

Fuck.

11 - DANITA

"*H*ave you told him yet?"

I sigh into the phone as Vanessa pesters me, pinching the bridge of my nose and counting to ten before I answer, "No. Like I said, it's not that easy."

"Bullshit. You're just afraid."

"And?"

"You're dying anyway. Why do you care if he's mad at you?"

"Vanessa!"

She laughs. "Too soon? When can we joke about your imminent departure anyway?"

"It doesn't bother me, although I'm sure many people would find our attitude about it rather morbid."

"Right, but you know what I say."

"Fuck 'em!"

We say this in unison before snickering, then she sobers and says, "In all seriousness, Dani, you've gotta tell him everything. I know from what you've said it sounds like he still cares for you, but it'll only get harder the more you let it go on."

"I know, I know."

She jabbers on as my mind wanders off.

It's been four days since our interlude in the dining room, and I've barely seen him thanks to his work.

I thought having time to myself would be a good thing, but without him around, I'm lonely. The only people to talk to are the staff, and of course, they praise Ryker up and down. According to them, he's a saint, and he keeps them on simply because they had these jobs before he got here, letting them perform their duties — such as cooking and serving him all the meals — like they had before he got here, even though they all know he could do it all himself.

Most of them are loyal and shy away from my questions about him, directing me to seek my answers from him, and I have to admit I admire them for it. It reassures me they don't blab their bosses business to anyone and everyone, meaning my screams aren't likely to be talked about...well, outside themselves, of course.

I continue to blush like mad every time one of them walks by or stops to speak with me, but every single one of them is kind and I feel foolish being embarrassed, as I'm sure Ryker's proclivities have to be well known since they said he bought the house over eight years ago.

A thought which, quite strangely, makes me jealous and is absolutely absurd since I certainly had my fair share of sex partners during my misguided attempt to deal with my issues by looking for love in all the wrong places.

"…Dani? You're still breathing right?"

Her voice jerks me out of my thoughts. "Yeah, of course."

"I asked if the sex was amazing. Are you paying attention?"

"Sorry, I was daydreaming."

"About the amazing sex?"

"Yes." I laugh as she sighs dreamily. "I might've been his first, but he's sure learned a lot since then. He's…he's just great. I'm so screwed."

"In more ways than one, huh? I'm jealous."

"You've got Frederick!"

She scoffs, and I imagine her flipping her hair as she stares down at her nails with annoyance. "Yeah, I do, but he's so…vanilla. I love him, but he's not adventurous at all."

"Do you tell him what you want straight out?"

"Oh god, no! I joke, hoping he'll take a hint, but he doesn't. He'd be horrified, I think, to find out the things I wanna try."

I stand up and move to look out the window of the living room as I chuckle. "He's not a damn mind reader, Ness. Maybe when you say it jokingly, he thinks you aren't serious and is afraid to agree with you."

"Oh." Her end of the line goes silent, and then she asks, "What do you think I should do then? Just get stuff for what I want and be like 'let's get it on'?"

"Yes. The worst thing he could is reject you, but at least then you know."

"How come I'm older than you, but you seem so much wiser some of the time?"

I don't answer her question because it's rhetorical. We both know why I grew up so fast.

Grimacing as a shot of pain hits me, I tell her, "I'm gonna go take my meds and lie down. I'll talk to you later okay?"

"Sure thing. Take care of yourself, Dani. I'm gonna go shopping — and once you see him later, you tell him everything!"

"Yeah, yeah. Love ya."

"Love ya too."

Walking toward the steps which lead upstairs, I take in my surroundings for what is probably the hundredth time since my arrival.

Ryker's house, if one were to describe it in one word, can only be describe as humongous. I don't want to call it a mansion, but it certainly hovers on the border of being one.

Not for the first time, I wonder about why he purchased it. It's not in the main town where we once lived side by side, but a little bit outside of it. I have yet to go into town. I'm not sure I can, even if I wanted to, which I don't.

The only good memory I have of this place resides in this house with me, and even that will end up damaged by the fact we had a child together and he knows nothing of it.

One of the staff — the housekeeper, Henrietta — is

heading toward me, a smile on her face, when a shot of pain has me gasping. I grab on to the railing of the stairs, but soon I'm doubling over as she runs to see how she can help.

"Miss, what's wrong? Do you need something?"

I shake my head as I use one arm to hold myself up, and the other to cradle my stomach. "Find someone to help me to my room, please?"

"Yes, right away, I'll be right back."

She takes off at a run as I slide down to the floor to wait while the ache spreads through my body and tears stream down my face because I've a feeling things are now going to begin heading downhill…and fast.

Fourteen years and four months ago…

"HE'S LOVELY."

My father's wife, Trisha, sits next to me as I lie in the hospital bed, holding my son in my arms.

Ryker's son.

I'm not in any pain even though I ended up having a C-section, but as I stare down at my son, one thing they told me sticks out and tears slips down my cheeks.

I've been diagnosed with Non-Hodgkin's Lymphoma and have to start treatment immediately, since I refused to begin treatment while pregnant.

I'm only sixteen.

Now I have to deal with cancer…and giving my son to someone else to raise because I simply can't do it.

He's sleeping, but soon I'm sobbing, clutching my son as my stepmother rests a hand on my arm and tries to console me.

But nothing will ever comfort me.

In this moment, I wish I could call Ryker, but my family told me they spoke to his parents, who want nothing to do with the child or me. They refuse to tell Ryker and forbid me from calling him, said I already ruined his life enough.

I don't understand as I cry harder, holding the child I love with the boy I love in my arms.

"Oh sweetie, it'll get easier. You'll get through this, all of this, and you can see him any time. You know I will love him like my own."

I nod as if I agree, but I don't.

Because nobody will ever love my son like I do.

But I remind myself it could be worse; he could be going to someone who would never let me see him.

And I'm pretty sure if that were to happen, I'd just let the cancer kill me anyway, because I already lost one love of my life, I really can't lose the second.

I give my son a last kiss from mommy to son, whisper 'I love you, Sterling' — a name she has promised to keep as his first one — then hand him to Trisha before rolling over and crying myself to sleep.

12 - RYKER

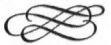

"*Y*ou'll never guess who showed up on my doorstep the other day."

My mom tosses me a smile over her shoulder as she opens the fridge door and pulls out a soda, then closes it and turns back to me. "Probably not since you know so many people, so just tell me."

I stopped by on the way home from work as I do every day.

Something I've done since my father passed away four years ago.

I would've told her days ago but I wanted to make sure Angel was sticking around before I opened my mouth.

"You remember the girl who used to live next door?" I nod out at the window at the now empty lot where Angel's house used to be before I had it torn down six years previously. "The one I was crazy about?"

She frowns as she takes a sip, then chuckles. "The pretty

91

little white haired girl who used to sneak in your window in the middle of the night?"

"Yeah, that's her. Did you know the whole time?"

"Of course I did." She waves a hand dismissively. "Your father and I trusted you, and we knew it was pretty innocent."

"It started that way."

Making a face, she shakes her head. "I don't want to know. All I know is one day she was here, the next she was gone, and you were pretty damned depressed about it. What happened to her?"

I debated on how much I should tell her, especially with the new knowledge about her awareness of my teenaged activities, then decided to tell her it all from start to finish. By the end her eyes are filled with tears and she has her arms wrapped around me in a hug, while I awkwardly pat her back. "Mom, it's okay. I'm not sure I'm the person in this story who needs a hug."

"You're my son, I'll hug you any time I want." She pulls away. "And I say good fucking riddance to that scumbag. That poor girl."

"Agreed."

We're silent for a few moments before she adds, "How come you never heard from her again? Seems she would've called you. Called us. We never moved or anything."

I shrug. "I don't know. She had her name changed and stuff. I think her father just wanted to protect her after all that. I can't really blame him, or her, since she was a minor and a victim."

"Has she told you anything?"

"No." I run a hand through my hair in frustration. "I get the feeling she's afraid of my reaction. As if she's afraid to tell me what happened, or what she's gone through, or where she's been."

She nods, staring out the window with a thoughtful look, then moves her eyes back to smile at me. "Now I understand why you bought that house and tore it down. Perhaps showing her what you did will get her to talk."

"Maybe."

I've thought about her every moment since she arrived, and although I've been busy the last four days, it's a fucking joy to go home and find her sleeping in my bed. I strip and lie next to her, then bring her close as possible, and in the morning, I leave her sleeping just the way I found her. And my worries are growing.

"I think she's sick, Mom. Something's wrong with her and she won't tell me. So I hope you're right."

"She doesn't sound like a girl who has ever been able to trust many people, and you two were just kids, Sterling." I smile as she calls me by my middle name, something she did once my father had been released from prison when I was four and hadn't been amused at her choice of name for me. "Doesn't really seem like she wanted to end up on your doorstep either."

I know she's right and I fucking hate it.

Angel is staying with me because I didn't really give her any other options.

I'm glad I did, and I won't change my mind, but I made shit ten times harder for myself.

I open my mouth to reply when my phone rings, the caller ID telling me it's from my staff. And since they never call me, I'm on my feet and shrugging on my jacket as I answer.

"What's up?"

"Oh sir, she collapsed at the bottom of the steps," my housekeeper bawls into the phone. "She said no hospital, but she can't move, and when we tried to take her upstairs, she started screaming in pain—"

"Call an ambulance and ignore her protests," I order her, cutting in. "Tell them I'll meet them at the hospital since she's under my care. Give them the paper she signed in my office, top drawer."

"Yes, sir."

I hang up and my mother's eyes are wide. "I'm coming with you."

I don't argue, glad to finally have someone in the know and on my side, and in seconds we're speeding toward the hospital.

I COULD KILL HER RIGHT NOW.

I stare down with disbelief at the papers the doctor handed me as he looked at me with sad eyes, saying how sorry he was when I showed him the paper that gave me power of attorney over everything including her medical care.

A paper I made her sign the morning after the night she agreed to stay. She hadn't been happy about it, but I told her it was just in case of an emergency since she had no one else and lived in my home.

I know she hadn't thought I'd use it otherwise.

And I'm sitting here fucking wishing I hadn't and glad I have at the same time.

I skim the documents as the ugly words scream at me from the page.

Non-Hodgkin's Lymphoma. Non-responsive to treatment. Aggressive. Four to six months.

Four to six months to live?

And nearly a month since she found out.

She's dying and she hasn't told me.

She's *dying*.

What the fuck?

"Excuse me," I say to my mother who sits next to me with a sad look in her eyes since I read the words out loud, her mouth in a grim line. "I need some fucking fresh air. And to punch something. I...I'll be back."

I rush outside as my chest aches, the first roar of pain ripping out of me as I head away from the doors.

I know I should go in to her but I can't.

I don't want to look at her and know soon she won't look so healthy.

She'll waste away in front of my eyes when I finally have her back in my fucking life and I'll lose her.

All fucking over again.

How dare the fucking world *do* this to me?

To us?

Haven't she and I suffered enough?

I pick up pace, and soon I'm running across the parking lot straight toward the trees, and once I'm among them I pick up a solid stick. Hitting everything and anything I can, I'm sure anyone looking on would think I'm a fucking madman, but I can't contain my anger.

My hurt.

My stupid desire to scream how fair this isn't.

As if life has ever fucking been fair.

My stick finally breaks. "Shit. Shit. Goddammit. Fuck, fuck, fuck!" I pick up another as I continue my useless abuse of the tree trunks.

I don't know how long I do this, but it's the soft voice from behind me saying my name that has me dropping to my knees and putting my head into my hands as I break down for the first time since Angel's mother killed that bastard.

My mother places a hand on my shoulder and says, "They said you can go in and see her now."

Then, nothing else, because in the end, there's nothing more she or anyone can say.

And once I've composed myself, we head inside.

I'M SITTING IN THE CHAIR NEXT TO HER BED WHEN SHE finally wakes up.

I have her hand gripped in mine, and she flinches as she turns her head, her eyes meeting mine.

She opens her mouth, then closes it. I expect her to say something, but it's not what ends up coming out of her mouth. "Sorry."

"Angel…I—"

She shakes her head, pulling her hand from mine, and turning her face away to stare at the windows. "Don't. I never wanted anyone to see me this way. Or how I'll be in a very short time."

My reply is swift as I swallow, tamping down my grief and heartache, as I snatch her hand once more. "You need taken care of. I'll take care of you until the very end. But, are you sure there's nothing that can—"

"Stop it!" Her head whips back toward me, eyes glaring as she spits out the words. "Don't you think I've done everything I can? This is the *third* time. Nothing, *nothing*, can be done this time, so just stop!"

"Third time?" I know my voice is incredulous because I don't remember reading that in her medical files. "When…?"

"Second time was when I was twenty, first…" Her voice breaks, tears sliding from her eyes as she whispers, "First was at sixteen."

My mouth drops open, but before I can form a coherent reply, Angel's face whitens, her eyes going wide for a moment before she barks at someone behind me, "Get out! Get out now!"

Whipping my head around, I see my mother standing

there frozen with confusion on her face, while Angel's screams escalate.

I stand up, blocking her view and forcing her gaze to mine with one hand, her body trembling as I hold her down with the other. "Hey!" I cut in through her screaming with a loud bark, and she quits with a whimper. "Why in the fucking world are you screaming at my mother? She came here with me."

"Make her leave." Her voice is small, her eyes filled with pain and considering how high her pain meds are right now, I gather it must be emotional. "I don't want her here."

"Danita…" My mother doesn't get to finish what she was going to say as Angel cuts in.

"No." She pushes her hands against my shoulders and I move out of her way with a sigh, as she goes back to glaring at my mother. "You don't get to talk to me. I want nothing to do with you. I didn't even want to see him. I just want to die in fucking peace!"

"I don't understand…"

Angel doesn't say another word, crossing her arms over her chest and looking away from both my mother and I, as I stand here completely fucking confused.

"I will go then." My mother walks over to me and hugs me. "Don't worry about me, I'll take a cab, Sterling—"

Angel's sudden wail has me jumping away from my mother and rushing over to the bed where she is curled into a ball, hands covering her ears as she sobs and bawls as if she's dying. When I try to pull her hands away, she sobs harder, and I draw her into my arms.

"It's all their fault," she cries into my chest. "I loved you. I wanted to talk to you, but they told my parents that I needed to leave you alone, that I ruined your life."

Snapping my head up, I find my mother looking dumbfounded as she shakes her head, and Angel's pleas growing louder. "Please. Please make her leave. I can't...I can't breathe...hurts so badly..."

"We'll talk later," I say to my mom and she nods before walking out, then I turn my attention to Angel. "Talk to me. You're making everything harder than it has to be. How can I be mad at you for anything?"

She continues sobbing into my chest while I stroke her hair, but even after the tears subside, she doesn't say anything else.

And once she falls asleep, I place her back into the bed, sitting by her side through the evening as I wonder what the hell just happened.

*H*is hovering is annoying me.

It's been three days since I left the hospital, which kept me for two in order to do some tests to see if and where the cancer has spread, and now I am back at Ryker's.

Ryker, who has decided to work from home as much as possible, doesn't seem to ever leave my side now and it's pissing me off. If I'm in my room, he's sitting in the chair. If I'm in the living room, he's sitting nearby in a chair or by me on the couch. And on and on.

It's enough to make me want to choke him.

"Can't I get some time alone?"

He looks up from his laptop and cocks his head a bit as he stares at me before shaking it. "I'm not leaving you alone if I don't have to."

"Well, you do have to." I stand up with a huff and cross my arms over my chest while contemplating my chances of outrunning him and locking him out of my room before he can catch me. "I don't want to always be around you, or anybody. I need time to myself."

"For what? From what I was told, you mostly sit around here and mope anyway."

"What I do with my free time is my business. And what I want for my free time is to be left alone."

"Too bad. You can't always get what you want. I know I sure I don't."

I throw my hands up in the air, even as I ask the question I shouldn't because I already know the answer. "What do you want from me? I don't have anything to give you."

He purses his lips, removing his computer from his lap and placing it on the table, then stands up and walks over to me. Leaning in, all I can smell is his combinations of scents that make me wet with wanting him in an instant as he whispers, "I want you. All of you." He moves the hair that falls into my face behind my ear before wrapping an arm around my waist and hauling me against his body, where I feel all of him, including his strong heartbeat beneath the palm of my hand which is now on his chest. "I want to know why you reacted that way to seeing my mother, I want to know about all the scars on your body, and mostly, I want to know that you will spend what little time you have left with me."

Part of me wants those things, too. Too bad life is way more complicated than that. "Why aren't you angrier at me?"

"What good would being angry at you do for either of us? I wish you would've told me, but you didn't." He frowns down at me and I feel guiltier than ever before. "I don't know what I did to make you trust me so little."

I drop my gaze. "Nothing. You did nothing. I simply don't trust anyone except a few people, and they earned it."

No response from him; instead a heavy sigh as his arm tightens around my waist, the hand on my face moving into my hair. I wait for the delicious pull, the sting that will change his embrace from one of coaxing to one of domination, but it's as if his willingness to use force has been wiped away by learning I have cancer.

And I hate it since fulfillment of my desire for being hit is the only thing I really control anymore.

I want it, and I need it, and we haven't had sex in over a week now.

Apparently, it's up to me to make it happen.

"Don't treat me like priceless china," I snarl, shaping my hands into fists before hitting his shoulders with them. "This is why I didn't tell you. Pull my hair, slap me, do what I *need* you to do!"

His clasp in both area tenses, but he doesn't do as I ask. I can't do much from my position except pound on him with my fists as he stares down at me with compassion, which only makes me angrier. So, before he can react, I slide my arms around his neck, stand up tip toe, and use my teeth to bite him on a very sensitive spot of his neck. Hard.

I land on my ass on the floor as his natural reaction is to push me away and grab his neck where two little pearls of blood rise up. His eyes widen as I scramble up off the ground and back away.

"What the fuck, Angel?"

"Don't be nice to me!" I scream as I stomp my foot like a frustrated child. "I don't deserve it. And if you can't do what I want, I'll leave! You're the one breaking the rules, not me."

"You know what will happen if you leave."

"Your threat means nothing. I stayed because I wanted to before, not because I was truly afraid of you turning me in. I'll be dead by the time anything happens anyway. So do it. Fucking do it because if you don't give me what I want, I'm leaving."

I whirl and head to exit the room, but before I can leave, he's spinning me back around and pushing me flat against the door.

"Why," he says in a rough, low voice as his hand comes to rest around my throat, "do you insist on making everything so fucking difficult? Tell me why you don't deserve my kindness, if it's that fucking important to you that you don't receive it." He squeezes a little and I whimper with excitement. "Tell me all your fucking secrets and maybe, maybe, you'll get the treatment you want so badly without me giving it a second thought." He drops his hand and takes a step back. "Until then, feel free to leave. I won't fight for someone who doesn't want to be fought for."

He walks back across the room as my mouth drops open at what he said, where he picks up his computer and heads back toward me, and I step aside as he opens the door. Then before passing through, he turns to look at me, his mouth in a flat line. I open my mouth and he shakes his head and says, "Just remember, sweetheart. I'm not the one who walked away then, and I won't be the one who walks away now if you leave. This time though, the only person you'll have to blame is yourself."

I can't even speak as he walks through the door and leaves me standing there without a backward glance.

IT'S TWO DAYS LATER AND I HAVEN'T LEFT.

But I haven't seen Ryker either.

Antagonizing him had been childish, especially biting him, but I liked seeing him lose his cool for a few seconds.

Anger or annoyance is way better than the compassion and empathy. It's better than him treating me like I'll break any second and making me feel as if I'm nothing more than the cancer spreading through my body, instead of a human being with needs.

Desperate needs not being fulfilled because of my inability to tell him what he wants to know.

I'm to the point I either give in, or I find someone else to give it to me.

Problem is, I don't want to walk away. The first time, I felt I had no choice, and this time, I know I'm simply being too fucking stubborn.

After all, who do I have left that really cares?

Nobody, really, except for a few friends like Vanessa.

My father and his wife are dead.

My mother, dead.

Ryker is here for me, wants to continue being here for me, and what am I doing when I should be trying to enjoy what little time I have left?

Being a bitch because…well, I could count the ways but I won't bother.

Truth is, I'm afraid.

What happens when I tell him about our son, the child I gave birth to just over fourteen years ago, and who now lives with my sister?

Will Ryker forgive me for never finding him to tell him once he became an adult, or will he understand I was so messed up it had been the furthest thing from my mind once my father and Trisha took our son in?

They never adopted him.

I couldn't deny I knew the father, and it was illegal to give the child up without the father's consent.

My son knows I'm his mother, but he's always lived with my family — first, my father and Trisha, then my sister. I refused in the past to take him away even once I went into remission, fearing the worst, which came true at age twenty, and now…again.

He deserves stability and he comes first, no matter how much it hurts to have him living a separate life from me, even if he's always understood. Loving him means doing what is best, even if it's painful.

I just hope his father is as understanding.

Making my decision, I stand up from the desk where

I'm sitting and head to where I know Ryker is right now — his office.

As I approach the door and open it, his attention to me is instantaneous. "If you want to talk to me because you've decided you're staying, and you've got a few things to say to me, I'd prefer you come toward me on your knees."

I don't necessarily want to be stubborn right now, but 'on my knees,' really? I smile because I know he expects me to not do it, lowering myself to the floor after closing the door, then my eyes connect with his as I crawl toward where he sits in the chair. When I reach him, I pause, sitting up straight on my knees and back on my heels, hands folded in my lap.

I like games.

I don't like the fact I don't know how this evening will end.

"I will start from the beginning," I say in a low voice, swallowing as I close my eyes to avoid his intense stare. "But you can't interrupt me, no matter how angry you are."

I open my eyes when he says nothing to see him nod, one hand curled around his drink, the other resting in his lap. He is a bit disheveled with his tie loosened, his shirt's two top buttons undone, and his belt unbuckled. I want to touch him, but I keep my hands in my lap as I look down and speak up.

"The night I left, I found out I was pregnant." I hear him suck in a breath, but he stays silent as I requested. "For three months I hadn't had a period, but I was in denial until I took that test. I knew I had to leave though. I couldn't even risk staying another day because I knew I'd be showing sooner rather than later. I wanted to tell you, and I planned on it, but I got to my father's house and they took me in. With everything going on, they said I shouldn't trust anyone; that I should change my name to protect myself, and they received custody of me. They wouldn't let me call you, and they kept an eye on me *all* the time, until I was about six months and they told me I should just wait until the baby is born just to be safe. I…"

Tears spill down my cheeks as I pause for a moment and take a breath. "I didn't want to not tell you. But they said I wouldn't be able to take care of a baby, and once we found out I had cancer, they persuaded me to let them take our son, because they said they called your parents and they told me not to call them again, and to leave you alone. I was only sixteen, I was sick, and I believed them."

"Our…son?"

I can hear him choking up, but I can't bear to look at him as I nod my head and continue. "I got treatment, went into remission, and sort of just…went wild for a while. I dated, and had sex, and did everything you're not supposed to do because I figured it was just a matter of time before something else went wrong. I was miserable, but I hurt so badly on the inside I didn't care. I wanted to feel loved, and no matter how hard I tried, nobody could love me like you did when I needed you to."

I feel his hand on my hair, but I still can't look up. "Then, at twenty, the cancer came back and it was like being punched in the face in the middle of a fight. You knew it would probably happen, but you didn't *expect* it to. I hated myself even more because I felt like I brought it on myself. So, I received treatment again, and after that, put my life back together. I finished high school, I went to college, I got a good job…I did everything right, but in the end, it didn't matter. I thought as the years passed by, the chances were less and less. All this time…for nothing, because I'm going to die anyway."

Lowering my head into my hands, I let the sobs take over, and within seconds, Ryker hauls me on to his lap and into his arms. Cradling my head against his chest, he strokes my hair in an attempt to console me as my body shakes and trembles with the force of the emotions I can no longer keep inside.

*S*he had a baby.
        Our baby.

A son.

I have — had? — a son!

As I sit here holding her in my arms while she cries, I try to wrap my head around that fact.

And I'm angry, but not at Angel.

At her father and stepmother for not letting her tell me from the very beginning.

And my mother?

Did she know all this time?

She said she had no idea why Angel yelled at her in the hospital when I visited her yesterday, but now I can't be sure she hadn't lied to me, and that pisses me off.

I'm not sure what to say, so I don't say anything, not even as her sobs turn into hiccups and sniffles.

I want to ask about our son. I want to know if he's still

alive or if something happened. He'd be…what, fourteen now?

Fuck. I had a child at age eighteen and I hadn't known.

But most of all, I hurt for Angel.

Because she had one rough thing happen to her after another, and I hadn't been there for her, even though I would've been had I known.

I hug her tighter, and her palms slide up my chest until she's wrapping her arms around my neck, placing her head on my shoulders into the crook of it, and I move enough to kiss her cheek.

Then I ask the one question I want to know more than anything as I slip a hand up into her hair at the nape of her neck, whispering, "What's his name? Is he…?"

"Y-yes, he's fourteen now." Her voice is so tiny, so fragile and I can tell she's forcing the words past her lips, her breath against my neck. "His name…is…is…Sterling."

Aw, hell. "You named him after me."

"He was all I had left of you."

"Where is he now? Why isn't he with you?"

She tightens her arms around my neck, shaking her head a little as she sighs. "My father and Trisha had guardianship of him, until they died a few years ago. Now my sister has him." Her voice cracks as she admits, "I've never had him with me. I had all those issues, I wanted him to have stability, and even once things got better, I didn't want to uproot his life."

I can't imagine the world of hurt she's in right now and always has been, if she considered our child the only piece of me she had left, and she hasn't ever truly had him with her. I've just discovered I'm a father, and while I'm upset I didn't fucking know, I don't think it compares to being separated due to circumstances and trying to do the right thing.

"You did what you thought was right," I tell her with a kiss to her temple. "That's all that matters."

"How can you be so calm?"

"I'm not, but I don't have any trees to hit right now."

"Huh?"

Keeping my hold on her hair gentle yet firm, I drag her head away from my shoulder and cover her lips with mine. Her mouth opens under mine in an instant, and as much as I want to yank her head back and shove my tongue down her throat for her behavior, I don't. I can't.

I know she wants me to act like I did before I found out, but at this point, that won't happen.

She whimpers her need, sliding her hands up into my hair and tugging on it to try and encourage my own reaction, which only makes me pull away and smile against her lips, my words a brush against hers, "We have a son. I…I never would've imagined."

"Yes." She's panting, rubbing what she can of her body against mine in a blatant attempt to gain my touch, as she presses kisses along my jaw.

"Angel." I bend her head back until she can't touch me with her lips, then ask, "Does he look more like you or me?"

"You."

Her eyes are shut, her neck bared, and in this moment, she's the most beautiful I've ever seen her.

And I can't bear to lose her again.

I won't say anything right now, but soon I will convince her she needs to try one more time to save her life. If not for herself, then for me and our son, to give us all a chance to be the family we didn't get to have all these years.

Her lips move as I stare at them, and I move my focus from my thoughts to her words. "...Kids?"

"I'm sorry. What?"

Her mouth curves up as her eyelids flutter open, her gorgeous blue eyes shining at me with amusement. "I said, it's been a long time. Did you ever get married or have kids?"

"Oh." As my grip lessens, she moves her face closer to mine until our breaths mingle and I'm hoping she'll come even closer as I respond, "I was married once, but we divorced over two years ago. No kids. She couldn't have children."

"I'm sorry."

"I'm not," I rejoin with a grimace. "We were married eight years and the last three of those were miserable because it was all she wanted, and she blamed me. When I finally persuaded her to get some testing, she threw a fit at the results."

"You were married awful young."

"I loved her," I said, gazing into her eyes even as I frown, "and didn't want to risk losing any time with her."

Not like with you, I want to say, but I resist the urge to do so, especially since we'd just been teenagers.

"So what happened?"

I don't want to talk about this, but since she was open with me, the same is necessary in return. Moving as close to her as possible until our lips brush light against one another, I say, "She ended up cheating on me with…" My lips quirk up as Angel puckers hers against mine quickly as I finish with, "the pool boy."

She busts into laughter before sobering. "How cliche! I'm sorry, I shouldn't have laughed."

"Nah." Shaking my head, I chuckle. "It was cliche, you're right. And I'm over it."

We quit talking, her perched on my lap as I give in to the urge to kiss her, showing her my love without saying it because I know she isn't ready to hear it yet.

Then, I pull away after a few minutes and ask, "Are you up for going out? I want to show you something."

At her nod, I remove her from my lap and stand up, then take her hand and lead the way out of the house.

I BLINDFOLD HER BEFORE WE GET IN THE CAR, AND WHEN we're almost there, she reaches over and grabs my hand tight.

"Don't be nervous." I squeeze her hand with mine, lifting to kiss the back of it, letting her feel my grin against it as well. "You'll love it. I'm sure of that."

"Okay."

Her voice is small, so painful in its intensity I decide to distract her. "Will I get to meet our son?"

She stiffens, turning her head toward me even though she can't see, and gives me a sad smile. "If you want. I'm sure he would love that."

"I see." I don't like the way she worded that, as if she wouldn't love it, but I file it away for later to ask for sure. "I would love it, too."

She says nothing, and I turn the corner while announcing, "We're here!"

Parking the car, I exit my side and head over to hers, helping her out before slamming the door. Grasping her elbow, I walk her toward our location, leaves crunching beneath our feet as she laughs.

"What's with all the mystery?"

"Well," I begin, stopping in front of the entryway before moving behind her, and placing my hands on her shoulders, "you can take the blindfold off and find out for yourself if you want."

She does, the mask falling to the ground as her hands cover her gasp of surprise before she whirls around, tossing her arms around my neck. I encircle her waist with one arm, while the other cradles her head against my shoulder. She pulls back and turns her head to the cottage, her mouth wide as she grins. "You fixed it up!"

"I did more than that," I say as she turns her eyes, glistening with tears, back to mine. "I bought this land to prevent it from being torn down."

"Why?"

"Because if I ever found you, I wanted to give it to you. You deserve to do what you want with it."

She's staring up at me as if she doesn't comprehend. Then her eyes widen and she pushes on my shoulders. When I remove my hold, she takes off at a run toward her old house and I chase after her.

When I catch up, she's standing on the edge of the creek, staring at the land where the house used to sit, now filled with nothing but green grass. Placing my hands on her shoulders, I say nothing because I know she will when she's ready.

"I'm so glad I don't have to look at it," she whispers after a few minutes, shoulders slumping. "When did you…?"

"Almost two years ago." I turn her around and gaze down into her upturned face. "I saw it every time I came to visit my mother, and I couldn't handle it. It was a reminder of you…and the way I failed to protect you by keeping my promise to you about not saying anything."

"You didn't fail me." Her words are vehement, her eyes filled with unshed tears as she beams up at me. "You…you kept me going even when I wanted to give up." She glances around for a moment before returning her eyes to mine. "And, in the end, that bastard got what he deserved."

"I know," I admit with a grin. "I was there."

"Wh-what do you mean?"

"I thought you were home because I heard a commotion from your house a week after you left, but when

I entered, your stepfather had your mother against the wall and was choking her." Her eyes widen, but she doesn't move, barely breathing as she waits for me to go on. "He… he said some nasty shit to me after I told him it was me who told your mother about what he did to you, and I punched him. We were fighting when your mom came back in the room with the gun, and he tried to convince her it wasn't what she thought. But then she shot him twice when he tried to take a step toward her."

I expect her to look horrified, or sick, or something.

But she doesn't. She stares at me for what seems like forever which makes me ramble on as I glance away.

"Your mother, she stood up for you. I know it was too little, too late, but she didn't know. She told me you were okay but she couldn't say anything else, and she made me leave before the cops showed up. They never doubted her self-defense story, especially after she told them what she learned, and—"

"Ryker," she cuts in, and when I look back at her, she's grinning. "You punched him? Really?"

"I did. A few times. And I enjoyed every fucking second of it."

She jumps into my arms, throwing her arms around my neck, her lips seeking and finding mine before I can even blink.

Not that I'm complaining.

Wrapping one arm around her waist while using the other to cradle her head, I groan into her mouth as she opens up to the thrust of my tongue, making me wish we were at my house in my bed. But we're not, and at the cat call of someone passing by, I rip my mouth away and gaze down at her.

"I know you don't want to, but we should go speak to my mother while we're here."

She tosses a look at my mother's house, worrying her lip between her teeth in a show of anxiety, then brings her eyes back to me. "Are you asking, or telling?"

"Suggesting."

"I don't know." She sighs, the emotions on her face going from fear, to torture, to desiring the truth in whatever form she can find it in, and finally, she shakes her head. "No. I can't right now."

"Angel—"

Dragging herself from my arms, she crosses them over her chest, and walks around me, back toward where we came from. "I'm tired. Will you take me back to your place, please?"

From the corner of my eye, I see my mother standing in her window, and I wave back with a nod when she waves at me. Then, I follow Angel back to the car to head back home, where I will make sure she's napping before I make a few phone calls to try and find help for her.

15 - DANITA

*R*ising from my nap, I take some pain meds before hopping into the tub — well, okay, it's a jacuzzi.

And honestly, I love it.

It's strange going from my life where I couch surfed to having one place to stay. I did live with Ness on and off, but you can only impose on your friends so much before you feel like a burden.

Which is why I never liked staying in one place for long.

Even my old job used to involve traveling because I didn't want to call one place home.

Home meant roots. It meant building a life, and I always felt if I never built a life, it couldn't be taken from me. My job had provided stability in the financial department, but it hadn't afforded me the luxuries I found here at Ryker's.

As I sit in the hot water and it bubbles around me, I am amused by the size as usual.

There is enough room in here to fit three to four people, of Ryker's size *with* their legs stretched out, and not for the first time, I wonder why anyone would need a jacuzzi this big.

Laying my head back against the edge, I close my eyes after putting in my headphones, and play the music on shuffle.

Ryker had surprised me with the cottage, along with him getting rid of my mother's house, and I hadn't known how to respond. Then, when he'd told me about how he'd punched my stepfather, I couldn't resist kissing or hugging him.

I'm glad I didn't have to see it. I'm not sure I would've reacted in any good way and have been avoiding going to town because of it.

And I know he wanted to go talk to his mother, see if they actually had received a phone call from my father and stepmother, but I'm afraid I already know the answer. I just don't want to face her because of the most important detail of all — if she never got that phone call, then nobody knew about the baby at all back then, except my family.

So, if that's the case, then they lied to me, but I don't understand why.

They knew how much I loved Ryker, and with all I went through, they should've realized how much he meant to me. I think things would've been much easier on me if Ryker had been there for me, as I know he would've been.

I do regret not telling him before I left, and I have every single day since, but I made my choices even if they weren't the right ones in the end.

And as long as he's not mad at me, then I can live with myself.

After all, I've not got much longer to do so anyway.

But, what hurts the most, is knowing he will want me to keep fighting…and I'm just not sure I can anymore.

I've made peace with it so I can live without crying every day, wondering why happiness seems so elusive for me, and why it seems things get better for a while only to get worse again.

I don't want to die…but why should I fight my fate when I've got such little time to enjoy what's supposedly left of my life?

And that's what I wish he would realize.

What I wish everyone would realize, like Ness, who makes me laugh every time we talk and jokes about it with me.

With a sigh, I get to washing off so I'm not late for dinner.

"YOU ARE SO BEAUTIFUL."

I know my cheeks go pink at his compliment, even though I should expect it by now, as I pick up my water and sip it. "Thank you."

He grins at me, then lowers his gaze and continues

eating. Pushing the food around my plate as usual, while occasionally taking a bite, I examine him, and can't help but think of our son.

Sterling is a 'spitting-image' of his father in every way. The same eye color, the near identical height, and the hair, although fourteen-year-old Sterling reminds me more of sixteen-year-old Ryker in build than the nicely muscled thirty-two year old at the table.

And although it's only been a few weeks since I've seen him, I miss him.

Even though we both have each other's number, we don't speak on the phone often, preferring to save conversation for when we're together in person.

I'm due to see him in a few days, and know Ryker will want to go with me, which means one thing.

I pull out my phone as Ryker finishes eating, who scowls at my barely touched food per usual, and lifts a brow as I smile at him. "Would you like to see a picture of…of our son?"

I hate the hesitation in my voice, but I'm nervous. However, he hides his surprise swiftly and nods, holding out his hand. When I scroll to the picture and go to place the phone in his hand, he shakes his head.

"No." He brings up his other hand and covers mine. "Come sit on my lap and show me."

Tugging, he scoots back his chair, forcing me to stand up and move along with him, then tugs me down into his lap. Now I'm sitting sideways on his lap, my legs dangling over the arm, and he rests one arm over them so I can't move or readjust my position.

"Now you can share the pictures," he murmurs into my ear, before lowering his mouth to kiss my exposed shoulder, which turns me on and makes it hard to focus.

After all, it's been over a week since we've had sex and I'm nearly bursting with the need for it.

Figuring that giving him what he wants might get me what I want, I lift my hands from my lap where they are resting with the phone, and press the button to wake it.

Holding it up, he removes his lips from their path of kisses along my jaw and neck, using the hand that locked down my legs to grab the hand cradling the phone and stares at it.

"Wow." His exclamation is soft and filled with wonder. "It's almost as if I'm looking at pictures of me from high school."

I laugh, using my thumb to scroll to the next picture, then another with his encouraging squeeze as I say, "That's my thought too. He looks just like you did…"

Moving his hand away from mine, I expect him to lower it, but instead he brings it up to cup my face and turn my head until our lips barely touch.

"Not quite. He has my coloring, but he's got your eye shape, and lips. And your nose," He notes with a chuckle. "He hit the gene jackpot between the both of us."

Then before I can respond, the phone drops into my lap, forgotten as his mouth crushes mine. His hand slides back into my hair at the nape of my neck, his tongue seeking and gaining entrance with no effort as I open up for him because his touch is all I want. When I moan with the pleasure of it all, though, he pulls back and loosens his grip.

"Are you all right? I don't want to cause you more pain, so—"

Placing my hand over his mouth, his eyes flare as I growl in frustration. "If I'm in pain, you'll know. Stop treating me like something precious, and fucking fuck me already. It's been too long."

When I remove my hand, he grins. "I thought you didn't like having sex in the dining room."

"At this point," I say while wrapping my arms around his neck, getting as close as I can in this position, "I will take whatever I can get from you."

His eyes darken, his abrupt gathering of me in his arms making me squeal and snatch my phone as he stands up, then walks us out of the room and up the stairs. Placing me on the bed with extreme gentleness, I lie back as he covers my body with his, taking one hand out of my line of sight and pulling my shorts and panties down.

"In a hurry?" I ask with a giggle, pulling my shirt over my head while he finishes removing my bottoms, then takes off his own shirt.

After unbuttoning the fly of his pants, I yank them down as much as I can from my position as he remarks, "Aren't you?"

He moves off me briefly, shoving his pants the rest of the way off, then spreads my legs and after using two fingers to make sure I'm wet enough — which, I always am, and foreplay is usually *not* necessary — places his cock at the entrance to my pussy and shoves inside with one smooth thrust while on his knees.

Wrapping my legs around him, he captures my mouth, our moans of pleasure mingling while he puts almost all his weight on me. Grabbing one hand, he intertwines our fingers and locks it against the pillow above my head, then does the same with the other. Then, our mouths are mingling once more, his tongue exploring my mouth as he rocks into me, and he's all I feel around me.

His weight is so nice; I've missed it.

My hands are pinned to the bed, his grip tightening as he withdrawals to the edge, then slams back into me. My gasp in reaction to the pleasure shooting through me is lost between our locked lips, and he chuckles as he does it again. And again.

We don't part. He takes and takes from my mouth as he gives and gives with his cock, not pausing, not stopping, until I can't think, tingles of pleasure shooting through me as my body tightens up to prepare for orgasm.

Normally I would panic, but his pace makes it hard to breathe, let alone think and one more thrust has me whimpering as I come; unable to cry out, unable to stop it, unable to do anything but feel.

And when he follows me moments later, making sure to roll off as to not crush me, I turn on my side and lay against him, listening to the crazy beat of his heart as tears of happiness and sorrow mingle, trickling down my cheeks.

Because in this moment, I feel more than I have any

other moment in my life, and the imminent terrifying threat of death — the one I thought I've come to accept — has wrapped itself around my heart once more, reminding me that soon, things like this will no longer be.

That it's my heart that will stop beating.

That *I'll* no longer be.

And the thought of making Ryker — or my son or my sister or Ness or anyone else — grieve my death has Ryker turning and taking me into his arms and comforting me, cradling me in his arms as I burst into tears.

I hate being unable to focus.

I sigh in my head as this fucking moron on the other end blows up at me for something me nor my businesses have anything to do with. But there is no point in telling him that until his rant is over, so I pay enough attention to hear him, but not listen to a damn word he says.

Usually my secretary would deal with this, but she went to lunch and I always field my own calls during that time. Sometimes it's great; other times, like right now, I know why I have a secretary and make a note to give her a raise. Again. She's worth every cent.

Instead, I think about last night, and Angel.

I don't know why she started crying after we had sex, but even when I asked while holding her, she wouldn't answer me.

She's really good at not telling me things.

Which leaves me unsure of what to say or do, so I end up saying nothing even though I really want to know what the hell is going on. And what really pisses me off is that, for some reason, she doesn't seem to trust me.

Not now, and not even in the past, truly.

Not enough to tell me she was pregnant with our child, or that she was leaving, and while I'm not angry at her for that — matter of fact, I'm really proud of her for getting away from that bastard in any way she could even if it left me in the dark — I'm absolutely fucking pissed her family lied to her all those years ago.

My mother, who I went ahead and spoke with about it earlier this morning, has absolutely no idea about what Angel said and was devastated to learn she had a grandchild she knew nothing about. She swore up and down that neither her nor my father were ever contacted by Angel's father or stepmother, and I believe her.

Not that it solves anything. There's nothing any of us can do about it now, but I'm absolutely determined to get to know my son.

My son.

Simply thinking those words is fucking amazing.

The man finally finishes his rant, so I finish up the call with him, then dial a doctor friend of mine — my last option after my failed attempts yesterday while Angel napped to find some information to help her.

"Ryker!" Percy — yes, that's his name, poor guy! — answers with his usual annoying cheer. "How goes it? Haven't heard from you in a few weeks."

"Eh, it's fifty-fifty, Prissy. How's the missus?"

He chuckles at my use of his college nickname. "She's fine. Nesting. All excited for the baby. You would think it was her first, not her fifth."

"Fuck, it's gonna be your fifth? You do know what causes pregnancy, don't you?"

"Har har, funny. You callin' me for a reason, or you just wanting to be a dick today?"

"I'm a dick every time I call. That's why you love me."

"Yeah, yeah."

I wave at my secretary as she opens my door to let me know she's back, and she exits with a nod as I fill in Percy on the situation from start to finish. By the time I'm finished, he's tapping away on his keyboard, searching for what I hope will save Angel's life.

"Well," he says with his super serious doctor tone, "I would probably be able to get her into a clinical trial near you. It involves thirty-six weeks, where she would be given two medications that have never been used simultaneously, together. She's a little under the expected survival requirement, but I may be able to convince them to overlook it due to the direness of her situation. She'll have to consent, which sounds like that might be an issue, but you've always been rather charming so I'm sure you'll persuade her one way or another."

We both chuckle at that, after which he asks, "Do you have her information so I can give them the details requested?"

"Yeah, hold on." Breathing my first sigh of relief since

finding out, I open up my desk drawer and pull out the files her doctor gave me. "What do you need to know?"

I give him everything he needs and once that's done, Percy prods for more info on Angel. "So, this is the girl you went on and on about for the first two years of college?"

"Yeah, it's crazy." I take a deep breath. "You'll never believe what I found out a few days ago."

"Nothing that involves you ever really shocks me."

"Well…I've recently discovered I have a fourteen-year-old son. With her."

The sound of Percy coughing like crazy — in shock, of all things — has me laughing. When he recovers, his words are wheezy. "Fucker, don't pull my leg. You do not!"

"Yeah, I do. No fucking joke. His name is Sterling."

"Wow. I…I don't know what to say, other than what the fuck?"

"She was only sixteen. You know what went on with her at home; I told you." I fill him in on the rest, finishing with, "I suppose I'll be meeting him soon. I think she's a bit worried."

"Honestly, there's nothing like being a father, Ryker. Nothing like it, man. I'm sure it'll be fine." He pauses, then after a bit of shuffling around, says, "Really fucking sucks though, having the love from your teenage years come back into your life, then tell you hey you have a kid, only to find out she's dying. Sorry, man, that's rough."

"Thanks, but she won't be dying for long…not if I can help it."

After a few more moments, he hangs up after assuring

me he'll call back later with the details, and I spend the rest of the day trying to come up with the best way to convince Angel to try and save her life…just one more time.

THE QUIET WHEN I ENTER MY HOUSE IS A DEAD GIVEAWAY that Angel isn't having a good day, or so I've learned.

My staff, who were all informed about Angel's health and keep an eye on her for me, tiptoe around, doing their work while making as little noise as possible so she may sleep undisturbed.

Taking a seat in the living room, I set the papers Percy faxed me to share with Angel aside for later, and stretch out on the couch to watch some TV — specifically, *Kitchen Nightmares*. This show makes me laugh like no other. I know most of the drama is made up, but it provides great entertainment value while reaffirming my excellent business skills, especially compared to those on the show. I'd be embarrassed if my businesses looked like theirs do, and I'm not even involved in the food industry. Ick.

It's amazing though, how many of their problems really started with or involve their boss or co-owner, etcetera. If they just communicated, perhaps most of their problems would've been solved without Ramsey's help.

Hmm. Maybe I should make Angel watch this and show her how communication is better than keeping it all inside.

Of course, this makes me wonder if Angel has ever

watched this show, and realize even after all that's gone on, I still don't really know what she likes or enjoys as an adult.

I'll have to remedy that immediately.

"Sir?"

At the sound of Henrietta's voice, I sit up and look over at her standing in the doorway, wringing her hands and making me instantly worried. "What is it? Is Angel awake?"

She shakes her head. "You…uh…have a visitor."

I didn't even hear the doorbell ring, but that doesn't matter. "Who is it?"

Henrietta doesn't even get to answer as the very last person I ever expected to see again enters the room behind her.

"Hello, darling! I've returned!"

Ah, fuck. Shoving a hand through my hair, I stand up as my ex-wife approaches, placing my hands on her shoulders as she attempts to hug me. "Don't touch me, Ver. What the fuck are you doing here? Shouldn't you be with husband number two?"

"Oh him?" Veronica — or Ver, as I always called her — sticks out her lip in a pout, stepping back out of my reach, then walks over to the window to look out before tossing me a grin and turning to face me once more. "That's over. He's a cheater, and broke. I don't want to date a broke cheater."

As always, her logic astounds me. "So you'd date a cheater as long as he's rich?"

"Don't be crass."

"Me? Crass." I watch out of the corner of my eye as Henrietta exits the room, but makes sure to leave the door wide open. She'll definitely get a raise. "Interesting. I'm pretty sure you're the one who was fucking the pool boy in our bed." I hold my hands in the air, palms facing up as I shrug at her angry look. "It's not my fault you didn't realize pool boys were *poor* and his mama was the one buying his fancy clothes for him at the age of twenty-eight."

"I'm sorry," she says, drawing out the word sorry in a whiny high pitched tone that ticks me off. "It was only twice!"

"Wow. Only twice. That made it so much better." I point at the door and look away from her. "Get out of here. You are not welcome, and I don't care for your apology. I divorced you for a reason."

"No."

Stalking over to the window, I take her by the elbow and start walking toward the door. She resists the whole way, attempting to yank herself free but failing, as I stop outside the room and glare down at her. "If you don't leave, I will call the cops, and you'd just love that, wouldn't you? Perhaps you might actually convince them I hit you against your will this time."

I release her arm and she steps back, glaring at me for a moment before smiling, her whole face lighting up. "Aw, come on, they knew I was just mad. I love you Ryker. Give me another chance. I won't fuck up this time and—"

"Not a chance in hell," I interrupt, pointing at the front door and nodding, as I slip my hands into my pockets to keep from forcibly removing her on my own. "Get out before I have you removed."

Her lower lip wobbles as she tosses a glance at the door, then back at me. "You're so mean. You ignored me, and only noticed me when I did something stupid because I was lonely. You didn't love me once you knew I couldn't give you a baby, and—"

"That's fucking bullshit." I step toward her, my voice raising, even though I know I shouldn't respond to her manipulative tactics, but I hate her continuous spouting of lies. "You became a damn psycho, obsessed with having a child, *obsessed* with keeping up with everyone else. Even when you slept with him, we were still having sex once, sometimes twice a day. How much more attention could I possibly have given you while continuing to keep you in the lifestyle you wanted to maintain so badly? I had to *work*, Veronica, which is something you still know nothing about since you've never worked a damn day in your life."

"I'll—I'll get a job. I'll do whatever you want me to do, just please give me another chance!"

As she stands there, clutching her arms to her chest, pleading with me, her brown eyes shiny with unshed tears, I've never been more disgusted in my life. I wonder how I ever loved this woman, who thinks of nothing but herself and even now, can't accept responsibility for her part in the destruction of our marriage. I hadn't been a perfect husband — who was? — but I certainly hadn't deserved her cheating on me, or her allegations of abuse near the end when she didn't get her way, and had ramped up once I served her with divorce papers. I need her to leave, now.

"Veronica, I swear if you don't leave right fucking now—"

"What?" She steps forward, laughing. "What will you do? Will you hit me? You like to do that, don't you? Hit women—"

"Be quiet!" I whirl on my heel and head back into the room, pulling my phone out of my pocket to call the guard at the gate, who was going to get a talking to for letting her in, but I don't even get to dial as she comes up behind me and smacks my arm, knocking it out of my hand.

As my phone flies across the floor, I'm pissed and I grab Veronica, lifting her with her arms trapped, crossed over her chest as they are, and she cries out when her back meets the wall even though I'm not forceful at all.

And, of course, because I have all the fucking luck... that's how Angel finds us when she enters the room seconds later.

I stop short as I enter the room, my eyes widening at the sight of Ryker holding a dark-haired woman against the wall.

I thought I'd been imagining him arguing with someone as I came downstairs — you know, hallucinating from my meds, which happen to be a side effect I have yet to experience — but obviously, I hadn't imagined a thing.

Unsure of what's going on, the first thing out of my mouth is, "What the hell are you doing?"

He tosses me a look of exasperation and nods his head toward the floor. "Pick up my phone and call Adrian, the guy at the front gate, will you? Tell him my *ex-wife* needs escorted off the premises before I call the cops on her for assault."

"Assault?" She laughs, turning her head to face me, and smiling brightly. "He's such a kidder. He's always liked playing rough. Sorry you walked in on our foreplay."

Oh, dear.

Without saying anything, I walk over and pick up his phone, scrolling through his contacts until I find Adrian's name. I would think he'd be right up front, but I see Ryker has over five hundred contacts in his phone. Yikes.

"Adrian," I say when he answers, turning away from the stare of both Ryker and his ex as I continue speaking, "Ryker would like you to come to the house and uh…escort his ex out."

I hang up after he says he's on his way and turn back around. "He said it'll be a few minutes."

"God, Ryker, let me go." She squirms, and I hide a smile as Ryker moves his body away from hers, causing her to stumble as her feet touch the floor. "Thanks for doing it gently, asshole."

When he comes to stand next to me, she looks from me, back to him, then at me once more. "Oh, I see. You're his latest whore."

"That's a rather bitchy thing to say." I really want to stoop to her level, but I refrain as Ryker puts his hand on the small of my back. "You don't even know me."

"Don't need to," she remarks. "You look like you could use a good meal or two though." She looks at Ryker and laughs. "Don't know how you went from fucking this," she sweeps a hand down her rather voluptuous form, "to screwing waifs. I didn't know you were into boy-like women, or I'd've starved myself more."

Wow, this woman is fucking special.

"The pool boy kinda looked like a woman with his long hair and sounded like one too," Ryker pipes up with a chuckle. "I always wondered if you were truly a lesbian."

"Looking back, he seems like your type." She tosses me a dirty look, dropping her eyes from my head to my toes, then focuses on Ryker again. "I get it now. You were jealous. If you wanted to join in, all you had to do was say so."

I can't help it — laughter bubbles up and out of my mouth, and she twists her lips in disgust, only to glare at me when Ryker starts laughing, too.

"Yeah, laugh it up," she rolls her eyes as I wipe the tears from mine, her smile nasty as she takes a step toward us. "But you're just his whore. I was his wife. He at least married me before he fucked me."

Okay, fuck it. I'm stooping to her level.

I ignore her and look up at Ryker's face with a happy grin. "Tomorrow is the day I go see our son. You want to come with me?"

The gasping, choking sound that comes from her is totally worth it, even as Ryker's eyes widen with surprise. "Of course I do."

"Excuse me?" She takes another step toward us and Ryker steps in front of me as her voice rises. "What did she mean by 'our son'? You don't have any children!"

"Not with you, I don't."

He doesn't say anything else, and as Adrian arrives in the room, taking his ex by the arm, she starts to cry. "See?

You didn't love me. You moved on quick enough to have a son! I couldn't have hurt you that badly, so why won't you give me another chance?"

"He's not a baby." Her eyes widen as I step around Ryker and cross my arms over my chest. "He's a teenager. And he won't give you another chance because you're a cheating liar, so give it up."

I can see the moment it clicks who I am — I know enough about Ryker to know he would've told her about me all those years ago during all the previous relationship talk most normal people engage in — because she sucks in a breath, her eyes moving back and forth between us as she screeches, "What?"

But she doesn't get a chance to say anything else because Ryker cuts in. "You aren't welcome here. If you step on my property or in my house again, I'll have you arrested for trespassing. Leave me alone, Veronica. You've no need to contact me — ever."

Adrian escorts her from the room as she screams obscenities, but I stop listening. Ryker turns to face me and drags me into his arms, wrapping them around my waist and hugging me close as he leans in close to my ear.

"How are you feeling?"

"Mmm." I slide my arms around his neck, slipping my hands into his hair and gripping it while he nibbles my neck. "I had a good nap, but I wasn't expecting to find your ex-wife in the living room with you."

"Neither did I," he says between kisses on my neck.

"She showed up out of nowhere. That's the first time I've laid eyes on her in two years."

"I may've made an enemy, but I'm sure once I'm dead she'll approach you again."

I meant it as a joke, but he jerks his head back and glares at me, which only makes my smile widen as he says, "She may want me, but the only person I want is *you*. Veronica had her chance and she fucking blew it. She'll be lucky if I even acknowledge her in public if I happen to run into her after her little stunt today."

I love the absolute look of possession on his face, and decide to mess with him even though I know the answer would be a resounding 'no' because Ryker is a loyal man. "Would you have been tempted to leave her if you had run into me?"

"What kind of question is that?" He frowns as he releases my hair and steps back, running a hand through his own.

"An honest one." I cross my arms over my chest and drop the smile. "Do you ever wonder what might've happened had I contacted you? Your poor wife, who can't get pregnant, learning about a child you had with your teenaged girlfriend many years ago."

"Once I married her, I gave up on you, but I can say with certainty that Veronica would've been as devastated then as she was just a few moments ago. She wouldn't've believed I had no idea." He shrugs, walking over to pick up some papers off a table, then comes back toward me, holding them out for me to grab. "These are for you."

I take them in my hand, but keep my eyes on him as I ask, "Are you mad at me for saying it in front of her?"

He shakes his head and points at the papers.

Sighing, I look down and instantly, upon seeing the words 'clinical trial,' I stomp over to the table and slam the papers down upon them. "No. Absolutely not."

"Angel—"

"Why can't you respect my wishes?" He steps toward me and I hold up a hand, which thankfully, he doesn't ignore. "What don't you get about what I've said?"

"Don't you want a chance?"

"A chance at what?" I spit out, throwing my hands up into the air as I head toward the door. Stopping right before I would walk through, I turn to face him. "To spend the last few months of my life feeling sick and tired, instead of enjoying life up until the moment I can no longer get out of bed?"

"No." He slides his hands into his pockets and simply stands there, staring at me with his mouth in a grim, straight line. "A chance with me. With our son."

I wince at his words, at the desire to say yes, even as I shake my head. "This *is* your chance with me. I'm taking you to see him tomorrow. You'll have lots of time with him, especially after I'm gone. But, sorry, I'm not going to spend what little time I have left being filled with drugs or whatever just so I *might* somehow magically beat this for a third time." Unable to stop the tears from sliding down my cheeks, I swipe at them with my fingers before saying one last thing as my heart squeezes with the pain I'm feeling and the pain I know he's experiencing as well. "You can be mad, or sad, or upset, but imagine how I feel. Either way here, I lose if it doesn't work, and I don't want to spend my last few months giving anyone any hope. I just can't. I've accepted it, and you need to accept it, too."

Then I whirl around and run back up to my room.

18 - RYKER

*W*ell, yesterday officially landed in my 'that was a shit day' category.

My ex-wife…well, her actions speak for her all on their own. I don't know what happened to the sane woman I married, and later divorced, but she's completely lost her mind. That much is obvious.

And Angel…

Hell. Angel didn't even look at those papers past the top phrase.

After she stormed off following her little speech, I didn't even see her the rest of the evening, as she'd locked herself in her room and refused to open it.

Sure, I could've let myself in with the master key, but I think it's clear that's not the way I should deal with her.

Even if every minute she refuses to consider getting help one more time is another minute she's closer to death than life. Which is really fucking depressing me.

Now, we're on our way to see Sterling.

With Kevin driving, we should be talking and laughing back here, especially since I'm excited and nervous, but we're not.

Oh, she smiled at me this morning at breakfast, and she's been perfectly polite, but it's like any progress I've made with her flew out the window.

Fucking great.

I alternate between staring at her — which she doesn't even notice because she's focused her gaze out the window the whole time so far — and nervously scrolling through my phone trying to occupy my time, and get my thoughts away from fucking her right here in the car.

I figure it would be disrespectful to muss her clothing and show up there with flushed cheeks, but the more she ignores me, the more I want to do exactly that, merely to get a reaction out of her.

Any reaction.

I cough, and she ignores it.

I shuffle my feet, readjust my position, and cough again.

She lifts a hand to her hair, taking a strand and wrapping it around her finger, then twirling it round and round while still staring out the window.

It's strangely cute and erotic at the same time because she uncrosses her legs, bared as they are as she's wearing a sundress, and in that moment, I have to know if she's wearing panties or not.

I lift my hand and tap the window behind me, Kevin automatically shutting it and blocking us from his view.

Then, I move over to her, spreading her legs open before she has a chance to stop me, and placing myself between them.

Her hand drops as she turns her head until her gorgeous eyes meet mine. "What do you think you're doing?"

"Tell me," I murmur, ignoring her question as I slide a hand up her leg and fondle the hem of her skirt, "did you wear this skirt just to tease and flirt with me, thinking we'd be in a car and I wouldn't touch you?"

"Maybe. Maybe not."

I keep my gaze locked on hers as my fingers continue their trek under her skirt and up her leg, and when the curve between my thumb and forefinger meet the apex of her thighs, I have my answer.

She's wearing panties, but they are barely a scrap, making it easy for me to move them to the side and shove a finger deep inside her without warning.

Gasping in surprise, she raises a hand and grabs the handle above the window, the other coming up to rest on my shoulder as her eyes flutter, but I'll hand it to her, she keeps them open. She keeps them on me and thrusts against my hand with a lift of her hips, curving her body to encourage my invasion, making my cock harden to the point of pain at the mere thought of giving in and fucking her this second.

"It's not nice," I begin with the addition of another finger inside her, "to refuse me, to refuse this, like you did last night. Maybe you've accepted what you see as your fate, but I haven't, and I won't." Her eyes widen, and I curl my fingers up, stroking and caressing her g-spot enough to make her wiggle, yet not enough it will get her off. "I know you think you showing up on my door was just a coincidence; that you were so drunk, in your stupor you believed you should look up my address, and come see me…and then you did. But it didn't *mean* anything, it just happened. However, I don't see it the way you do."

She slams her eyes shut with a moan, her pussy tightening around my fingers as I withdraw them and thrust them in once, twice, then resume stroking her while using my thumb to tease her clit.

"Way I see it, Angel, you came to see me because deep down inside, you wanted me to know everything." I move and readjust so I'm able to keep my fingers deep inside her while aiding the touch of my thumb with the stroke of my tongue. My movements are languid, perhaps even lazy, and for a minute or two, I say nothing. Just licking, sucking, and fucking her with my fingers, until her hand slides up to my head and she grasps a handful of my hair, tugging on it as she begins begging with her mouth, her words incoherent.

I feel her body tighten, preparing to come as my touch inches her closer and closer, so I move my mouth away, sliding my body up until she and I are face to face. Her head lays back against the seat, her eyes closed as her mouth hangs open a little, her breath quick and shallow as she alternates between panting and moaning.

Cupping her jaw with my free hand, I bring her head

up and kiss her lips, saying against them, "Open your eyes and look at me if you want to come."

She does, her eyes hazy and filled with need, and when she moves her hips to ease the ache, I laugh as she begs, "Please."

I pull my fingers out to the edge, then thrust back in, making her cry out. As her hand tightens on my hair, I slide my hand into her hair, wrap it around and close my fist, yanking her head to bare her neck and she sobs with all her need and wants, keeping her eyes open as I demanded.

"You're a lot of things to me. You were the friend I cared about, and the one person I would've done anything in my power to protect. You were my girlfriend, my first love, and as I've recently discovered, the mother of my child." I stroke harder, faster as the tears slide down her cheeks, and I finish what I need to say so I can please her even as she refuses to please me. "As the boy who loved you, you didn't let me save you. Hell, you didn't even let me try. You did what you needed to do to save yourself and I'm so fucking proud of you for that, but you're not that girl anymore, and I'm not just the boy who loved you. I'm a man who would do anything to protect you, to *save* you, to help you heal so you can give us the chance denied us all these years. I want my family. I want my son. I want *you*," I spit out through clenched teeth, "and the least you could fucking do is give me the chance to have you for more than a few moments. Let me hope if I want to; just fucking give me, the man, the chance to save you, the woman, like the boy couldn't do for the girl."

Then, as she breaks out into full on sobs, I stroke nice and hard. She falls apart in my arms, her orgasm ripping through her, and as I hug her to me, she wraps her arms around my neck and cries into the crook of my shoulder.

Somehow, I feel victorious and like an asshole, all in one.

And that perhaps, maybe, just maybe, she heard my own pain at this whole situation cutting through her own.

AS WE WALK UP THE STEPS TO THE SECOND FLOOR apartment where Angel says her sister and son live, I ask the one question I haven't yet.

"Does he know I'm his father?"

After my little stunt in the car, and once she'd stopped crying, she'd gone back to ignoring me for the rest of the drive. However, she can't ignore me now, so she turns her head to look over at me before facing ahead again and saying, "It's complicated."

"How so?"

We reach the landing and she walks ahead of me. Even though I could catch up, I don't even try, because it's quite a nice view from behind. When I whistle low, she throws me a glare over her shoulder, which merely elicits a chuckle from me.

She stops in front of a door and smooths her skirt, then her hair, and it's really endearing.

"You look lovely," I say, leaning in to kiss her on the

cheek, to which she respond by elbowing me in the side. "Ouch!"

"Keep your hands off me, especially while we're here, okay?"

"What am I walking into, Angel?" I ignore her demand, turning her to face me as I wrap my arms around her and hug her close so she can't escape, kissing the top of her head. "Tell me why it's complicated."

"I didn't want him mad at you…ever. I told him I didn't know who his father was." I feel her whole body wince against my chest as she ducks her head, clutching my shirt in her fists as she sniffles. "But I promised him I'd try to find out."

I don't know whether to feel horrified or amused.

But since she seems ashamed, I go with the easygoing option, and laugh. "Well, now you can tell him you found me, and he'll never be the wiser."

She lifts her head away from my chest, her gaze rising until her wide watery eyes are staring into mine, and whispers, "You're too nice to me considering all I've done."

Stroking her cheek, I lean in and give her lips a gentle kiss, murmuring against them, "You're too harsh on yourself considering all you've been through." Then I pull back and smile. "See what I did there?"

"I…"

She doesn't get to finish her sentence as the door opens and a familiar voice says, "Oh, there you are! Why didn't you knock? I was—" I hear her suck in a breath as I turn to look at her, and the color drains from her face as her very recognizable green eyes widen.

Because wouldn't you know it…I'm staring into the brown haired, glasses-free face of my damn secretary.

What the fuck?

I drop my hands from Angel and step back, pointing a finger at her sister. "You better fucking explain yourself. Right now."

"Huh?" I see Angel glance between her sister and me, not understanding, and I know her confusion is real. She may have trouble telling me things, but lying well is not a talent she possesses. "What are you talking about Ryker? What does she need to explain?"

"Your *sister* has been working as my secretary for the last *six years*." I hiss out the words, taking a step toward Felicia — well, if that's her fucking name — and she gives me a nervous smile. "And I've got no doubt she knew exactly who I was when she was hired, so again, she better fucking explain herself!"

Angel gasps, covering her mouth with one hand, and glares at her sister.

"Uh…" She steps back, dropping her gaze, and nods toward the interior of her place. "Why don't you two come inside? Sterling isn't here right now, but he'll be back in a little while…he, um…he went to a friend's house."

I stride into the apartment first as Angel trails behind me, and take in the surroundings. It's a pretty nice place, which doesn't shock me since I pay my secretary a pretty fucking high salary, and at least a little bit of me — you know, the part not seething with anger in this moment — is happy my son doesn't live in a dump.

Taking a seat on the couch, I put my arm around Angel's shoulders as she sits beside me, unable to keep myself from touching her. And when her sister is seated in the chair to the side of us, I lift one brow and say, "Well?"

She flushes, averting her gaze into her lap, and I almost feel sorry for her.

Almost.

My sister has been working for Ryker for six years?

The thought boggles my mind as I stare at her while she keeps her eyes focused on her lap, picking at her fingers on one hand with her other hand, and biting her lip as if trying to find the right words to say.

But really, what can she say?

I had no idea where she worked because honestly I didn't care about such a detail with all the other things I had going on. She would have to drive roughly an hour and a half to get to work every day, and to get home.

Why in the world would she do such a thing? She hadn't even had guardianship of Sterling at the time.

I have so many questions, yet voice none of them as she finally speaks.

"Just so you know, my name *is* Felicia Melbourne." She nods at me as she looks at Ryker once more. "She will verify that. I was married once and decided I liked the last name better than Barlow, so I didn't change it back after my divorce."

"Um, yes." I smile at Ryker as he gives me an expectant look. "That's true."

"Go on," he says, returning his gaze to Felicia. "You know what I want to know."

"Yes." Letting out a heavy sigh, she holds her hands out in front of her, palms up. "Look, it was innocent at first. I was getting divorced and needed a job, you were hiring, and I was curious. Sterling was only eight at the time, but I could see the resemblance right away."

"An hour and a half is a long fucking way to drive merely to satisfy your curiosity about me."

She shakes her head. "Sterling's always lived in this area with my mother and father, but once they died, I moved here to keep him in familiar surroundings."

I admit, I'm fascinated, especially as Ryker's arm tightens around my shoulders; a deliberate move I'm sure. My sister's eyes flash from his arm back to his face, and she frowns.

"Are you two together?"

"No."

"Yes."

The 'yes' comes from Ryker and I elbow him in the side while shaking my head at my sister. "No. We're not. I'm sure he'd like to be, but we're just having sex, actually."

As Felicia's face falls in utter dismay, I get a sick feeling in my stomach, especially since I only meant it as a joke.

And Ryker must've gotten that feeling too because he

stands up and grabs me by the hand, which I take and once I'm on my feet, he points at her and says, "You're fired."

Both my sister and I gasp, her eyes filling with tears and spilling over as she asks, "Why?"

"Because." He looks at me, then back at her, and points at me while keeping his gaze locked on her. "I didn't know where the fuck Angel was, or I would've contacted her a long time ago. *You* knew though. You worked for me, knew who I was, *and* knew I had a son. Therefore, you're fucking fired."

"But—"

"No. Where is my son? He is going home with us."

"Ryker." I place my free hand on his arm, stepping in front of him to make him look at me, and try to calm him down as my sister sobs behind me. "Please. She isn't totally to blame here—"

He clenches his jaw, removing his hand from mine, and pulling his arm away. "I need some fresh air. I'll be right back." He points at the door as he glances at me, his mouth in a grim line. "If he comes back while I'm outside, try to have an honest conversation with the boy, will you?"

Stalking away and out the door before I can reply, I whirl on my sister with an angry growl of frustration. "What the fuck is wrong with you? How could you work for him and not tell me?"

Felicia swipes at her face, getting rid of the evidence of her tears, and straightens her back, looking every bit the haughty bitch I know she is. "Please. Like you would've fucking cared or noticed. You should've warned me you were bringing him."

"Why would I warn you? I came to see *my* son like I always do, and I brought his father to meet him. Was I supposed to somehow know you were working for him, in addition to apparently having the hots for him?"

"It's not like we fucked or anything, *Angel*." She goes from the sweet version of herself to the mocking one I've always known. "How ironic he calls you that when you're anything but. And he wants to take Sterling home…'with us'? So, now you're living with him? Yeah, that won't end badly. He does know you're dying, doesn't he?"

"Of course he does."

"Why is he mad at me and not mad at you?" She pulls out a cigarette and lights it, taking a long drag before smirking at me. "You're the one who gave birth to the damned kid, after all."

"Maybe it's because I spent fourteen fucking years believing his parents prohibited me from speaking with him when I needed him the most?"

"God, you believed that? You're such a dumb ass. My mother wanted a new baby so bad, she'd do anything to get it. I had no idea she fed you such a lie, but you're stupid for not questioning it."

"I had a lot going on—"

"Oh shut up," she cuts in, waving a dismissive hand as she walks over to the sliding doors and opens them, stepping out onto the balcony. "I know all about everything you had going on; you were the center of fucking attention."

"That just killed you, didn't it?" She turns to face me, leaning back against the railing, and shrugs as I advance on her. "It's pathetic you were jealous of me, and apparently, still are. It wasn't *my* fault I knew nothing about my father until I was fifteen, and happened to need his help at a time when all you cared about were boys and your social life. Sorry the abuse I endured, followed by my pregnancy, and then my cancer took the spotlight off of you. God fucking forbid your life was inconvenienced in any way by reality."

She twists her lips, stumping out her cigarette under her feet before stabbing me with a finger on my chest, as she leans in close. "It wasn't just then though, was it? You run around and do stupid shit after your treatment, then get cancer again. Okay, fine, you turned your life around for a while, but the only person you cared about is yourself, and now, once more, it's all about you and how you're dying."

I laugh, because this is absolutely fucking absurd, and then say, "You're being an idiot. And, if you hated me so much, I don't know why you'd take on my child, instead of just saying, 'no thanks' after your parents died and not taking guardianship of him in case something happened to me."

"Because I care about him, unlike you, and have been a mother figure to him while you just dumped him off on others."

"Dumped him?" My voice is loud and screeching now,

but she's gone and pissed me right off. "Fuck you! You offered! And you damned well know that I would've given anything — *anything* — to have had him with me all this time, but I did what was best for him. He needed stability, and a home, and people around him who weren't fucking sick all the time. Besides, even though he was only five when I went into remission, you don't just pull a child away from those he spends all his time with and loves just because he's your child, even if you hope it won't come back. I had hope but I'm not a fucking moron to believe it wouldn't return." I back away as tears stream down my cheeks and she stands there, arms crossed over her chest, eyes hard. "You can't understand because you're not a mother, but I did what I thought was best. And I spent as much time with him as I could."

"Mom?"

Felicia's eyes drop to stare at the ground as I whirl around and find Sterling standing inside the sliding doors... and Ryker right behind him.

20 - RYKER

I bump into Sterling on the way back inside.

Literally, which is rather embarrassing because I've been looking down while walking, and didn't see him heading toward me. He didn't see me either because he, too, had been staring at the ground, ears plugged with his headphones and not paying attention to where he was going.

I grab his arm out of instinct to keep him from falling or tripping, and when he lifts his head to see who is touching him, his eyes — so like his mother's — go round, his jaw dropping. It only takes me a few seconds to sweep his form from head to toe, where he looks just like his picture, and discover that while he's a bit skinny — taking after his mother there, too — he's as tall as me.

Something tells me he knows exactly who I am, but I act as if nothing is out of the ordinary. "Headed inside, are you?"

He blinks, then blinks again, before relaxing his stance and smiling, taking out his ear buds. "Yeah. My mom's probably waitin' for me, but I'm guessin' you know that."

Smart kid. Probably a bit of a smart ass, too, and I couldn't be more proud as I grin back at him. "She's inside with your aunt, who happens to work for me, by the way."

Shit! Probably shouldn't have said that, but he either doesn't notice or doesn't care, shrugging as he opens the door and steps inside. I follow as he takes the steps two at a time, then enters the apartment without looking back at me.

But, the yelling inside reaches my ears, and I find myself copying his two-step-at-a-time routine to get there faster, recognizing Angel's voice as the angry, loud one. As I walk in, Angel is slowly backing away from her sister while screaming, and Sterling is right inside watching her. As I walk up behind him, he says, "Mom?" and she whirls around with a horrified look on her face.

"Sorry I'm late," he says as she re-enters the apartment, and stops right before him. "I missed the first bus."

"It's...it's okay." Her eyes go from him, to me, and back to him where she gives him a wobbly smile. "I need you to get your things." She tosses Felicia a look over her shoulder, but I can't make out what it is, before facing us again. "Your aunt Felicia isn't able to take care of you any longer."

"Does that mean I'll be with you now?"

I watch her take his hand in hers and squeeze it, her gaze and all her focus on him even though I know she's upset, and wish I knew what they'd been arguing about. "Yeah…we'll…we'll work things out for later…somehow."

"Mom…"

She interrupts him with a big smile, shaking her head. "Let's not talk about it right now. Go get your things, okay?"

Sterling glances back at me, then over at his aunt, before returning his attention back to Angel with a shrug. "All right."

When he's gone from the room, Angel heads into the kitchen, while Felicia returns inside and sits on the couch, glaring up at me. "Am I still fired?"

"Yeah, you are." Crossing my arms over my chest, I shrug. "But that's only because I no longer trust you. It may not've been your place to say anything, but the fact you could keep such a secret makes me wonder what else you could possibly hide from me." She opens her mouth, but I shake my head as I continue, "You will receive six months pay and a reference. That should be enough to find yourself a new job."

I don't even want to give her that, but I'm not a total asshole.

She purses her lips in thought before nodding after a few moments. "That's fine. Thank you."

"Sure. Pick it up Monday."

At that, the sound of something shattering in the kitchen has me running in, only to see Angel clutching the edge of the counter, knuckles white, and her feet surrounded by the glass I'm assuming she was drinking out of. Her eyes are filled with pain as she looks up at me.

"Sorry. Don't know what happened."

"It's just a glass," Felicia says from behind me, voice filled with annoyance. "But of course, it's not the first one you've broken, and I'm sure it won't be the last."

Well, if her tone is any indication, I'm betting she started the argument Angel was finishing when I returned. I lose my temper a little and snap, "Way to be a bitch, Felicia. She's obviously in pain."

"Isn't she always?" She mutters as I grab the broom and swipe what I can away from Angel's feet, before handing the broom to her so she may finish cleaning up, and grabbing Angel into my arms.

"Five month's pay," I amend before carrying Angel from the kitchen and toward Sterling's room. Once I reach it, I look in to find him zipping up a bag. "Let's go. Anything you need, I will get for you later. Your mother needs to rest."

I expect him to argue, but he doesn't, worry clouding his face instead as he takes in the fact his mother is in my arms. "Okay. I got all my important stuff anyway."

Soon we're in the car and on our way home.

It doesn't take long for Sterling, who is sitting across from me as I hold his sleeping mother, to ask the obvious question.

"You're my father, aren't you?"

I almost want to ask 'what gave it away' in a smartass retort, but I remember he's fourteen and refrain. "Yes."

"Hmm." He glances out the window for a few seconds, then returns his focus to me. "I always knew she knew, but I never said anything. She had more important things going on than me bugging her about it."

"What makes you think she knew?"

He gives me the 'don't treat me like I'm stupid look' every kid, in my experience, has perfected. "Ever since I was a kid, she's always been a terrible liar."

"You're pretty intuitive then," I say with a grin, liking this teenager who happened to be my kid more and more by the minute. "Your mother is definitely not a good liar."

"Yeah." He runs his fingers through his hair, which is styled in a crew cut, before blowing out a breath and giving me a pointed look. "You didn't know about me, right?"

"Not a clue," I assure him, making sure to make eye contact before looking down at his mother. "She left and didn't tell me, but she had her reasons. Don't be mad at her."

"I'm not. She's my mom; how could I ever be mad at her?"

I laugh at that. "Oh, it's possible."

"Nah." His fingers fidget with his music player. "The kids at school always complain about their parents, but they have them both around all the time. I think they're a bunch of pussies."

Quickly covering my chuckle of surprise at his language

with a cough, I have to agree with him at the same time his statement makes me a little sad. "Most people don't know how lucky they are."

"Why do you have a driver?"

Although abrupt, I'm glad for the change of topic since I might as well prepare him for where we're going. "Well, years ago when I bought the house I live in, it came with a whole bunch of staff. I keep them on because that's their jobs and Kevin here drove for the last owners who died."

"Oh."

"Your mother asked me nearly the same question after she arrived."

"So she lives with you now? What about Vanessa?"

Can't tell him the truth, so I go for a modified version. "Vanessa is fine, your mom talks to her all the time. I simply can take better care of your mother, and have people around to watch her when I'm at work in case something happens."

"I can watch her, too."

"Don't you have school?"

"No. Summer vacation." He goes back to looking out the window, even as he asks, "You know she's dying right? She told me a few weeks ago."

"Yes."

"Sucks, doesn't it?" When I don't say anything, he looks at me and clarifies, "So many bad people and *she's* the one who is going to die? It's not fair. She always cried every time she left me, and I know she loves me so she doesn't want me to watch her die...but she doesn't get it. It would be way worse if she died and I wasn't there to say goodbye."

It's one of those moments where I can see the man he'll be, but am also witness to how much of a child is still in him, because his words wobble along with his lips, and his eyes tear up. He takes a shuddering breath, though, and swipes at his face, looking out the window to pretend I can't see, even if we both know I can.

So I do what I think anyone would do when they know they need to say something, but they don't want to intrude upon someone's private feelings — I change the topic to something I'm sure he wants to know.

"Your mom and I met when she was thirteen and I was fifteen, when I moved in next door, although she wouldn't talk to me at first." I know he's listening because he tilts his head a bit even as he continues to look out the window and his fingers stop fidgeting in his lap. "Then, one day, we became friends, and soon after, we were dating."

"Why did she leave?"

"I can't say." I give him an apologetic grimace as he looks over at me. "It's not my place; you should ask her. All I'll say is she didn't have a good home."

Angel stirs in my arms and seconds after I look down, her eyes flutter open and after a weak smile, closes her eyes once more and snuggles closer to me.

After a few moments, Sterling says in a hushed voice, "Sometimes, I feel like she doesn't live, like she's just waiting to die. And it doesn't matter how much we love her...she's given up."

I can't do anything except nod in agreement, because to me, his statement is the most honest fucking one I've heard all day.

*I*t's three a.m. when I wake up, as the glaring clock next to the bed shows.

I don't remember much beyond when we left my sister's place, but what I do recall…well, it makes me grimace with disgust at myself.

I hate Felicia for saying what she did, and even though I know I did what was best for my son, I suppose I could see it from her point of view, too.

Not that I asked for my life to take the turns it did. I hate that she resents me for needing a lot of attention because it's not like I was enjoying myself. Quite the opposite, since I've spent most of my life being miserable and waiting for the other shoe to drop, which it inevitably did.

Then, to hear Sterling talking to Ryker in the car, and to know he thinks I've given up on life hurts so much. I didn't think I'd given up, but have I? Is not wanting to continue fighting something that keeps coming back really giving up, when the other choice is to spend what could be my last months fighting for a potential nothing and feeling sick the whole time?

If it is, such an example is not something I want to set for my son, but I'm still not sure I can put myself through more treatments that may end up doing nothing except wasting what little time I have left.

But I'm also not sure I could sit here with my son and Ryker and let them watch me die without trying either.

With a sigh, I roll over to find Ryker sound asleep. He's lying on his side and facing me, and while the moonlight through the window makes it not completely dark in here, I can't really make out much more than his form.

I want to reach out and touch him, but I don't want to wake him since I'm not sure when he fell asleep. Instead, I get up as quietly as possible because I'm hungry and head to the kitchen.

Which is where, of course, I discover Sterling sitting on a stool at the middle island eating a bowl of cereal, ear buds in, scrolling through his phone. When I tap him on his shoulder, he jumps a little, his head swiveling to see who is touching him. Upon seeing me he smiles, pulling out the buds at the same time he says, "Hey."

"Shouldn't you be sleeping?" I step away toward the fridge, opening it up to see what there is to eat, and pull out some strawberries — the only food that really looks tempting right now. "It's three a.m."

"I was playing video games," he informs me, taking a

bite and crunching his cereal for a moment before continuing, "and then I watched a movie, and when I went to lay down, I realized how hungry I was so I came to get something to eat." He waves a spoon in the air, dropping milk on the counter, and I glare at him when he laughs. "It's not like I have school tomorrow, Mom, geez. I'll go to sleep after I eat, kay?"

He sits there, still holding the spoon in the air as milk drips on the counter, his eyes twinkling with amusement, and as he practically radiants happiness at me, the realization this is the biggest smile I've seen on his face in a long time has my heart clenching with sadness.

And it's very clear that all my efforts to protect him only really did one thing: it robbed both him and me of moments like this.

Moments I'll never get back now.

A thought which has tears springing to my eyes and I turn away as his smile melts from his mouth. I hear the spoon clink as it hits his bowl, and within seconds, his arms are wrapping around me as he whispers, "Don't cry, Mom. It's just a little milk."

"I'm sorry," I sob into his shoulder, the pain from my sisters mingling with my own sense of inadequacy in a blubber of near incoherency, "I've not been a good mom. And—and, I...I never meant..."

"Shh." He shakes his head, his arms tightening as his own voice thickens with tears. "Not bad. You're just my mom, and you always made me feel loved. Isn't that what a good mom does?"

"Y-yes, but—"

"No." He pulls back and looks down at me with his own red-rimmed eyes as a tear slides down his cheek. "You're my mom and I'm your only kid, and so, what I think about you as my mom is the only thing that matters."

"Well, your aunt was pretty upset at me—"

"Screw aunt Felicia. She's always grumpy."

"Sterling!"

He laughs and gives me a quick hug, then pulls away and goes back to eating his cereal with a lift of his shoulders. "What? She is."

"Doesn't mean you can say it out loud."

"Why not? It's true!"

I smile without answering, carrying my strawberries over to the sink to wash them off, and then pull out a knife to remove the hull before popping it in my mouth. I turn around and lean back against the counter after preparing a few more, staring at him until he lifts his head and quirks his brow — a move which makes him look *very* much like his father. And I ask the question I should've asked earlier even though he really hadn't had any options.

"Are you okay with being here? With…you know." I wave a hand, my face flushing with embarrassment because of what I'd told him about his father. I should've known that would come back and bite me in the ass.

He stands up and brings his bowl over to the sink, rinsing it out before returning to sit down, and folds his hands on the island as he nods, then asks, "Why'd you not tell him?"

Grimacing, I shake my head and turn around to put the container of strawberries away, but he doesn't say anything. He just waits, and I try to figure out what the hell to say.

"He…he said you didn't have a good home. But why not tell him? I know you knew all along. You're a bad liar."

My heart pounds, my shoulders slump, and my mouth going dry as I stand facing away, not knowing how to respond.

"Do you love him, Mom?"

"I've always loved him." I turn back around and walk over to stand on the opposite side of the island, folding my own hands and leaning in. "But…life got in the way, and once I had you, I started treatments for the cancer. I…" Sighing, I lower my head and rub my temple and he sits there waiting patiently, until I look back up at him. "I wanted you to have stability. Things…things happened."

I don't want to tell him about how my father and Trisha most likely lied to me. That's simply not necessary. "I loved you more than anything else though and have always thought I did the right thing. I also tried not to talk about it, because you deserved a mom who spent quality time with you and made sure you knew how much I loved you. After a while, I didn't think about your father. I always knew it was wrong, but from where I was standing, I didn't think I had many options and as time passed…"

"He said he wasn't mad."

"Yeah." With a sad smile, I sigh. "I expected him to get angry, but he surprised me. He's taken everything pretty well."

"That's 'cuz he loves you."

I straighten up, my head jerking back a little as his statement slams into me. "What? No, honey, he doesn't."

"Mom." He rolls his eyes, pulling his phone back out, and scrolling through it as he sighs with exasperation at me. "Look at this."

He holds it up and there is a picture of Ryker holding me in the car in what looks like a very uncomfortable position for him.

"Kevin had to carry you upstairs," my son informs with a chuckle, "while…while uh…well, while he sat in the car unable to move 'cuz his leg went numb on the drive."

"I'm not that heavy!"

"You're heavier than his leg?"

We both jump at the sound of Ryker's laughter as he walks into the kitchen wearing a t-shirt and boxers — I file away my thanks to him for covering up for later — and stands beside me. "I think even that may be debatable, son." He puts a hand on my lower back, and when I shy away by sliding a bit down so he can't touch me, he frowns. "You should be resting."

"I did rest. Now I'm wide awake."

"Uh…" My son stands up and grabs his things. "I'm gonna go to bed now. Bye."

He leaves the room so fast I nearly laugh, but Ryker bears down on me and traps me against the counter. "Is there a problem?"

"You mean besides me?" Giggling at the immediate scowl on his face, I slide my arms up and around his neck, interlacing my fingers to lock my arms around his neck as I lean back a little to gaze up into his eyes. "I'm kidding. No problem. I just…I'm not comfortable with PDA in front of him."

"Ah, I see." Ryker curves his body over mine, sliding one hand into my hair and getting a good grip on it, while pressing his lips to mine, locking me against the counter with no escape in sight with his other hand on my ass. After a few slow, deep kisses, which I give to him quite happily, he barely removes his mouth from mine before whispering, "I thought maybe you were still mad at me for…well, for everything sounds about right."

"No." Disconnecting my fingers from each other, I slide my hands up into his hair and ruffle it before sliding them back down and onto his shoulders, where I hold on for dear life in advance of what I know is coming soon. "I don't hold grudges…for long."

"Thank fuck for that." His right hand — that would be the hand cupping my ass — moves to my left thigh, his fingers spread as he slides it down to the hem of the skirt, then under it until he's cupping me between the legs. "And I'm glad you're still wearing this, because I want to fuck you on this counter with it on. Up for it?"

"I don't think so. Not with…"

"He went to bed."

"So? He could come back any second."

"I doubt it. He ran out of here like his ass was on fire." He slips his hand under the band of my underwear with a chuckle, gliding his fingers down until he's stroking me with one finger, followed by a second as he groans. "You're so fucking wet, as always. I love it." He inserts both fingers at the same time, capturing my gasp with his mouth and tongue, swallowing my moans of pleasure as he grinds his hips against me, making his own arousal known.

He releases his grip on my hair and adjusts me until I'm laying back with my lower half hanging off, and shoves my shirt up with one hand. Cupping a breast with his free hand, he strokes my g-spot with the other while taking one of my nipples into his mouth and sucking it in deep. Catching it between his teeth, he bites it hard enough to sting, and I gasp, taking his hair in my hands and keeping him in place.

Not completely forgetting my objection, I manage to get out, "Okay fine, but make it quick."

His only response is to laugh, because we both know I'm trapped here, and he'll take as long as he likes.

I close my eyes and hope my son doesn't come waltzing back into the damn kitchen because right now, I just can't deny how the very idea of doing it with Ryker like this thrills me.

Moving his mouth to the other nipple, he gives it the same treatment, until it's standing as tall, proud, and glistening as the other. Then, pulling his fingers out of my pussy, he brings them up to his mouth and sucks on them, before putting them up to my mouth and commanding, "Taste yourself."

"Mm-mm," I say with a shake of my head, compressing

my lips and locking my jaw, even as he runs his fingers along them anyway while laughing. "Jerk."

"You taste so sweet, and since we both know by the end you'll be licking your lips…" His grin is as naughty as the gleam in his eyes. "Well, you'll see why I'm never able to resist you."

"Resist me? Ha! You never even try to."

"That's because I'm not stupid enough to resist someone I love—" His grin doesn't falter even as his eyebrows raise, followed by him whistling. "Whoops. Guess that's the cat out of the bag."

I probably would've stiffened if my son hadn't pointed out — okay, what should've been obvious to me but wasn't — how Ryker feels about me, but instead I lock gazes with him and give him an affectionate smile. "As if it were ever in the bag anyway."

"Angel…" He nips at my jaw, down my neck, and across my collarbone, alternating with sweet kisses. "You mean so much to me. You always have. And even though I loved someone else when I thought you were gone forever…I never stopped loving you."

"I know." My words are a whisper as he keeps up his affectionate barrage on my senses, and then I laugh. "Although you have a funny way of showing it."

"I never would've turned you in," he assures me, nibbling his way up to my ear and taking the lobe in his mouth. He flicks his tongue once, twice, then sucks on it until I'm wiggling from the tingling going down my leg, and releases it. "But it worked like I hoped it would. Sort of."

A sadness I know he doesn't want me to hear creeps into his voice, and I know what I have to say — no, what I have to do — even though it goes against what I originally decided to do. Maybe it was the argument with Felicia, or the fact my son is now with me, or the looks Ryker gives me when he thinks I'm not paying attention; I don't know.

All I know is, both Ryker and Sterling deserve for me to fight one last time. So I will, with one caveat. Before I tell him however, I want him to finish what he's started here.

"Ryker?"

"Hmm?"

"Don't make me wait any longer."

He captures my mouth while his hands leave me completely, and soon, the tip of his cock teases me right where I want it the most. Taking hold of one thigh, he keeps me secure so I won't fall, then enters me slowly. Tortuously. When he's all the way in, he grips the other thigh and our mutual moans blend in our mouths at the same time our bodies completely unite.

The sudden prick of tears catches me off guard and I slam my eyes shut as he withdraws to the edge, holding himself there to tease me. I feel his lips curve up against mine.

"Open your eyes." His eyes are intense on mine, and if he notices how mine are a little watery, he chooses not to say anything. "That's better." He licks my lips, making me laugh at how it tickles, and then asks, "Fast or slow?"

"Fast." My answer is immediate and swift, like how I

want him to fuck me, and I wrap my arms around his neck. "Hard."

He gives me what I want, our mouths locked to catch any and all sounds, and right as my muscles tighten and my body prepares for my impending orgasm, he rips his lips away from mine and slaps me just as I like.

Moments later, after his orgasm follows mine, he sort of rests on top of me while we try to catch our breaths. I don't know how long we stay that way, but soon, he's pulling away and helping me off the counter. He holds out his hand, and as I interlace my fingers with his, I take a deep breath before letting it out slowly.

Then, catching his gaze with my own, I say the words he wants to hear, and which will mean no going back for any of us.

"Show me those papers for the clinical trial, please?"

*a*t her request, I immediately lead her to the bedroom where I had placed the papers in a drawer, and turn on the light as she sits on the bed. Bringing the information over, I take a seat beside her and stay quiet while she reads them. Which is pretty fucking hard when I want to jump up and down with joy.

"So," she says after a minute, looking up from the papers to me, "they are mixing two drugs that've never been mixed before. I receive one three days before the other drug, which only happens once a week every other week four times, then every eight weeks for the final four. They stop if the treatment doesn't prevent it from spreading."

At my nod, she swallows and blinks rapidly, and I cover her hand with mine. "You don't have to keep going. If it gets worse, it ends…and we…" It's my turn to fight emotions as I spit out the rest of the horrible sentence, "We prepare for the inevitable."

"That was going to be my condition." Her smile is sad as a tear slides down her cheek. "The moment we know it's not working, I wanted it to end."

"See? They knew how difficult you were and therefore, made sure they were ready to take you on," I tease, leaning in and licking up the tear before it trickles off her face and down her neck. "I'll make the call in the morning. You ready to go back to bed?"

She tilts her head, smirking as she places the papers down beside her, and wraps her arms around my neck. "Not really. I want to know what you and Sterling talked about."

"Simple. We talked about you." Wrapping my arms around her waist, I pull her onto my lap with her legs spread, leaving her vulnerable to any touches I want to make. "We've got one hell of a kid, Angel. And he adores you."

"I know. Out of all the decisions I made, the ones I made for him were the right ones, at least."

Tightening one arm around her waist, I bring the other up to gather in her hair, and stare into her eyes to make sure she's paying attention. "You did the best job you could've done in your situation, and all that matters now is you're here, with both of us. You don't worry about a thing anymore. Let me do the worrying and you enjoy being with me, being with our son, and if in the end….well, a few months is better than none…" I swallow as her eyes go misty at my words, and unable to resist, I crush her lips under mine.

She lets me in without me even asking, moaning into my mouth, touching her tongue with mine. I suck on it, following it up with a nip, and a chuckle as she pulls it away in protest. Taking her lip between my teeth, I give her a little pain with her pleasure, and our tongues are battling once more.

Removing my hand from her hair, I bring it down to her leg and slide it up her thigh, then under her skirt. She rotates her hips in my lap, and my cock strains against my boxers, ready to go for round two. When my fingers find her pussy wet and waiting for me, I decide denying either one of us what we want would be a fucking sin.

Releasing her lip, I skim mine down her jaw, murmuring, "Lift up sweetheart," as I free my cock. Angel's hands slide down to my shoulders, and when she does as bid, I guide my cock to the entrance of her pussy. She glides down bit by bit, and when she can lower herself no more, her moans mingle with mine when I devour her mouth once more. I hold her hips as she moves up and down, staying completely still as she gasps into my mouth and pleasures herself.

The most beautiful sight of her is when she rips her lips from mine, and tilts her head back, the tips of her long and gorgeous hair brushing the top of my knees, mouth hanging open as little mewls of pleasure erupt from her throat as she slides up, then drops back down with a sharp thrust of her own.

"God Angel, watching you fuck me…" My words are cut off by her downward descent, a long moan replacing whatever I'd been about to say, as her nails dig into my shoulders.

"Ryker." My name is a whisper of breath, but from her, it says everything.

I slip a hand between us, circling and teasing her clit while she rides me, and she tilts her lower body into my hand even as she keeps up her pace.

"Oh god," she cries after a minute of my sweet torture, nails digging even more as she sobs with pleasure, "I— I…ooohhhh!"

She comes with my hand on her and my cock seated deep inside her, her head thrown back. And when her orgasm subsides, she slides her arms around my neck and places her head in the crook of my shoulder, kissing me over and over with quick ones in between her panting. A moment or two later, she raises her head and stares into my eyes with a beautiful, wide grin.

"There's something you need to know," she says at the same time she clenches her pussy around my cock, which twitches in response, and makes me laugh. "Something huge and important."

Her smile makes me believe she's teasing, but the tone of her voice is serious, and I decide to hover somewhere in between with my response. "Huge and important." Gripping her hips, I thrust up as I hold her still and she slams her eyes shut with a gasp while I chuckle. "Seems to me that's something you're quite acquainted with already."

She rotates her hips, and squeezes around me again, which has me sliding off the couch and onto the floor while holding her in my arms. Placing her on it, I cover her body, thrusting in and out with a speed that has us both moaning and barely able to speak.

"Come for me," she manages to whisper, lifting her hips and bringing us even closer together, her legs wrapped around me tightly as she begs. "Please…"

I'm close to giving her what she wants, but first, I want to know what's so important. "Tell me, Angel. Tell me what you need me to know, and I'll give you what you want."

"I…"

"Open your eyes. Look at me and tell me, Angel."

She does as bid, her blue eyes burning into mine. "I…I love you Ryker. I always have."

"I know," I assure her with one final thrust, lowering my head and invading her mouth with my tongue as I fill her with my come, giving her exactly what she begged for as I groan against her lips a final time and pull my lips away to murmur, "I love you, too."

Her lips curve under mine. "I know. You'd be a fool not to."

Laughing, I roll off and cradle her body against mine, enjoying the feeling of having her in my arms.

And scared to fucking death of losing her again.

ANGEL IS SOUND ASLEEP WHEN I ROLL OUT OF BED AGAIN AT eight a.m.

Knowing how much she needs her rest, I leave her there

and head down to the kitchen, and find my cook making breakfast as usual. Meg smiles at me, then frowns as I pull out some cleaner from under the sink, and a paper towel.

"What are you doing?"

I spray the counter — which is thankfully not the one she is using to prepare the food — and give her a grin. "I'm washing the counter. I uh…I forgot to last night after I had a middle of the night snack."

"I already did that," she replies with a quirk of her lips. "You think I would ever use any surface in *any* house without cleaning it first? I am married, y'know."

Not many people manage to embarrass me, or make me blush, but Meg somehow manages both as I wipe off the cleaner and place it back under the counter. "Smart lady."

"The fact you acknowledge that is one reason I continue to work for you." She laughs and begins cooking, looking up at me after a moment with a curious expression. "I notice there's a new person in the house this morning."

"You don't miss a thing, do you?"

"It's my job to know how many people I'm cooking for before you tell me," she teases, then adds. "I'm all ears."

"Right." I open the fridge and pull out the orange juice, grabbing a cup as I tell her the details she wants to know. "You'll notice he's a teenager, about my height. Kinda looks like me, but has his mother's eyes."

"Ah. I see."

"He'll eat everything you make and more, no doubt. Probably takes after me in that regard." I put the orange juice away and turn back to her, taking a drink before I continue with a wink. "We both know I'm always hungry."

"And this teenager, does he have a name?"

"Sterling."

She doesn't even blink, even though we both know she's well aware of the name my mother calls me. Instead, she merely smiles and goes back to cooking. "If he's anything like you, sir, then we'll probably need to double the food budget."

"No doubt."

"I have a teenage son," she offers up without looking at me. "During the summer, he sleeps 'til noon, and is up pretty late. And messy. Teenage boys are messy."

"I know. I was one once."

"Hard to imagine. Henrietta's always complaining you aren't messy enough to warrant how much you pay her," she jokes. "Now she'll have to work for it."

With a chuckle, I sit down at the table as Meg brings over the food. "Thank you. You're the best."

"Don't you forget it."

"How can I when you're always reminding me?"

She laughs as she turns to do the dishes, and that's when Angel walks in, rubbing her eyes. Taking a seat across from me, not even a second passes before she's got her arms folded on the table, resting her head upon it.

Meg turns around before I can speak and approaches the table, placing a hand on Angel's arm to get her attention. "Would you like some breakfast, Miss Danita? The pan's still hot and all."

Angel lifts her head, blinking her eyes rapidly as if confused while staring up at Meg — which instantly has me worried. "Uh…you don't have to."

Meg clucks her tongue. "It's my job. How about some coffee? Or juice?"

"Um…" Angel shakes her head, keeping her eyes averted from mine, before looking down as she answers. "J-juice, I guess?"

"Sure."

Meg walks away as I reach an arm over to Angel and use two fingers to lift her chin, making her eyes meet mine. "What's wrong?"

Her smile is weak, her eyes glossy as she grimaces. "I woke up in a lot of pain. Had to take meds to even get out of bed. Not good on empty stomach."

"Why didn't you ring the bell I had set up for you?" I'm unable to keep my mouth from flattening with disapproval, and her eyes tear up at my obvious annoyance, so I soften my words and tone. "Everybody here understands, Angel. No need to be so damned stubborn about needing help."

Meg returns with the juice, and when she sets it down, I say, "Please make her some food real quick, Meg. She took her meds and needs to eat."

"Absolutely."

Angel takes a sip of her juice, and when she looks up at me, I hold part of my banana out to her. "Here. Have some of my banana. I know you'll like it."

She busts out laughing, which makes me feel ten times

better as the confusion flees her face, and takes it from my hand. "Thank you."

Within minutes, Angel has a plate full of food in front of her. Even though I've finished eating, Meg brings me a cup of coffee while I wait for Angel, who picks at her food as usual, but eats more than I know she wants to in order to please me.

Hiding my satisfied smile behind the rim of my coffee cup, she pushes the plate away and announces, "Sorry, but I'm done. And thank you Meg."

"You're welcome."

Standing up and carrying our dishes to the sink, I come back to the table and hold out my hand to Angel. "Time to get ready to go."

She grimaces, placing her hand in mine and rising, any pain she is feeling less obvious now than when she arrived earlier. "So soon?"

"I think you know time is of the essence here. They are expecting us."

"Okay."

Fuck. I know she agreed to treatment, but her easy agreement catches me off-guard. "Do you want to wake up Sterling to go with us?"

"No. There's no need for him to witness the treatments. And he was up late. Let him sleep."

"Meg?"

She turns around from the sink with a smile, nodding her head before I've even asked the question. "You go on ahead. I've got no problem staying to make sure he's taken care of."

"Thank you. I'll let you know when we're on our way back, so keep your phone close." Nodding toward the door, I tell Angel, "Okay, let's go."

After a quick shower — where I managed to keep my hands to myself even though I didn't want to — we both dressed and headed to the hospital.

She held my hand the whole way there, but it's hard to tell which was of us was being comforted or reassured by the other.

I guess in the end, it doesn't matter, since we'd get through this together.

And she'll live, because if this doesn't work…

Well, then I'll need a hell of a whole lot of trees to beat the fucking shit out of.

23 - DANITA

The one thing I hate about chemo — and hated every time I needed to receive chemo — is how absolutely tired and drained it makes me feel.

So I lie here in bed with Sterling sitting in a chair to the side with a sad look on his face, because he brought me food and I won't eat it. Not only am I too tired, I'm not all that hungry, and I ache all over.

It's day five since I entered the trial. The first day, they gave me the initial medication which is used to reduce the risk of infection, then yesterday, the chemo. And this is what I'll keep receiving, eight times each over the next thirty-nine weeks, as long as the cancer doesn't progress.

From where I'm lying and how I'm feeling at the start, thirty-nine weeks seems like a fucking eternity.

But I'll do it, because I love my son and I love Ryker, and I promised them I'd try one more time.

I just wish it didn't hurt so damn much, and the meds only help so far.

"You look tired, Mom. You should get some more sleep." He readjusts my blanket, then takes my hand in his. "I'll sit here and listen to music, play on my phone, in case you need me."

My eyes are closing even as I squeeze his hand in mine and say, "No...I've got the bell. You should go do something fun."

I'm sure he says something in response, no doubt a reply to my suggestion which would break my heart because I don't want him to sit here and watch me go through this, but if he does say anything, I can't be sure as I drift off to sleep with him still holding my hand.

THE NEXT TIME I OPEN MY EYES, RYKER IS SITTING NEXT TO me holding my hand, and my son is standing at the window looking out.

"Sterling," Ryker says while keeping his eyes locked on me. "Go ask Meg to bring up some food for your mother, please."

"Yeah, sure."

I hear Sterling leave the room, shutting the door softly behind him, and within seconds, Ryker has captured my lips with his. It's a sweet, soft kiss full of his love and devotion, and only lasts a few seconds, yet it makes me feel ten times better while reminding me exactly why I'm torturing myself this way once more.

"I know you're probably not that hungry," he murmurs as he pulls away, "but you have to eat something, and I made sure Meg prepared something especially for you. Some soup and crackers; should be light on your stomach." He reaches down beside his chair and holds up a bucket. "But, if not, I got this just in case."

"Thank you." The words are rough, pushed past the lump in my throat at his thoughtfulness, and I clear my throat before asking, "Has Sterling been in here all day?"

"No. Meg says she made him eat, and kept him busy by talking to him for a little while." He grins, lifting my hand to his mouth and kissing the back of it. "She also has a teenage son and said they seem pretty alike, so if he wants to, she'll introduce them. Maybe he'll make a new friend."

"That's great. I don't want him to be lonely."

He nods, then stands up and leans over me as the door opens, my son and Meg entering the room. "Let me help you sit up."

Perhaps it's because I didn't eat earlier, but my stomach grumbles as Meg places the food in front of me on a tray, and I actually want to eat. Meg smiles as she steps back.

"Smells great, Meg. Thank you."

"Enjoy." She scowls at Sterling and then Ryker. "Both of you need to let her eat in peace and come feed yourselves as well."

Ryker waves a hand in her direction, releasing his hold

on mine so I can eat, and sits back. "You and Sterling can go eat. I'll be down in a little while."

Meg doesn't bother to argue, instead giving Sterling a bright smile as she walks toward the door. "You heard him. Growing boys need some good food."

"How do you know it's actually good food?" He calls out after her, and after tossing me a smile over his shoulder, he follows her. "Just because *they* say it is doesn't mean—"

His words cut off as the door shuts behind him, and Ryker chuckles. "He is definitely my son."

"Yes." I take a sip of the hot soup, closing my eyes to enjoy the deliciousness of it before opening them, and smiling at him. "It's amazing how many of your qualities he has even though he wasn't around you."

"That's because being a smartass is a natural born talent, not a learned skill."

It's a good thing I haven't put any more food in my mouth, because my laughter would've had me either choking or spitting it out. But he doesn't say anything else as he sits beside me, his eyes filled with amusement while watching me. And once I'm done eating he removes the tray, sits on the edge of the bed, and takes my hand in his again.

"Angel," he begins, his face going all serious, "there's something I need to tell you. Something you need to know."

"Uh…" I'm sure I should be amused at him using my words from the other night back at me, but his face and tone indicates this is important, so I merely smile and nod. "Okay. What is it?"

"Well, you see, when I was fifteen, I met this amazing girl who had more strength and determination than anyone else I knew. I would've done anything for that girl, and when she left without a word, seventeen-year old me was devastated. But I understood." He holds up a finger to my lips as I open them to speak, and shakes his head. "Then, fifteen years later, she shows up at my door, only she's not the girl she once was. She's been through so much, she simply wanted to end her life before the pain became too much, and when she told me what she's been through, and was still going through, I couldn't blame her."

He squeezes my hand, and I'm fairly sure his eyes are shiny with unshed tears, but I can't see through my own blurry ones to know for sure.

"But, you see, I saw something in her. I saw that same strength and determination, and her will to do what was right for those she loved, whether or not it went against something she wanted. I was ready to fight for her, make her see things my way no matter what it took, but she surprised me by wanting to fight for us, too. And thats when I decided, I won't let her get away again. Whether we have months, or only a few years, or decades — which would be my fucking preference, honestly — I want her next to me the whole time."

He reaches down into his pocket, and pulls out a box, releasing my hand only long enough to open it up and show me the ring inside. "So what I'm wondering is…will you marry me, Angel? Will you be mine, for however long we have together, which is hopefully a really long fucking time?"

My answer is yes, a big, resounding yes.

But wouldn't you know, dinner didn't like me so much after all, and the word that comes out of my mouth in reply instead of 'yes' is, "Bucket!"

Lucky for both of us he has quick reflexes and hands me the requested object in the nick of time.

There's two reasons my work day was screwed from the moment I woke up this morning.

The first was when nobody answered the phone at work, which means either they didn't find me a new secretary as I requested, or the person is incompetent and doesn't realize they're not allowed to leave their desk until I arrive.

Good news is, people can be trained. Bad news is, I don't have fucking time to train someone, so human resources and I are going to have a chat if they did hire someone and the person doesn't know what the hell they're doing, because I've got enough on my plate to deal with.

Problem is, the instant I walk around the corner to my office, the second reason my work day is fucked is glaringly obvious when I catch sight of the person sitting in my secretary's chair.

A person who happens to be my ex-wife.

Veronica's the last person I expect or want to see in my office.

Right as I decide to turn around and work from home, it's too late, and she spots me.

Shit!

She stands up, smoothing down her skirt, and giving me a nervous smile.

Fuck. No.

Scratch having a chat with human resources; someone is going to get fired!

Scowling, I stalk up to her, and I have to give it to her, she doesn't even fucking tremble. She just looks up in my face and asks, "May I get you some coffee?"

"No." I point to where I just came from and shake my head. "No fucking way. Get out of my sight, right now. How the hell did you get hired?"

In her usual manipulative manner, her lower lip begins to wobble as she swallows, taking a step back. "I applied like everyone else, and I might've told them you said it was okay if they hired me."

"What?"

She winces at the bite of my question, yet stands her ground, lifting her chin and crossing her arms over her chest. "You said I've never worked a day in my life, and you're right. Problem is, at my age, who is going to hire me with no experience?"

"Not my problem. Go flip a burger or something."

"Ryker, please," she pleads, grabbing onto my arm, which I free with a simple tug as I open the door to my office and head inside. Of course, she follows me. "Give me a chance to show you I can do this job!"

"You don't *deserve* a chance, Ver!" I slam my briefcase down on the desk, and she jumps, taking a step back. "Especially not at the expense of me or my clients, when none of us have the time for your incompetence."

"Why are you so mean to me?" Instead of yelling, she asks it in a whisper, tears streaming down her face. "I said sorry for what I did. And you're right. I need to work, and live in the real world. I applied for this job and got hired. I'm not a total idiot, Ryker. Why won't you even give me a chance?"

"Because I don't trust you." I throw my hands up in the air, frustrated out of my fucking mind with this whole thing, and point to the door. "Go sit out there; I need to make a few phone calls."

"Okay." She nods, then before turning to exit, says in a subdued voice, "I really hope you'll give me a chance, Ryker. I won't let you down like I did before. I swear it."

All I can manage is a growl, but it's enough to make her scurry out of the room, closing the door behind her.

Then I pick up the phone and dial the one person I know will give me something to smile about and perhaps some perspective on this whole thing. She answers on the first ring.

"Ryker." Angel says my name with such happiness, even though I can tell she's barely awake. "Miss me already, I see."

"Of course I miss you, Angel."

Even though I think I'm keeping my voice steady, she must hear the annoyance or something in my tone. "What's wrong?"

"Well, right now I'm enclosed in my office, and outside sitting at my secretary's desk is my ex-wife, who somehow managed to convince human resources to give her the job."

"Oh, Ryker. That's hysterical!" She cracks up laughing, and even though I'm highly annoyed, hearing her laugh cheers me up a little. "Did you tell her to get the fuck out in your usual fashion?"

"I did, but she practically begged me for the job, and promised me she wouldn't let me down." I sigh, running a hand through my hair, and trying to figure out what the hell to do. "Either way I go, there isn't a chance in hell this will be good in any form."

"Why would she want to work with you when it's clear you don't like her?"

"She doesn't have any skills and she's never had a job. I suppose it's because she's hoping I'll take pity on her and let her gain some experience so she doesn't have to work in fast food or retail."

"Oh."

"The cynical part of me doesn't believe that though. I'm pretty sure she simply wants to work here to be close to me."

"Well, it's up to you. Do you think she'll learn if trained?"

"You wouldn't care if my ex-wife worked for me as my secretary?"

"Hmmm." She drags it out, as if she's thinking real hard about it, then giggles. "Pretty sure I'm lying in your bed, got engaged to you last night, and have had lots of sex with you recently. Not really worried over here."

"Nor should you be, but I wanted to make sure."

"Because you're going to give her a shot? You're a nicer person than I am, Ryker."

"I know." I sigh, feeling as if I'm going to regret making this decision, but at least if I'm working with her, I can keep an eye on her. "But I doubt she'll last two days, let alone a week or months. She won't find this job easy at all."

"Oh, so you're going to scare her away with all the hard work." Angel yawns on the other end. "Ry...I love you but...I'm gonna go back to sleep now. I'll see you when you get home."

"Yeah, you will. Love you too."

She hangs up, and I press the button on my phone, saying into it, "Veronica, come back in here please."

A few seconds later, she comes back inside my office, eyes wary as she approaches my desk and stops just before it. Her reticence irritates me because if she came in running her mouth, I would've changed my mind and told her to get lost, which I really want to do.

"Between the two of us, one of us is an asshole, and that person is not me," I say in a quiet voice, and she grimaces, but doesn't smart off, which is one point in her favor. "As of this moment, you are my employee." Her eyes widen, and when she opens her mouth, I hold up a hand to quiet her. "I don't trust you as far as I can throw you, but at least this way, I can keep an eye on you. If you fuck up though, you're gone. I'll have one of the other secretaries show you what to do, so you better learn fast."

When I pause, she simply says, "Thank you."

"Don't fuck with me, Veronica." I turn my head to gaze out the window, stopping for a moment to figure out the best way to say this, and get the most enjoyment out of it. When I face her once more, I'm smiling, and she beams back at me, no longer hesitant as she thinks she's won. "You are not my ex-wife here. There will be no mention of our past, and if anyone here even so much as breathes a word of you saying anything about me that isn't in regard to work, you will be fired. Got it?"

At her nod, I continue with what she needs to hear. "Sometimes you will be required to go to functions with me. You will do as I say, when I say it, and keep it one-hundred-percent professional. Also, if at any time my fiancee calls, you are to put her through immediately—"

"Your fiancee?" Her voice rises as she cuts in, but she keeps her hands clasped in front of her, and her face neutral.

All the same, I enjoy the slight break in her facade and my smile turns into a full-on grin. "Yes, as of last night. My son, Sterling, may also call and he, too, is to be put through immediately. You are to be respectful at all times, and again, no discussing any of our personal history at any point in time. Any problems with this?"

I can see her trembling, holding back what is no doubt her irritation, yet she doesn't give in and snap at me like I fucking hope she does. Instead, she takes a deep breath, smoothes her skirt, and looks me dead in the eye. "No problem at all. Anything else I can do for you?"

"Yeah. Let Deirdre know I'll need her assistance until you've got the hang of things, and she's to help you until I tell her to stop. You may also leave me alone for now. Don't forget to bring me my coffee in fifteen minutes."

I deliberately look away, dismissing her, and she leaves as quietly as she entered.

Ex-wife being hired as your secretary?

Pain in the ass.

Deciding to let her stay on because you're not a complete asshole and agree she needs work experience if you want her to leave you the hell alone in the future?

Probably idiotic.

The unavoidable rise in her voice when you've put a damper in her 'secret' plans to get you back by announcing you have a fiancee?

Absolutely priceless.

Something tells me this may be more fun than I could've imagined.

"*A*re you ready?"

We pull into his mother's driveway as Ryker asks me that question, and I swallow, nodding even though the anxiety I feel rises. I know it's all from my mind. She knows all about our son, she knows what I've thought the truth was all this time; that I just took the advice of my parents. Most of all she knows Ryker loves me. I shouldn't be anxious at all, but I am.

Perhaps it's because Ryker insisted we not tell her about our engagement until we could do it in person, and well, here we are. He wants to marry before my next treatment. Even though the wedding won't be anything big at my insistence, he wants his mother there for the ceremony. Which is fine with me, of course.

Ryker puts the car in park and gets out, coming over to my side to help me out. I'm feeling fine at this point. Although it's been a week since my first treatment, and my second will be in a week, everyone still wants to do as much for me as they possibly can. It's nice, and I appreciate how much they care, but they're treating me like I can't even walk on my own. It's rather irritating.

However, I keep my mouth shut and when Ryker opens the door, I place my hand in his and climb out with a smile. Sterling gets out as well, ears plugged with his buds blaring music, and I give his music player a pointed look. He pulls the buds out and puts the whole thing in his pocket, sighing even as he shrugs.

As we walk to the door, Sterling blurts out, "Why does she live here in this tiny house? You've got that big one and all."

"She's lived here since we moved when I was fifteen. Just me, her, and my dad," Ryker points out with a chuckle, opening the screen door and knocking on the main one. "This is her home and she's comfortable here."

"Oh. Well, someone should tell her she'll be more comfortable in your big house. I mean, it looks like it would fit in your living room."

"Sterling…" I start with a laugh of my own, unable to fathom why he cares so much, when the front door opens.

His mother steps back to let us in, her eyes widening as she takes in Sterling who stands behind me. Once we're through the door and standing in the living room, I see her eyes are bright and shiny with tears.

"Oh god, Sterling," she says with a smile at Ryker. "He looks just like you."

"You'll need to call me Ryker when he's around, Mom. Otherwise you might confuse him."

My son rolls his eyes. "I'm standing right here."

"Yes, yes you are."

"You're not going to pinch my cheeks, are you? Because I'm too big for that."

"No, but I am going to hug you." She steps forward and envelops Sterling in a hug. He puts his arms around her in reciprocation after a slight hesitation, and tosses a 'help me' look in my direction. "By the way, you're never too old for a hug, so don't forget it."

"Yes, ma'am."

"Miriam," I say, trying to rescue him from what he sees as torture. When she releases my son and turns toward me, all I see on her face is happiness. "It's been a long time."

"If you don't count the hospital."

I wince as she laughs, then say, "Yeah, sorry about that."

She waves a hand, continuing to smile, and shakes her head. "Don't worry about it. Ster—Ryker told me all about what they told you, but I swear I'd never do such a thing, and I know you need to hear that from me." She nods at the couch. "Go on and sit down. I'll go get the tea."

"I don't like tea."

Miriam laughs at Sterling's comment and tips her head toward the direction of the kitchen. "Well, come on with me and get something to drink then. I'm sure I've got something you'll drink, but you've gotta get it yourself."

She walks off before he can reply. He's quick to follow

her, and once he's left the room, I take a seat. Of course, Ryker sits as close to me as possible on the love-seat.

"See?" He murmurs into my ear, his voice filled with amusement as he trails a finger up my arm. "Wasn't painful at all. How do you think we should tell her?"

Since Ryker's been holding my left hand, the ring has stayed hidden from Miriam's view, and I shrug even as my lips curve up. "We didn't bring a sign, so I think simply telling her straight up will have to do."

"That's kind of boring. What about jumping on the couch, Tom Cruise style?"

"Do you want to get laid later?"

He chuckles low into my ear, nipping at the lobe. Sucking on it before releasing it, he whispers, "I most definitely want to fuck you later." His hand slides down my arm and onto my leg, then sidles up under the hem of my skirt until he's cupping me through my panties. "I would do it right now if I could."

I slap at his hand, my cheeks warming even as the naughtier part of me is enjoying what he's doing. "Get your hand out of there. We're on your mother's couch!"

"Don't worry. I've got one eye on the door." He moves his fingers, pushing aside the fabric until he's gliding one finger between my lips. We both moan at the same time he slips a single digit inside me. "Ready as always. This excites you even though I know you're highly embarrassed right now."

"Ryker..." I pause, licking my lips as he kisses my neck, unable to deny what he's said. "You're a tease."

"Not at all. I plan to deliver later." He curls his finger up, stroking me in the way he knows I enjoy. Our hands are still clasped between our bodies. I squeeze his, compressing my lips together in an attempt to stay quiet as pleasure swirls through me. "More than once, for sure. It's been too long."

"It's only been a week," I manage to get out through barely parted lips.

"That's six days and forty-five minutes too long," he jokes, making me laugh as he removes his finger and puts my skirt back into place. "They're coming back."

I lift my free hand to my hair, taking a piece of hair and twirling it around as Miriam returns, taking a seat in the chair to the left. Sterling follows a moment later with a soda in hand and a grin on his face.

"Mom," he says, taking up the little space left next to me on the love-seat, chugging from his soda before continuing. "Why is your face red? It's not hot in here. Are you okay?"

Miriam's eyes widen as Ryker lets out a laugh beside me.

"I'm fine. Just feeling a little warm." Miriam pours a cup of tea and holds it in my direction, but before I can take it myself, Ryker leans forward instead and hands it to me. "Thank you."

"How's everything going?" After giving Ryker some tea, and taking some for herself, Miriam sits back and takes a sip of hers while keeping her gaze on me. "My son said you've joined in on a trial?"

"Yes. It was his idea."

She nods, smiling over at Sterling who has sat back and crossed his arms over his chest, a bored look on his face. "I'm so happy you're both here. I wish I would've known. The day Ryker told me…I couldn't believe it."

"There's something else you won't believe," Ryker jokes, holding up our entwined hands with the ring up. It takes his mother a few moments to register what she's seeing, her eyes going wide as he grins. "We're getting married."

"Oh." She brings her hands up, clasping them together as her eyes tear up once more, her eyes going from our hands to our faces. "That's such terrific news!"

"You didn't think they just wanted to come over for tea, did you?"

That came from Sterling. Miriam laughs while I blush in embarrassment at his penchant for saying whatever comes to mind. Ryker joins in his mother's amusement with a chuckle of his own.

"You're cheeky," Miriam notes with a fond glance at Ryker. "Just like your father was at your age."

"Was?" I lift a brow at both of them. "I'm pretty sure he's still a smart-ass."

Ryker brings my hand up his mouth and kisses the back of, winking at me. "Like I said, natural born talent." Then, he smiles at his mother. "We're getting married tomorrow and want you there."

"Tomorrow?" At his nod, and not even blinking at the speed of which we're getting married for obvious reasons, she asks, "Where at?"

"At the house. Family and my staff. They are looking forward to it."

"I bet. They probably find Danita amazing compared to Ver—" Her words cut off and she brings a hand up to cover her mouth.

"Yes, they do," Ryker says simply. "But nobody finds her more amazing than I do."

Miriam lets out an 'aww' while Sterling rolls his eyes with a disgusted sound, and Ryker leans in to give me a kiss.

And I smile because in this moment, I know I'm completely surrounded by people who love me for the absolute first time in my life.

$\mathcal{I}$'m nervous as fuck as I stand in front of the mirror, preparing to walk down the aisle for the second time in my life.

Sterling sits across the room in his suit, totally oblivious to everything else around him with his earbuds in. I can't blame the kid for spacing out.

No matter how either of us look at it, today is a heavy day, being sixteen years in the making and all.

Does it matter I thought I'd never see her again? Nope, not one fucking iota. I love her, she's about to become my wife, and I'm going into it knowing I may lose her.

Not trying to put a damper on my wedding day, but I'm a realist. We don't really talk about it, and take things day by day, but it doesn't mean I don't think about it. It's hard not to think about it, yet I try real hard to push it aside until I have to deal with it, which I fucking hope I don't.

I'm marrying her because I'm hopeful for a future, but

that's not all. I'm also marrying her because I want her to know for sure I'll take care of her and our son, no matter what. In sickness and in health; she can be sure of that from the get go.

As I finish dressing, there's a brisk knock on the door. Without the person seeking entrance giving anyone time to respond, the door opens. A woman with black hair and green eyes slips inside, shutting it behind her, then grins at me as she steps forward.

"You must be Ryker," she says, tossing a glance at Sterling before focusing on me. "I'm Vanessa, or Ness as Danita calls me."

She holds out her hand and I take it with a nod. "Nice to meet you. Have you been to see her?"

"Nope. I wanted to introduce myself before I go surprise her." She releases my hand and turns to Sterling who has pulled his buds out of his ears and stood up. "And you! Look at how much you've grown!"

"I'm not that big since the last time you saw me."

Vanessa rolls her eyes and steps forward, arms open. "At least two inches. Give me a hug before I go see your mother." When her arms are around him, she squeezes and I laugh as he grunts like she's killing him. "Such a kidder, as always."

Letting him go, she smoothes her dress, flipping her hair over her shoulder before smiling at both of us. "You both look quite handsome. And so much alike."

"My mother said the same thing."

"I met her downstairs. She's bossing all the staff around

like she owns the place."

"My first wife wanted everything her way and didn't let my mother help with a thing. Angel was more than happy to let her handle things today, although my staff could've taken care of it all on their own. I'll let her feel special, though." Winking at her, I button my cuffs and turn to Sterling. "Don't tell your grandmother I said that."

"I'm fourteen, Dad, not a seven-year-old tattle tale."

Vanessa gasps, which has me glancing back over at her with a quizzical look. "What?"

She shakes her head, eyes tearing up alongside her wobbly smile. "Nothing. It's just so sweet — and odd — to hear him call you 'Dad.' Not used to it after all this time."

"You guys are too sappy for me," Sterling says with a roll of his eyes, stepping toward the door. "I'm going downstairs now."

"See ya later, kiddo," she says and snickers as he leaves the room, turning her smiling face back to me. "Love him, such a good kid."

"He is."

"How'd you do it?" She rushes to explain as I raise my brow at her, unsure of what she means. "Get her willing to try treatments again. She'd given up, and I was so upset even though I know the decision was hard for her."

"Ah." Adjusting my cuffs a final time, I step toward her and the door with a smile as I rest my hand on the doorknob. "It wasn't simple. She fought me the whole way, but in the end, I think it's because she finally got back everything she lost. She saw she still had a chance at happiness with me and our son."

Tears threaten to leak from her eyes as she nods. Stepping forward, she pulls me into a hug before I can blink, leaving me with nothing else to do except pat her back awkwardly. "Thank you, for everything. She deserves to be happy. She really does." She lets go and I open the door, letting her step through first as she says, "I should go shock the shit out of her now."

Nodding, I chuckle and tip my head toward the door down the hall. "She's in the room at the end to the right." I look down at my watch real quick as she starts to walk away and say, "Tell her she's got twenty minutes."

She acknowledges what I've said with a wave. Closing the door behind me, I head downstairs to see if my mother needs any more help and wait on Angel to make her appearance.

My mother is running around like a crazy person when I get downstairs, and I laugh as she pulls me into a hug, then steps back.

"You look so handsome," she says with tears in her eyes, fidgeting with the lapel of my jacket for a second before dropping her hands. "And so happy."

"I'll agree with the happy part."

She rolls her eyes in an exaggerated manner like she did when I was a child and said something we both knew was dumb. Then, she slaps me on the side of my upper arm in mock disgust, the smile on her face giving away her joy for me as she teases back, "You're right. You're a troll."

"Thanks Mom, I'm always glad when you tell me how you *really* feel."

Wrapping her arm through the crook of my offered arm, she says, "Everything is ready to go."

"All right then. Let's go wait on the arrival of the bride. Vanessa is with her now."

"Oh is she? I met her when she passed through…"

She rambles on and on while my thoughts drift Angel and what I'll do to her when we're all alone later.

Can't wait.

*W*hen the door opens, the last thing I expect to see is Ness.

It doesn't keep me from squealing with delight as she closes the door behind her and runs over to me, hugging me to death.

"I thought you couldn't make it!"

"Well, I worked it out, so surprise!" She releases me, holding my upper arms as she steps back and gives me and my dress the once over. "You look stunning. He'll love it!"

My dress is a simple sheath ivory gown. It's sleeveless and smooth with a strap on one shoulder while the other is bare, and the skirt touches the floor. I grin at her and turn toward the mirror with a roll of my eyes. "The man would love me in a dirty potato sack."

"Lucky." Her sigh's filled with envy, and I laugh as she says, "It's like a fairy tale."

"More like a tragedy," I joke with my morbid sense of

humor, knowing Ness would understand, and turn back to her. "It only turns into a fairy tale if I live."

"Which you will, Danita, or so help me…"

"Or what? You'll spank me?" I lean over, facing the mirror once more, putting my hands on my knees and wiggling my butt at her. "Come on, do it now and get it over with."

"As nicely clad as your ass is right now — no really, it's pretty fine," she insists as I bust out laughing. "Get that ass away from me, girl. Ask Ryker to smack it later, will ya?"

"Oh, I will." It comes out as a groan and she lifts a brow at me in question as I straighten. "It's been a bit since we had sex. I'm jumping his bones tonight since I feel all right. It'll be another two weeks before it happens again I'm sure."

"Not even married and he isn't even sexing you up properly? You sure you wanna marry him?" She throws her arm around my shoulders and gives them a squeeze, bringing me close to her side as we both gaze into the mirror. "It's not too late to back out."

With a snort of laughter, I shrug off her arm and pick up my veil, handing it to her. "It was too late the moment I showed up on his doorstep."

"So true. There's no chance that man will ever let you go without a major fight." Making sure the veil is on and in place, she steps back and says, "I saw him before I came in here. Both he and Sterling looked quite handsome, and I about cried when Sterling called him 'dad' and all."

Lifting the veil so it falls down around my face, I take

her arm and pull her close, tears in my own eyes. "I'm so glad they got to meet before…well, before I go, if that's the case. But…" I pause, and she waits without a word for me to finish what I'm going to say, and I sigh. "Is it terrible that I wish my mother was here? And to wonder if she'd be proud of me?"

"No, of course not. Terrible as things were, she was still your mother. And in the end, she killed that motherfucker, didn't she?"

"Yeah, she did. Ryker said she stuck up for me, that she didn't know. I had no idea he was hurting her though. Shouldn't I have known?"

Ness places her hands on my shoulders and glares at me in the mirror. "No. You were a child who was experiencing hurt yourself. Your mom probably hid it from you because she didn't want to burden you."

Even though I know she's right, the guilt I've been carrying around for so long continues to weigh me down. The tears pooling in my eyes threaten to spill over as words spill out of my mouth. "I never saw her again, you know? Once I left, I never went back and she died while I was too messed up to care. I was so angry at her for failing to notice what that animal was doing to me."

"Danita, turn around." I do and she smiles at me before pulling me into a hug. "Your mother would be proud of you, just like I am, and Ryker is, and your son. You've been through so much. Even though it took all this time, you're back with the love of your life and fighting for the chance to spend many more years with him. Anyone who isn't proud of you is an idiot, and I don't see any idiots here today." I lift my head as she pushes gently on my shoulders and scowls at me once more. "Now get rid of those tears and get ready to become a wife."

"I love you, Ness."

"Not my wife, girl," she says with a wink as I laugh. "And I love you, too."

She holds out her arm and I take it as we leave the room, walking down the steps to where my son awaits me. He'll be walking me down the aisle today, and it seems I'll spend the day with watery eyes as they fall upon my son in his suit. Ness gives my cheek a kiss through the veil, then heads inside to take a seat, leaving my son and I alone.

Sterling loops his arm through mine with a smile and as we stand there waiting for the music to begin playing, he says, "Thank you, Mom."

His soft-spoken words have my heart speeding up as I look over at him. "For what?"

"For finally giving me the family I've wanted since I was a kid." He pulls me to him and hugs me close, his height making it so my head is on his chest. "I know you did what was best for me, but all I've ever wanted was to be with you. Please…" I hear him choke up, pausing for a moment before taking a deep breath, and continuing as I wrap my arms around his waist. "Please don't ever leave me again, not if you can help it."

I hate the pain in his words, knowing I caused it even with my good intentions. The tears I've held at bay all morning leak from my eyes as I tell him what we both already know, but needs said out loud anyway. "I won't, honey. You and your father are stuck with me for the rest of my life. I promise."

He hugs me tight, his sigh filled with the relief I didn't know he needed. A minute later, we separate and he takes my arm once more. "Ready?"

"Yep."

"Hey, Mom?" I lift my gaze back to his to discover the smile back on his face and in his eyes, where my own face beams back at me with our shared joy. "You're the most beautiful mom in the world. Just thought I should tell you."

I bring my free hand up to squeeze the arm he's looped through mine as I grin in return. "Thank you. You're a pretty handsome kid yourself, but you've got your father to thank for that."

He rolls his eyes, and before he can respond in his usual smartass fashion, the music starts.

Moments later, my eyes land on Ryker standing at the end of the aisle, and I'm sure the smile on my face is the biggest it's ever been.

*W*hat do men think about when the woman they love is walking toward them down the aisle?

I don't know what other men think, but what I'm thinking as she enters the room and heads my way is how fucking beautiful she is. How much I love her and hope she gets better. And, okay, I'm thinking about getting her naked later, because it's been too long. With her upcoming treatment, it will be a little bit again, so I want to use my time wisely.

But I'm good with that, because she'll be my wife. I'll get to hold her, sleep next to her, and do all I can to make up for the years we've lost. For me — and for her — I know that's enough.

Most of all, I'm happy. Fucking ecstatic, actually.

Our son has his arm looped through Angel's as he walks her down the aisle. The way Sterling stands tall and proud while walking beside her, as if a great weight is gone from his shoulders, makes me proud. I realize how fucking lucky I am to call him mine.

How lucky I'll be to call her my wife.

And I know I missed out on so much with both of them, but it won't happen again. I won't let any of us miss another moment.

When I focus my complete attention on her, she's giving me the biggest smile I've seen on her yet. I make a silent promise to make sure her smile is bigger by the end of the evening.

And even more so every day following today.

Her smile is so bright; it's as if she's not even wearing a veil. I lift my eyes from where they're focused on her lips until our gazes meet, then return her smile with a grin of my own.

I wish I could say I look at and appreciate her dress, but I don't, because I know she looks exquisite in almost anything. And in this moment, maintaining eye contact as she walks toward me is the most important. I'll get to examine — and remove her from — the dress later, after all.

Truth is, all I want and desire from her in this moment is the joy shining in her eyes. As she and Sterling reach the end of the aisle, I hold out a hand toward them. We've only eyes for each other as she places her hand in mine, moving until she's standing next to me, facing me. Sterling takes his seat next to Vanessa, leaving Angel and I alone at the altar with the Justice of the Peace.

He begins speaking, but I don't hear a word he says.

I've clasped Angel's hands in mine, and I don't want to let them go, so I don't. I take her in, all of her. This woman who is a mix of the girl I first fell in love with, and who had my child. Who kept going even when many would've given up. She looks healthy today with her glowing skin, bright eyes, and an impish lift at the corner of her lips, yet she isn't healthy at all.

And suddenly, I'm terrified, even in the face of the joy I feel at her becoming my wife.

Because even in my determination to keep her with me, it may not happen. This beautiful, vibrant, and kind woman who has fought tooth and nail to keep going; who is letting me try to save her one more time knowing it may be for nothing. She could be gone before we ever get to experience all the joys of finally spending our lives together. And the idea of losing her any time in the near future is the worst.

Holding up a hand to stop the justice of the peace from doing the normal vows, I say, "I want to say my own."

Angel's eyes widen, because I know she's caught off-guard by this, and the room is silent around us as I begin speaking.

"Angel, I don't believe in much, but when it comes to you, I'm willing to believe in anything." I lift her hands to my lips and kiss them, squeezing them tightly as I hold them against my chest, our gazes still locked with each other's. "The way you've persevered through the last fifteen years is nothing short of amazing. While I wish I had been with you through them all, I'm glad you're here today. We may have months, or we may have years, but either way, I'm yours. I want to spend every moment I can with you, even if it means doing nothing but lying in bed next to you, holding you close when you aren't feeling well."

The sniffles of other people in the room reach my ears, and I see Angel's eyes growing watery. I say what I need to say even if it's the mushy things I'm not supposed to admit to as a man. "I love you, and meeting you sixteen years ago was one of the best days of my life. The second was when you showed up on my doorstep after all this time. And the third is the day I found out you were the mother of my child. Our child. And the fourth best day of my life? Today. You marrying me. And I'd like to think that from now on, every day will be one of the best days of my life, because you'll be here. With me. And I hope it's a hell of a lot of days."

Tears are streaming down her cheeks as she tugs at her trapped hands, indicating I should release them, which I do. And then, before I can even gather what she intends to do, she lifts her veil over her head to uncover her face. Throwing herself into my arms, she wraps her arms around my neck as I slide mine around her waist to hold her close, and crushes her lips to mine.

The room erupts in laughter, everyone clapping while the Justice clears his throat and makes some comment about us being husband and wife. Neither of us are paying attention as we cling to one another, lost yet found in each other's arms.

"*D*id you enjoy your wedding day?" Ryker asks as he slides his arms around my waist from behind.

I'm standing in our bedroom in front of the window, watching as everyone leaves. Ryker gave the staff the evening off, so we'll be all alone. Ness, who will be visiting for a couple days, is going to a hotel room paid for by Ryker for the night, returning tomorrow to spend more time with me. Sterling has gone home with Ryker's mother. She wanted to spend some quality time with her grandson, one-on-one, and I'm so glad they are getting the time together.

"Mmhmm," I reply, leaning back into him, his arms tightening a little while I'm unable to resist teasing him. "Your mother is the best, and she can manage my wedding any time."

He nips the top of my right ear with his teeth, sliding one arm up as the other glides down the front of my body.

My soft laugh turns into a low moan as he growls, then says, "This is your first and only wedding, Angel. The only exception is if you ever want a renewal of vows. Is that clear, or do you need a more explicit explanation?"

Weighing my options in silence, my mouth parts, my breathing increasing as he uses his hand to scrunch up the dress in his hand. He raises the silky material up little by little until he exposes my leg to the cool air. He keeps the skirt hoisted up, teasing the lace trimming on the thigh-high stocking with his fingers, then glides his hand along the inside of my thigh. Seconds later, he cups my exposed pussy with his palm.

He murmurs his approval at my lack of underwear, slipping a finger through my labia, finding me slick and wet for him already. Not that it ever takes much. His simple presence makes me hot for him in milliseconds, his touch causing my body to quiver in anticipation. As one hand teases me below, he uses the other to steal inside the bust of my dress. He pinches my nipple between his thumb and forefinger, rolling and tugging on it. Arching into it, he chuckles while simultaneously sinking one finger, then two inside my pussy. Using the palm of his hand, he pushes against the front of my body to bring my ass closer to where I can feel how hard he is for me.

"I'd love to fuck you while you wear this dress, Angel. It's beautiful on you. I don't know if I told you that, but you make the dress; I'm sure of it." He moves his fingers inside me to the edge, then thrusts them back in, causing my brain to fog and another moan to slip through my lips. "But something tells me, you want to play tonight. It's been a while since I've done anything except be gentle with you, and you hate that, don't you?"

His name is a rasp on my lips. "Ryker. No. I don't hate it. I love when you're sweet and gentle, but I also love when you're rough and do the things I enjoy most."

"What do you enjoy the most, sweetheart?"

His hands are unmoving, yet my body is aflame. His touch increases my arousal as the seconds tick by, my body responding to him with a ferocity only he seems able to elicit from me. I want more. So much more.

And I know what I want. What I need. I'm also aware he knows what I need as well; he's simply waiting for me to voice it.

"I enjoy you inside me, giving me pleasure while taking your own." My tongue darts out, mouth opening on a gasp as he responds to my words with a thrust of his fingers, and a rock of his hips. "But I want you inside me while you give me the pain I crave. The pain I need."

Not only do I hear him suck in a breath, but I feel it since our bodies are so close. I know he's remembering the way I leaned over the table and he hit me with a belt; to do it while inside me would take things to a whole new level.

"I've got the perfect toy for that." He removes his hand from inside me, straightening my body so he can unzip the dress, and slips his hands inside to shove the dress down my arms. "Remove the dress, leaving your stockings and heels on, then lean over the bed."

He walks away, shuffling around behind me while I do

as bid. Stepping out of the dress, I lay it over the back of the chair in front of my vanity, careful to make sure it stays in place. I'm wearing the pieces he requested as I stand at the end of the bed and wait. The bed is a nice height, so when I bend over it, my position is perfect for what we're about to do, my bare back and naked ass awaiting his touch.

The room is rapidly darkening as the sun goes down. Because I've got my eye on the clock sitting on the nightstand, I know ten minutes passes before he returns to me. A shiver runs through my body as he places his hot hand on the small of my back. My skin is cool to the touch thanks to the air conditioning, a fact I'm sure I'll be happy about real soon.

Without a word from either of us, he drags his hand down and across my hip, then up across one cheek. Then his palm moves to the other before slipping between my legs. He pauses in his movements, cupping me in his hand. Moving a finger down and over my clit, he hits one of my ass cheeks with something at the same time.

Even though I'd asked for it, I didn't know it would come. The surprise slap of the material — and the subsequent sting — makes me hiss, jerking my body away and down toward the bed. In a matter of seconds, I register the fact he's using a whip, no doubt leather, but I'm unable to discern what would scrape my skin when it hit me. And any further thought on it gets pushed out of my mind when he slaps the other cheek.

"Back to your position, Angel. If you move again, I'll

stop." He slips two fingers inside my pussy as I follow his command, and he rewards me with a few strokes before simply cupping me once more. "Do you like the whip?"

"Yes, but there's one problem."

"What is it?"

"I feel like something is pricking me," I answer with a laugh, "and that something isn't you."

The removal of his hand from between my legs almost has me turning around to see what he's doing. But before I can, he glides his body over mine until his mouth is right by my ear. Dangling the object in front of my eyes, he chuckles while I study the implement he's chosen.

I was right. It is a whip — a cat-o-nine tails, specifically — and it is leather, but it's modified. Between the strands of the whip are secondary ones, braided with some sort of tiny pieces coming off them. I've no doubt these are what I feel scratch me.

"What is the material?"

"I've no idea, but it's neat isn't it?" He takes the whip out of view, lifts his body off mine, and drags it down my shoulder to the center of my back, leaving a tingling trail in its wake. "It leaves a mark, but doesn't break your gorgeous skin."

With that remark, he is quick to lift and bring it back down to slap my back, and there is no more talking. He covers every inch of my back, from top to bottom, and uses his hand to slap my ass at the same time the whip makes contact with my skin. And when I'm so turned on I feel as if I'm floating from the mix of pleasure and pain, he grips a hip with his one hand, and probes the entrance of my pussy with the tip of his cock -- something I'm more than ready for.

There is no focus, just feeling. As he sinks in inch by inch, every movement accompanies the whoosh of the whip in the air, followed by the slap of the strands against my skin. Every sting is so sweet when he's finally inside all the way, and every long stroke in and out of his cock hits me just right. Within moments, I'm lost, my orgasm upon me with no warning, so strong that if he spoke at all, I didn't hear him. I've lost all awareness, doing nothing but feeling in a way I haven't felt in so long.

Yet, it's only when he comes, when he slams into me one final time, that I realize tears stream down my cheeks.

And I don't know how he knows, but he pulls out, lifts me up and gathers me into his arms. Getting us both into the bed, he says in a soft voice, "Don't cry, Angel," as he lies down and brings me close to his side. Kissing the top of my head, he runs his hand up and down my arm, comforting me while hugging me close.

I'm incoherent, no sound from me at all, as the tears continue to spill down my face, unable to tell him they aren't tears of sadness, but of joy. Of how happy he makes me; how much I love him and never want to leave him. Words I need and want to tell him, but they won't come out.

So, I get on top of him, wrapping my arms around his neck, and place my face in the crook of his shoulder. With a sigh, he places a kiss to my cheek, keeping our bodies close by holding onto me.

Then he shows me how much he knows me more than I know myself as he says into my hair, "I love you too, Angel."

The knock at the door to my home office two days after the wedding is loud, distracting me from the work I've been focusing on for the last hour.

Keeping my eyes on the computer screen, I call out, "Come in."

"Dad." Sterling's voice is a bit on the whiny side as he plops into the chair in front of the desk, causing me to switch my attention to him and raise a brow. "My computer broke."

I'm still not used to him calling me 'Dad' but I enjoy it all the same and wouldn't want it any other way. Leaning back in my chair, I give him a smile. "Is it actually broken, or is it simply not living up to its normal operating standards?"

"Isn't that the same thing?"

"No." Laughing, I close out my work and log off,

holding out my hand. "Show me what's wrong with it and I'll see what I can do."

He passes the heavy laptop over to me and within seconds, it's clear the computer's a piece of shit.

"Damn. How old is this thing?"

"Um." He thinks for a moment, then throws his hands up in the air. "I dunno. Aunt Felicia got it for me years ago."

"This thing's a dinosaur. How do you get anything done on it?" At his shrug, I set the computer down on my desk, and stand up. "Come on, we'll go buy you a new one."

"You're gonna buy me a new one, just like that? Aren't they expensive?"

"For you, it is," I reply, chuckling as I head over to the door, not waiting for him to follow. "Me? I'm sure I can afford it."

I know he's behind me somewhere as I walk down the steps toward the living room. Sticking my head inside the doorway, I see Angel and Vanessa sitting next to each other on the couch.

"Hey."

In an instant, Angel's eyes find mine and she smiles, while Vanessa is slower to turn around yet the first to speak. "Aren't you the one who said you'd be working and you'd let us girls be?"

I answer her question while keeping my eyes on Angel. "I did. Just letting you two know Sterling and I are going to the store. It seems he needs a new computer."

Angel laughs. "Nice. You know he'll try to talk you into buying him more than that, right?"

"I might let him get away with it."

At that exact moment, Sterling walks up behind me. "Ready to go, Dad."

"Well, guess that's my cue to go." I take a step back, turning to face Sterling, who is standing by the front door which is now ajar. "Enjoy your time alone together, ladies."

"Buh-bye," Vanessa says in a singsong voice. "Make sure you bring me back something pretty!"

Angel bursts into laughter, then yells out, "Have fun boys!"

"We will," I shout back as I step outside, shutting the door behind me, and then slip into the waiting car.

STERLING EXAMINES THE COMPUTERS AS I WATCH HIM WITH amusement, his eyes wide while he takes in the various sizes and kinds. It's as if the boy has never seen so many in one place, but I know that's not the case. Probably more of a reaction to me telling him he can get whichever one he wants, something I'm sure has never been an option in his life before.

Angel didn't need to warn me about our son trying to convince me to get him more than a computer. Within reason, I'll buy him whatever he wants. He's a good kid and I figure even though I didn't know about him, I've got fourteen years to make up for.

This is the first time we've been somewhere together, just the two of us, since he and Angel moved in with me. I know I need to spend more time with him, so I promise myself I'll delegate more of my work to others so I can do just that, at least for the summer.

Sterling starts examining a laptop I recommended to him, but when I go to see if he has any questions, my phone vibrates in my pocket.

Taking it out, I look at the screen, sighing as Veronica's name flashes up at me. Not wanting to answer the phone, but having to since she works for me now, I tap the green button and put the phone next to my ear. "Yes, Veronica?"

"Ryker," she replies in a steady voice. "There's a Mister Ferguson here for you. Says you rescheduled with him last week, but I've no record—"

"Shit. I did. My mistake." Thinking real quick, I take a glance over at Sterling who is now looking right at me, waiting. "Give him my address and tell him to meet me there in an hour."

"Okay. Will do."

"Thanks. I've gotta go." I hang up on her without waiting for her response, and walk over to Sterling, pointing at the laptop he'd been checking out. "You want this one?"

He nods, pulling out his phone as it vibrates, and I find someone to help us. A few minutes later we're standing in line to check out when a girl wearing a baseball cap squeals my son's name and runs straight into his arms.

I figure okay, he must know her from living with his aunt; most likely someone he knew in school. He wraps his arms around her waist, throwing me a look that has 'sorry' written all over it, and I wonder why he's sorry for hugging what seems like an obvious friend.

Then she pulls back, takes her hands and places them on either side of his face, which makes him return his gaze back to her eyes...where she proceeds to press her lips against his.

Oh, shit. I turn away, facing forward in line as I realize this is what my mom must've felt like the one time she caught Angel and I kissing. A mix of 'aw hell' and 'fuck this is awkward' — or maybe that's just me.

"Dad?"

Keeping my face in what I hope is a neutral expression, I turn back to them.

Sterling smiles, nodding at his girlfriend who only has eyes for him. "This is Renee. My girlfriend."

"Hi!" Renee spares me a glance with her greeting, but doesn't even wait for me to reply before aiming all her attention at Sterling once more. "I can come over some time, can't I?"

I would wonder if all teenage girls are the same way, but she can't be more than fourteen or fifteen anyway, and I remember how focused I'd been on Angel from the moment we met. I'm not sure what I should do or say, if anything, because parenting is so fucking new to me. I'll have to have a discussion with Angel first so I don't screw anything up.

"Are you checking out, sir?" The voice comes from behind me and I turn back around, leaving my son and his girlfriend to their discussion as I nod at her, handing over the laptop. "Did you find everything okay?"

"Yes, thank you."

By the time we're finished, Renee has left, and as we head home, Sterling keeps glancing over at me then looking away.

"What?" I finally ask, figuring he wants to say something, but isn't sure if he should.

"We're not doing anything," he blurts out, his face turning a bit red as if he's embarrassed.

"I didn't say you were. I haven't said a word."

"But you're thinking it. Aunt Felicia had the same look on her face until I told her it wasn't like that." His words come out full speed, as if he needs to reassure me, so I say nothing as he continues. "We're both fourteen and all we do is…uh…kiss."

In for a penny…

"I see." I try to think of what to say next, and he turns to look out the window, his face turning redder by the second. "Do we need to have a talk about sex?"

Sterling looks absolutely tortured as his eyes shoot back to mine. "God, please no. Aunt Felicia tried once and it was terrible. We just kiss. I know we're too young for anything else, it could fuck up my future and—"

Holding up a hand, I cut him off as he recites something he's obviously been told countless times before. "First, your aunt is a female. As a boy myself, my father spoke with me about it, and there are things boys don't want to tell their mothers. Second, I don't care if you swear, but I hope you're keeping it out of where it doesn't belong, like when you're in school?" He nods in confirmation, his look of panic subsiding. "Good. And third, I'd be a hypocrite to tell you to wait, but you're only fourteen and I don't want you to think I'm not glad you're here—"

Now he cuts me with a roll of the eyes and a sound of disgust. "I know. That wasn't the same thing. I'm not gonna have sex with her any time soon, and if I do, I'll be smart about it. Are we done now?"

I lift my hands with palms forward in a show of surrender, lip quirking because his reply amuses me. "Yep. If you get it, you get it. I won't say another word."

In silence, he stares at me for another moment or two, then catches me off guard with his next question. "Do you think things would've gone differently if mom hadn't left? If you'd known about me?"

"Honestly, I don't know."

And it's the truth. I don't.

"Why not?"

His question is a valid one, and he's a smart kid. So I decide to lay it out for him, hoping Angel doesn't beat me to death for telling Sterling the truth, along with its consequences for all of our lives.

"Life isn't fair." He grimaces and opens his mouth, but I hold up a hand to cut him off. "I know everybody hates hearing that, but it's true. When it comes down to it, neither your mother or I got lucky. I can't say if it would've been different, because it's more complicated than that. We loved each other. Kids or not, our love was — and still is — real. I didn't love her just because I was young and wanted to have sex with her. We were friends before anything else, and we were friends *because* of her strength, her intelligence, and her ability to make both of us smile no matter the situation."

I pause, tearing my gaze from his to look out the window as I continue. "Your mother was young, and people lied to her while she was in a vulnerable position. She thought things about our situation that weren't true for a long time, so she did what she thought was best with what knowledge she possessed. Because of that, she never contacted me, and I never knew about you. We were robbed of years together, but at the same time, she was in a bad situation. So yeah, I'd like to say things would've gone differently, but that doesn't necessarily mean the results would've been any better than they are now."

"So you're glad she left even if it meant you lost years with us?"

"The only thing I'm glad for is the fact you two weren't lost to me forever. And that's all that matters."

Looking back over at him once I'm finished speaking, he nods, saying, "Me too." Then, he holds up the laptop box. "Thanks. It'll be strange to use something that isn't really slow."

"My pleasure."

And it is. Every single moment.

"*Have* you told Frederick you want to do weird things to him yet?"

Ness and I are sitting in the living room, and have been since Ryker and Sterling left an hour ago. She rolls her eyes at my question, lifting her hand and dropping her eyes to where she picks at her nails with her thumb.

"No. He's been working a lot. And whenever we try to talk, something comes up."

"You mean you're a chicken shit."

"Yes," she wails, throwing her hands up in what I take as a helpless gesture. "I love him. I don't want him to reject me because I want him to do things he's never done before."

"Ness, you two have been together for five years. He's not gonna dump you just 'cuz you wanna be tied up. And if he does," I continue, cutting her off as she opens her mouth to object in her usual absurd fashion, "then you have to decide if you can deal with not having that part of your sexual life filled. I mean, look at me. I like when I'm smacked and hit. Most men won't touch me, which made them not the men for me."

"But you've always been a freak." She laughs, and I join in, because it's true. "This would be new info for Frederick. I mean, we've got two positions…maybe three if he's feeling frisky."

I pull out my phone and once I'm in my contacts, I bring up Frederick's number. Ness sees what I'm doing and tries to grab for my phone, but I jump up out of her reach.

"Oh my god, Dani! Don't do it."

"I just wanna see how he's doing. He's my friend too, y'know." The grin on my face gives me away though and she doesn't try to take the phone again as I dial, her face flaming.

"Hey Freddie," I say with a giggle as he picks up. "How're you?"

"I'm all right. How's Ness? Congrats on your wedding by the way. Sorry I couldn't make it."

"No worries hon, I know you're a busy man." I wiggle my brows at Ness and say into the phone, "Ness is good. We're just sitting here watching this soft core porn movie on Showtime."

He sounds like he chokes on something, but covers it with a cough, while Ness' mouth drops open. "What? You're full of shit. Ness doesn't watch porn. She turns red when I turn on anything with nudity."

"Oh, does she now?"

"What's he saying?" Her words hiss out, eyes round like saucers, and I'd feel bad for her if I didn't think this was for her own good.

"Yeah, it's cute."

"Interesting. And here she sits, telling me she wishes you would spank her like the guy on the show did—"

Ness jumps up and snatches the phone out of my hand with a squeal before I realize what she's doing. Unable to contain my howl of laughter, I plop down onto the couch and she stands in front of me, Frederick's laughter coming through loud and clear from the other side.

"Freddie, I—" She stops, glaring at me as he speaks, then blushes. "No." He says something and her response follows with wide eyes. "Oh, really?" Mouth forming an 'o' shape, my grin widens as her face gets so red I'm afraid her blood pressure is going to make her head explode. "Uh… yeah, that would be nice. Love you too. See you later."

Ending the call, she tosses the phone at me. "Bitch." Then, with a laugh, sits down beside me on the couch and says, "I love you."

A phrase which tells me exactly what he said without her having to say a word.

"Ha! I told you."

"I know you wanna know what he said to me."

"Of course I do!"

"Too bad, I'm not saying." Enveloping me in a hug, I wrap my arms around her shoulders as she chuckles. "But seriously, you're the best."

"I know."

"You better call me when you find out whether the treatment is working or not, got it?"

As I pull back from her embrace, I flash her a smile, making her the only promise she'll accept. "You know I will."

She looks down at her watch. "Do you think I should call a taxi to take me to the airport?"

I didn't even need to answer her question. The front door opens and a few seconds later, Ryker's head pops into the room. I can't keep my lips from curving up with happiness at seeing him. "You're back."

"Yeah, I've got a client meeting me here in twenty minutes." His focus moves from me to Ness. "I forgot about meeting a client today at the office, but I didn't forget you need to get home in time for a meeting of your own. Kevin's waiting for you."

"Thanks. I'll go get my bags." She turns to me and gives me another hug. "I'll call you later."

"I'll hold you to that. Hopefully you won't be too tied up to actually follow through."

Walking away with a roll of her eyes, she tosses me a last wave as she exits the room, and Ryker moves toward me. He doesn't even give me a chance to blink after he stops in front of me, hauling me into his arms with one arm around my waist. The other hand cradles the nape of my neck as he lowers his head and covers my mouth with his hungry one.

I know it's cliche, but his kiss takes my breath away. His passion, love, and need for me flows out of him in every stroke of his tongue, and every slight pressure of his hand on my back as he tries to bring us as close as possible to one another.

I don't even get an opportunity to wrap my arms around his neck because he drags his mouth away and releases me with a heavy sigh, stepping back. Bringing my fingers up to my mouth, I touch my lips as we stare at each other, catching our breaths.

"I've got to go get ready to speak with this client." He snatches the hand I have against my mouth and lifts it to his lips, turning my hand over and pressing a kiss into my palm. "It might be a while, so you should have a chat with our son while I'm busy. See you at dinner."

"Why? Is something wrong?"

He squeezes my hand and then lets go, not answering my question other than with a shake of his head, and walks out of the room.

My question is answered a few minutes later when I'm standing in my son's room and he's waiting for his new computer to boot up. My son has a girlfriend and they've been together since they were both thirteen, apparently.

"It's not that big of a deal, Mom," he says right off the bat.

"How's it not? Why didn't you tell me you have a girlfriend?"

"I dunno, I guess 'cuz it's not important. You know, with what you're going through?"

"What?" The word comes out on a huff of exasperation. "Everything you do is important to me. I want to know what's going on with you, no matter what I'm dealing with."

Shrugging, he turns back to the screen as the setup screen appears. "Kay. Her name is Renee."

"You should invite her over for dinner sometime." He tosses me a look I can't decipher over his shoulder, so I clarify my statement. "You know, whenever you're ready."

"Okay."

He turns around and starts typing on his computer, and I know we're done talking for now.

Which is great because fatigue sets in all of a sudden and that means I need to go lie down and take a nap until dinner.

So I do.

*I*t's the day after Angel's second treatment, and instead of being home with her like I want, I'm in the office dealing with the aftermath of a client having a fit. Oh, and the fact Veronica is an hour late for work with no call.

I knew this would end up being a bad idea, but she has made it further than I ever expected so far.

With a sigh, I pick up my phone to call her again when my door opens and she steps in.

"I'm sorry! I know I'm late, but—"

"First strike," I say, cutting her off in a simple, straightforward manner as I slam the phone down and look away. "I should be at home right now, not dealing with all this bullshit because you didn't arrive on time."

"Ryker." Her voice soft and wobbling, she comes all the way inside the room, a soft click making it clear she's closed the door behind her . "I was gonna call but I figured it would be better if I got here instead of wasting time by phoning."

I stare at my computer screen, jaw clenched with irritation. "Why are you late? What was so important you couldn't make it to the job you desperately need on time?"

"Last night, Baron showed up at my apartment and—"

"Fuck, Ver, you're late to work because of your lover?" I know it's rude to cut in but the last thing I want to hear is *his* name, or any mention of him at all. "Unacceptable."

"He kept me up late," she clarifies, and I'm sure she's near my desk now, but I refuse to look at her. "I tried to make him leave but he ranted on for hours and short of calling the police, there was nothing I could do. I slept through my alarm because of it."

"I don't care 'bout your personal life, Ver. We both know it's a mess and you've never had control over it." I finally look her in the face then and it's clear she's making an effort to hold back her tears. "Doing your job is all I care about and if you can't manage to be here on time, you'll lose it."

She nods. "You're right. It won't happen again."

"Good." I take in her attire, which is suitable for our work environment, but not for the weather. It's eighty outside and will only get hotter and she's wearing long sleeves and slacks, both black. She's always worn skirts as long as I've known her, and it's strange to look at her and feel as if she's finally grown up when she's already thirty.

"Why are you wearing something designed for winter? Aren't you hot?"

"Forgot to do my laundry." Laughing, she wipes a tear which has escaped to trail down her cheek, and after another nod at me, turns back to the door. "If you want to go home now, I'll take care of everything here. Again, sorry."

"If only it were that easy," I mutter, picking up my phone to call Angel and make sure she's all right before I have to tackle the work. Work which has piled up and needs to be done by the end of the day and Veronica won't be able to finish on her own.

It's gonna be a long day.

THE NEXT MORNING, I FEEL ANGEL SLIP OUT OF BED AND GO into the master bathroom. Rolling over, I catch the alarm right as it blares, and shut it off as the sound of the now-running shower reaches me. Deciding to join in so I can give Angel a little impromptu pampering, which I know she needs since her treatment causes her to feel weak and sick, I slide my naked ass out of bed.

As I approach the door, that's when I hear her crying.

Shoving it open, I step inside to see her form through the glass door of the shower, leaning against the wall with her head in her hands.

"Angel? What's wrong?"

She doesn't answer with words. Instead, she slides the

door open a tiny bit and sticks her arm through. I walk closer to see what she has clenched in it, when she opens her fist and a wet gob of hair drops to the floor.

My heart drops into my fucking stomach as I realize her hair is falling out due to the treatment.

Fuck.

She was hoping this wouldn't happen.

And honestly, so was I, for her sake.

"Baby," I say, stalking to the door and stepping inside as she sobs harder. "Come here."

Enclosing us inside, I pull her into my arms and hold her against me as she cries, the hot water raining down on my back.

"I k-knew it w-would happen." Her face is buried in my chest, her stuttered words loud and filled with misery. "B-but I h-hoped—"

"I know, sweetheart. I know." I'm aware platitudes and such will do no good. She needs me to help her in any way I can right now, so that's what I'm going to do. "What can I do to help?"

"I need t-to c-cut it off." Although her words are still halting, she isn't sobbing anymore. She takes a few deep, shuddering breaths to calm down, then says, "I had a w-wig before. I don't like having my h-head bare."

"All right, I'll find someone to come here and do both. Anything else?"

She draws back a little, lifting her red, pain-filled eyes to mine, and raises her arms to her hair. Covering the crown of it with both hands, her lower lip wobbles as she whispers, "I love my hair."

"I love you," I whisper back, the suffering in her eyes fucking killing me, and give her a peck on the nose. "Hair or no hair. You're already hairless everywhere else, after all."

Her lip quirks for a moment at my point, but her misery isn't easy to overcome. Sliding her hands down her hair, she closes her eyes, not even looking when she reaches the end and puts her arms over my shoulders so the water streams over her hands and through her fingers.

I wish I could wash away her pain like the water rinses away her hair.

Pulling the loofa off the hook, I tell her, "Turn around. Let me wash you."

She does as I put body wash on the sponge and squeeze it, and right when I'm about to bend down and start with her legs, I hear her softly say, "I hope this isn't for nothing."

And even though her words are agonizing, I wonder if I'm the selfish one here. I know the answer is yes, I am, just a little, because I don't want to lose her again. It would hurt way fucking more than all those years ago.

"Less than a week," I remind her as much as myself, pressing a soft kiss on her neck. "We'll know if it's working when they test you before your next treatment. Hang in there, Angel."

She nods, taking in a deep breath as she straightens and responds, "Okay…okay."

Her voice is shaky, unsure, but in this moment, it's all I can ask for.

The rest…what happens next week…well, it's out of our hands now.

All I can do is beg the universe to have a little mercy on us both and hope it's enough.

33 - DANITA

"Felicia, it's Danita. I haven't heard from you in a while. I hope everything's going well. I'm starting to worry about you. Give me a call back, please."

I hang up the phone and sigh. This is the fifth message I've left her since the day at her apartment. Figuring she's just busy, I leave four or five days in between before calling her again. I even invited her to my wedding and nothing. No response.

So now I'm pretty sure she's simply ignoring me.

And Sterling said he hasn't heard from her either.

If she doesn't answer soon, I'll probably have Kevin drive me to her place to check on her, but with my luck she's just taken a vacation since she no longer works for Ryker. I wouldn't begrudge her that; she took on a child that wasn't hers for many years, after all. She needed time to herself.

I just want to know she's okay, especially after the fight we had.

Getting out of my bed, I walk to the bathroom and a couple minutes later as I'm washing my hands, I stare into the mirror.

I'm three days away from finding out if the treatment is working or not. An answer which will determine whether or not my life will be ending in the next few months, or if I'll have a chance at beating cancer a third time.

I'm not sure I could handle being told it's not working.

I have so much to look forward to, I have Ryker and Sterling and our family and friends. I have to apologize to Felicia for being blind to her problems because of my own. I have to improve our relationship as sisters and as friends. I want more time with Ryker. More time with Sterling. I want a lifetime with both of them.

Blessed, that's what I am. So blessed to have him again, to have married him, to have our son living with us, where we're all together as family like I always dreamed of.

And the woman in the mirror?

I'm so different than the woman I was just two months ago, when I wanted to die. When I tried to end it all.

And not just because my hair started falling out and I had it shaved off. Not because I'm wearing a wig that makes it look as if I simply chopped my hair off to my shoulders.

Not because I didn't have anything to live for — after all, my son had always been worth living for, which is why I tried so hard to make sure I did.

But because Ryker had given me my hope back, along with an opportunity to try one more time that I hadn't had available before.

And I want it to work. I need it to.

If it doesn't…well, I don't wanna think about that right now.

My stomach rumbles, reminding me I'm hungry, and I head toward the kitchen.

Male laughter drifts up the steps as I walk down them, and while I recognize my son's laughter, I don't recognize the other male's. Knowing it's not Ryker's by sound alone, and the fact he's at the office today, I stop right outside the door and listen for another moment.

"Dude, he's behind you! Kill his ass!"

The sound of gunshots, a third voice cursing from what sounds like through the TV, and Sterling and the person who is obviously his friend laughing like crazy has me smiling as I step into the room.

"What are you two doing?"

Both boys, who are sitting on the floor in front of the TV, cast me a glance. Sterling says, "Hi, Mom! Killing zombies!" and turns back around, while the other boy just nods at me before doing the same.

"Danita, you're awake." Meg's voice comes out of nowhere, and that's when I notice she's sitting in a chair off to the side. "You slept right through dinner. Take a seat and I will go prepare you a plate."

By now I've learned not to argue. It's her job and she, like every other employee here, takes it to heart. She loves to cook and serve, and I won't stop her even if I'm capable of doing it all on my own.

"Okay," I say with a simple smile and sit on the couch behind the boys.

Meg leaves the room, and I don't say anything. Sterling informed me before that he plays live, so there are other people in their group, and they are all able to talk with one another. They also can't pause the game since it's live, so I have to wait until they are finished if I want to talk and actually receive a response from my son.

I never interrupt him and have come to realize by watching him that he also never seems to die. He's careful and precise, but as I watch, I see the other kid isn't. He runs around, laughing like a maniac when he gets killed, over and over.

The game ends a minute later, and Sterling turns to me.

"Mom, this is Daniel. His mom is Meg."

Daniel turns a little to face me, a spitting image of his mother with his brown hair and big brown eyes, and smiles. "Hi."

"Oh! Hi, Daniel. Nice to meet you. Your mom talks about you all the time."

"Really?" He makes a 'ugh' face similar to one my son does once in a while. "I don't know why."

The cluck of Meg's tongue comes from the doorway, and I laugh as she says, "Because I'm your mother and I love you, maybe?"

With a roll of his eyes, he returns his focus back to the

screen and Sterling joins him, starting up a new game. Meg sets the tray across my lap and takes a seat beside me.

"How're you feeling?"

"Good." My mouth waters as I look down at my plate, which has rolled pork loin filled with apple-cranberry stuffing and grilled asparagus on the side. "Not in much pain at all for once."

"I'm glad to hear it," she says as I put a bite in my mouth and moan in appreciation. "That delicious huh?"

"You," I say after swallowing the scrumptious bite, "are a culinary goddess. I think I'll keep you."

"My husband said the same thing twenty years ago."

"Now see, I was only ten twenty years ago. I couldn't snap you up. That isn't fair."

She laughs and while I finish eating, we watch the boys play their game, commenting here and there.

And a little while later, Ryker arrives home and enters the living room, not saying a word as he takes my hand and leads me out of the room.

*T*he door to our bedroom isn't even shut a millisecond before I shove Angel up against the door.

She opens her mouth, but I can only guess at what for since it's under mine before she can make a sound. Her lips part in an instant to let my tongue invade it.

In this moment, I want to absorb her. I'd walked into the house after a long day and saw her sitting in the living room with our son, and Meg and her son, and it hit me. I wanted more days like this, where I came home and she was there waiting for me, in one way or another.

I want to walk up to her every day — like I did a few minutes ago — and have her turn her head in my direction. I want to see a smile creeping across her face as my appearance fills her with joy. I want to see the food tray with an empty or almost clean plate on it, knowing she's eating and keeping it down. Most of all, I want to stick my hand out and know she'll take it without question, and let me lead her away because she knows whatever I'm going to do, it'll be good for both of us.

Like right now.

My body has hers trapped against the door, my cock straining against the fabric of my pants, and I grind against her. When she makes a noise into my mouth and moves her lower body into mine, I slip my hands down her sides and grab her ass. Lifting her, she brings her legs up and around my waist, an action which has my cock positioned right where we both want it most.

Only problem is, our fucking clothing is in the way.

Carrying her over to the bed, our lips remain locked the whole way, until I take mine away when I lower her to the bed.

"Take it all off," I demand as her eyes fly open and note me standing over her. "I don't want anything in my way."

Her lips curve in a naughty smile I know is for my eyes only. She slips off the bed and into the tiny space left between my legs and the bed, dropping to her knees as she places a hand on the buckle of my belt. Looking up at me with her wide, desire filled eyes, she starts to undo the belt.

Covering her hand with one of my own, I shake my head.

She ignores me and I lift my hands in surrender.

Her removal of my belt is slow and deliberate through the loops, and when it's finally released, she tosses it to the side. Still on her knees, she unbuttons my pants and yanks them down until I have to step out of them.

"Angel…"

She takes my cock in her hand, wrapping her fingers around it and giving it a squeeze, then flashes a grin at me as I thrust into her grip. "Ryker…"

It takes all my self-control to focus on asking her something I should've before we began. "How are you feeling, love?"

"Never better."

Not waiting for me to acknowledge what she's said or anything, she licks the underside of my cock, then around and over the tip. She does it over and over until I rest my hands on her shoulders, my fingers digging in a little as she tortures me with her unhurried pace.

Lick, stroke, long strong lick, stroke, squeeze. What's she doing to me is maddening and exquisite all at once.

"Angel—"

What I was going to say flees from my mind as she takes me in her mouth and starts moving. Her pace is a little faster, but her mouth is tight and wet around me while she uses her grip to continue stroking me, and I'm sure I've died and gone to fucking heaven.

But nice as it is, I don't want to come in her mouth, so I pull away. The action results in a small 'pop' sound from her mouth, and as she stifles a giggle, I start unbuttoning my shirt.

"Now, get naked like I told you to before." It's still a command, but I say it low, knowing my voice is deep with the desire she's brought to an almost painful peak in me. "Then lie down on the bed and bring your legs up, bending them as you hold them up with your hands. Make that pussy of yours completely available to me."

Rising, she takes her time following my orders, giving no facial reaction to what I've said. Using her index finger on each hand only, she sticks them under the band of her shorts on each side and shimmies out of her shorts. Her panties come down at the same time, and after they drop to her feet, she steps out and kicks them to the side. Then, she pulls off her t-shirt over her head and tosses it in the same direction as her discarded bottoms.

Sitting back on the bed, she doesn't even scoot away from the edge as she falls onto her back, leaving her ass on the edge of the bed as she does what I asked her to. Her left leg bends and lifts, followed by her right one, and soon, she's open and waiting for me.

But she isn't watching what I'm doing at all.

Nope. Her head is flat on the bed, her eyes closed, one side of her lip held captive by the bite of her teeth. I've come to know this look; it's the one that says she's feeling everything. She's not focusing so much as trying to make sure she enjoys every sensation I give to her.

I ache to simply grab her hips, line my cock up at the entrance of her pussy, and thrust hard and deep enough in her to make her scream. But that's what she's waiting for, and I hate being predictable, especially when it comes to her. Surprising her with the ways I can make her happy is one of my greatest joys and I love to take advantage of every opportunity when one presents itself.

"What do you want?" I ask her this before walking over

to where I keep all our fun-time equipment and pull out the two things I plan to use on her while fucking.

"You," she answers, breathing out the word through her slightly parted lips before licking them. "Right now."

"Ooh, attempting to be bossy. How cute." Stepping close, I make sure she can feel what she does to me, rocking between her legs to tease her as I lean over her body, placing one of the items to the side. "I've got a surprise for you."

"You do?" Her eyebrows lift in her curiosity even as she keeps her eyes closed. "What is it?"

Instead of answering with words, I run my index finger from her belly button up to the undressed of her breast, then cup it in my hand. She arches into my hand, and after giving it a squeeze, I pull my hand away and flick her nipple.

She sucks in a breath as I lift my free hand and clip on the clamp to the nipple which now stands at attention. Her eyes fly open wide when I move to the other breast and repeat my actions, then step back with the dangling end in my hand. A slight tug on it has her moaning with pleasure, her eyes filling with a mix of delight and pain before she shuts them once more.

Chuckling, I tug on them again as I place the tip of my cock between her legs, sliding it up and down to make myself slick with her wetness. She lets out a sigh of delight as I enter the tiniest bit, teasing her along with another small yank of the chain. I know she's enjoying every second of it. She yearns for each pull of the chain which gives her the pain she craves, mixed with a sweet ache of pleasure from the exact same maneuver.

The fact I'm the one giving it to her is a delight all on its own.

"Ryker." The words are a plea, a begging, and an enticement as she licks her lips, her legs quivering from the effort it's taking her to keep them lifted. "Please."

"Do you like your surprise?" I sink into her a little more.

"Mmhmm."

"I have another one," I say before thrusting hard like I've wanted to since before we began, tugging the chain leading to the clamps taut at the same time.

She squeals a little in reaction, but holds her place. With how close we are, I feel her whole body trembling, and I know her orgasm is so close. And since my goal is to please us both and not to just torture her, I grab for the vibrating bullet I've placed off to the side and turn it on right as I place it on her clit, drawing back a bit to make sure it's touching her just right.

Knowing the silicone covered tips of the clamps protect her nipples from being hurt, and a tug on the stretched to the max chain will release them automatically, I do it at the same time the bullet touches her…and enjoy the fireworks.

"Oh god." Her arms drop to her sides as she clutches the sheets in her hands, the words flying from her mouth as I remove the toy from between her legs. She straightens them then, wrapping them around me as her cries of pleasure fill the room.

She's so beautiful, her body flush from her arousal and orgasm, that I don't resist the urge to cover her body with mine and capture her mouth with mine. Her arms steal around my neck, her hands sliding into my hair, clutching it in her fists as she opens up for me.

And what starts as a game of teasing turns into lovemaking with a slow and sweet, yet incredibly fucking hot ending.

35 - DANITA

"How're you feeling?" Ness asks me on our weekly phone call to each other.

"You ask me that everyday when you text. I'm fine, like every other day."

"Yes, but today is a new day. You might not feel well all of a sudden."

"Nah. Truth is, I feel better than I have in a long time."

She shrieks on the other end, I'm guessing with happiness, and says, "Good. That means tomorrow you should get good news."

"Or, it means my meds are working like they should." I point this out, not to ruin her happiness, but to keep a little reality in the conversation. "I don't want to get excited without knowing for sure first, that's all."

"Yeah, I hear ya." She shuffles around on the other end and speaks again after a few moments. "How's Sterling doing?"

"Ha. He's the same. He's good. He's been hanging out a lot with Meg's son, Daniel. They sit and play video games most of the time, but it's nice he has someone to spend time with."

"Ah. You said he has a girlfriend?"

"Yeah. I don't think he wants me to meet her, but Ryker did. He said she seemed nice, but more focused on my son than anything else."

"Ooh. Don't know much about teenage girls anymore. Been a long time for me."

"Right? I'm thirty and I'm not sure I understand teenagers at all. But Ryker said Sterling made it clear he wasn't going to have sex with her so…"

Her sigh of relief is similar to what mine was when I found out. "God, that's good. I mean, he's cute and all, but we both know he can do so much before that. However, it's likely he'll make you a grandma before you're forty."

"Wow. Let's hope not before I'm fifty, please."

She laughs. "That's a bit unrealistic since he'll be thirty-four then, but okay, let's hope."

"Speaking of babies, when are you and Freddy going to give me some god-nephew and nieces to cuddle?"

"Ha! Go have another baby of your—" She cuts herself off, and I hear her suck in a breath, then rush to say, "Dammit, Danita, I'm s—"

"Hey." I interrupt her with a laugh. "Don't apologize. I would fucking love to have another baby, are you kidding? And with the father actually around this time."

It sounds like she chokes on something as she chuckles

in response. "We're so inappropriate, you know that right? Joking about your life like this."

"I'd rather laugh than cry, any day."

"Me too." She clears her throat. "Do you think you will? Have another baby…ever?"

"I don't know. I…uh…I might not be able to, y'know?"

"Yeah. Well I hope you're able to, if it's what you want." Her voice perks up, making it clear her smile has returned to it. "Wanna know something?"

"Only always!"

"No babies in sight," she quips, "but how 'bout you being my matron of honor?"

My reaction is an instantaneous squeal of delight. "Oh my god, you're engaged! Ness, I'm so happy for you! You've been wanting to marry him since you two met."

"He proposed last night. Dinner, drinks, music, and down on one knee. God, it was perfect."

"I bet! So when's the wedding?"

"I haven't decided, yet."

"Because you don't know if I'll be a living attendee or visiting from the grave?"

We both bust into laughter at the same time. She's the first to catch her breath and says in her serious voice, "You'll be there alive, thank you very much. My date depends on your results tomorrow. It wouldn't be any good without you."

Eyes growing misty, I tell her, "You know I wouldn't miss it for anything. You're like the sister I never had. I love ya more than Freddy. He's lucky I let you be with him."

"Haha. I tell him that all the time."

We both fall silent for a moment, then I say, "Send me a text with a pic of the ring. I wanna see it."

"It's nothing compared to the one Ryker put on *your* finger. Does your finger hurt from all that weight?"

"Shut up. It's not that big," I say with a laugh, then joke, "Maybe it hurts just a little."

"Right!"

We both laugh again, then I realize how tired I am as my eyes start to feel a little heavy.

"Hey, Ness. I think I need a nap. But I'll call you after the appointment tomorrow, okay?"

"Absolutely. I'll send you a pic. Get some rest girl. Love you."

"Love you too."

I hang up and realizing I'm too tired to get up the steps, I lie down right on the couch where I'm sitting and pass out.

LATER THAT EVENING, AFTER WE'VE BOTH EATEN DINNER, Sterling and I head into the living room. Ryker is still at work, but sent me a text saying he'll be home in a little bit. I have learned not to take the messages literally; 'in a bit' usually means he'll be home around eight.

With a whole hour before then, and rested from my nap, I let Sterling convince me to learn how to play his game. He hands me a control and points to the buttons.

"You press this one to shoot, and use these ones to move. This one," he says, showing me the button on the top of the controller, "is what you hit when you want to use your boost. Got it?"

"Yeah, I'm pretty smart. Let's go!"

The game comes on the screen and when it starts, we're in a field and it's counting down. Three…two…one.

I take off running as soon as I can, shooting and shooting and shooting until…

"What the hell! I'm out of ammo, Sterling. There's one coming right at me and I can't shoot it!"

My son, who started laughing like crazy at the beginning of my freak out, catches his breath and says, "You have to find the boxes. It will have max ammo and random items in them. Run!"

Too late. I die.

"Aw, dammit."

Sterling chuckles as I revive and take off running once more.

Run out of ammo just like before.

Dead again.

"Shit. How the hell haven't you died yet?"

"Practice."

A boy's voice comes over the game. "Dude, who are you playing with? They suck at this."

"Somebody whose never played before," my son says before leaning over to whisper at me. "No need to tell them you're my mom."

"Okay," I hiss back at him in an exaggerated fashion,

which makes him grin before he returns his gaze back to the screen.

"Let's try again. Go!"

This time, I'm doing better right from the start. I decide to follow Sterling around instead of running off on my own, and I'm still alive moments later when I run out of ammo. He shows me a box to get it from and once I'm loaded up again, I go off on my own. Cheers come through from the other people when I take down a bunch of enemies myself, and this is when I realize we're all on the same team.

I get so caught up in finishing that game without dying, and taking on another board with a different layout, I don't notice it's almost eight until Sterling says, "Dad will be home any minute."

"Yep." I set my controller down with a laugh. "Are you trying to tell me you're done playing the game with me now and wanna play on your own?"

"No. I'm not gonna play either." He leans toward the game machine and turns it off after telling the other boys goodbye. "I gotta call Renee in a bit."

"Oh. Okay." Standing up, I give him a squeeze on the shoulder before turning toward the door. "I'm gonna go freshen up before your father gets home."

"Kay." I'm almost to the door when he says, "Mom?"

"Yeah?" Turning back around, I smile at him as he pulls his phone from his pocket and walks toward me.

"I'm gonna invite her over for dinner, I promise. I just…I wanna wait until after tomorrow. You know…"

I do. He wants to know which way my big thing is going before he does what he considers a huge thing of his own. I can't blame him. I'd probably do the same thing.

"Yes, I know. I can't wait to meet her though."

He rolls his eyes, morphing into the other side of the teenager I know and love; the one who hides the concern for me behind his mask. Being flippant is his way of coping. Which is something I understand completely.

Giving him a quick hug, I exit the room as he turns away and dials Renee, leaving him to his privacy.

36 - RYKER

She was late again.

I should've fired her the first time this happened, but I was trying to be nice.

Right now I'm trying to remind myself why I don't pick up the phone and fire her this instant. I gave her a chance the first time because she has nobody else. Her parents, the people who raised her to have zero work ethic and gave her everything she could possibly want without working for it, are dead. Her marriage to a man with no money and who liked to sleep with other people's wives has apparently ended. She has no friends because she's so self-centered and doesn't even know how to pretend interest in anybody else's life.

I knew this when we married. I knew she couldn't really help it when it's all she's ever known. I'd been in my early twenties when we got married and I thought having a housewife would work out well with how much I worked. I wanted her at home when I came home so we got to spend what little time we had together. I thought marriage with me and her having the freedom to figure out what she wanted would be a good thing. I didn't care about her not working, as long as she found something which made her happy.

And apparently, fucking the pool boy had made her happy more than me giving her the exact lifestyle she grew up in.

Which is probably where I went wrong. I hadn't made her work for anything either.

Now, things would go from bad to worse, when I honestly thought she's truly been making an effort to take care of herself for once.

Not to mention I'll have to find a new secretary, again. Dammit.

When my phone rings, I jump a little because I was so lost in thought, and frown at the unfamiliar number. Accepting the call, I lift the phone to my ear. "Hello?"

"Hello. Is this Mr. Redding?" The speaker was female, her words urgent sounding.

"Yes, it is. Who am I speaking with?"

"I'm a nurse at Valley Hill. You are listed as an 'in case of emergency' in Veronica Larson's phone and her medical documents. She's here in the hospital—"

Ah, shit. I cut the nurse off as I stand up. "What? Is she all right?"

"She's in pretty bad shape, sir. Assaulted, can barely

speak due to it, so she's unable to tell us who did this to her."

My mouth drops open, but realizing who probably did it, I snap my mouth shut and say, "Thanks for calling me. I'll be there as soon as I can."

I hang up after she acknowledges my response and dial Angel, who picks up on the first ring.

"Angel, I've got a bit of a situation to deal with." I try to keep the irritation and urgency from my voice, but I must not've done a good job because she gets right to heart of the matter.

"What happened, Ryker? Are you okay?"

"Yeah, I'm fine. Veronica was late again and I was all set to fire her, but then I get a call, and she's in the hospital. That rat fucking bastard beat the shit out of her."

She gasps loud and clear, then asks, "What? Who? Her husband?"

"He's the only person I know of who would hurt her." I run a hand through my hair in frustration and take a deep breath as I shut down my computer and consider who I can get to go sit with Veronica until I can get there. "God, I know she's my ex-wife and an utter bitch, but she doesn't deserve this. I'm gonna call my mom to see if she'll sit with her—"

"Go to the hospital, Ryker."

"What?" I can't believe she even said that. "No. Your appointment is in an hour. Your very fucking important appointment. I won't miss it—"

"Yes, you will." When I growl, she cuts in. "You told me

before that she doesn't have anyone else. They called you right?"

"Yes, but—"

"No. Honey, I'm fine. I've been through this twice. I can handle it again. I'll have Sterling with me as well. I'm strong. She isn't. We both know it. Go be there for her. It's okay, I promise."

I'm not sure what to say. I'm so unsure of what to say she speaks again before I can even spit out anything coherent.

"Ryker. I love you. The only people who have to understand this is me and you. And Veronica has nobody else except the man who probably beat her. She needs somebody who cares for her. And—" She raises her voice to stave off the objection she knows was about to come from my mouth, a tinge of amusement accompanying her next words. "While I know she did what she did, and you don't trust her or love her like that anymore, you care about her. Otherwise, you wouldn't have let her work for you to help her make a life for herself, and she's been doing a good job, hasn't she?"

"You're too nice, Angel. If you were anybody else's wife…" That's all I'm able to get past the rather unmanly lump of emotion in my throat at the amazing woman who is all mine.

"But I'm not. I'm your wife and I know *you*. And maybe I am too nice. Or maybe, just maybe, I know from personal experience that sometimes, the people who look like they don't deserve anything, least of all our compassion, well…they need it more than we can possibly know. And right now, that person is Veronica, and she needs you."

"*You* need me today."

"I always need you hon, but today is going one way, Ryker. I'm going to find out if I'll live or if I'm going to die. And either way, tonight, you'll be holding me in your arms whether I'm crying in relief or in despair." She clears her throat and says in a soft, sweet tone, "Go on. I love you. Make sure she's okay and get whatever bastard is responsible for it arrested. Then, come home to me. Okay?"

"Angel, I'm not going to the hospital. I'm going with you to the fucking doctor's office. You're the most important right now—"

"Ryker. If you show up at the doctor's after this, I'll tell them all not to let you in. You've made it clear you don't want to go to her, and I know you want to be with me and Sterling today, but please. This is my decision. Do it for me."

"Fuck. Fuck!" Placing my head in my hand while holding the phone to my ear with the other, I massage my forehead as I think about this bullshit, even though I know she's right. I do care about Veronica even though she frustrates the fuck out of me, and whether I like it or not, I'm the only safe person she has. Following a heavy sigh, and tamping down the urge to kick the crap out of something, I acknowledge how right she is about Veronica needing me, but I don't like it. "Fine. Dammit, I don't wanna deal with this shit, but fine. I'll…I'll be home as soon as I can. I love you, too."

"Good, and Ryker?"

"Hmm?"

"Don't go getting in any trouble, baby." She laughs, making it clear she knows how badly I want to find Baron and beat his ass, and says, "I gotta get going and so do you. Keep me in the loop. Love ya."

She's gone before I can say anything in response, and after letting loose another few select words into the empty air surrounding me, I head to the damned hospital, cursing this whole situation and its interference in my life the whole way.

*H*anging up with Ryker, I walk down the hall to Sterling's room and give a soft knock.

"Yeah?"

Opening the door, I stick my head and discover he's sitting at his desk, playing on his computer. "We gotta leave now. You ready to go?"

"Oh." He clicks a few times, then rises from his chair and closes the laptop. "Yeah. Now I am."

Sliding it into his bag, he shrugs it over his shoulder and walks toward me. Stepping back, I let him pass and then we head to the car, where Kevin is waiting for us.

But before we can get out the door, Meg stops me, holding out a plastic container with cookies in it.

"In case you get hungry," she says with a smile, her dark brown eyes shiny with what I'm sure is emotion for me and what I'm going to the doctor for. "You know, on the way home. Don't need you passing out."

"Thank you." I don't think she expects my sudden hug when I step forward and wrap my arms around her, but she accepts it and returns the embrace. "I'll be fine, Meg."

"I know you will." She releases me and steps back, swiping her hand at her eyes. "But either way, my chocolate chip cookies are delicious and you have to eat them."

"Yes, ma'am."

With a mock salute and a wink, I step out the door, which Sterling holds open as he waits for me. Walking toward the car, I hear him say something to her, but can't make out what it is. And moments later, we're both in the car with Kevin driving away.

"I want a cookie." Sterling holds out his hand and I hand him the container. He opens it, takes a cookie out, puts the cap back on, and then hands it back to me. He bites into the cookie and chews, making exaggerated sounds of enjoyment, and once he's done chewing, he says, "She makes the best cookies ever."

"What?" My gasp is fake and excessive as I place a hand over my heart. "Even better than mine? You're so cruel!"

He laughs and takes another bite, not even bothering to respond to my comments. He moans louder and louder until I'm covering my face in embarrassment, even though the only other person who can hear our conversation is Kevin.

"Renee would love these cookies," he says once he's done eating the cookie and I lower my hands to see him nodding at the container in my lap. "I'll have to save her one. Or have Meg make a whole bunch."

"You know she'll make you anything you want."

"Yep. She already does. That's why she's awesome... because she makes them just like you used to."

I was turning to look out the window but my head whips back to his face, catching his eyes — crinkled at the corners like his father's as he grins — with my wide ones. "What?"

"I asked her to make them how you used to. She asked me for the recipe and I said I didn't know, so she said to describe them. So I did." He shrugs, his eyes twinkling. "It took her three tries to get it right...well as right as I could remember."

Swallowing the lump in my throat, all I can manage to say is, "Sterling..."

"Mom." He glances out the window, then back at me. "Try one? Tell me if I got it right."

"Okay."

The word is said on a breath, but I lift the lid off and to the side, picking up a cookie before replacing it to keep the others fresh. Looking at it, it's easy to admit the cookie is perfect in shape, color, size, and smell.

God, I love cookies, but...

"It's been a while since I baked, hasn't it?"

Sterling nods, crossing his arms over his chest, waiting for me to tell him if the cookie is just like mine. So I lift it to my lips, taking a decent bite, but I'm only biting the cookie for his benefit.

Meg's cookie is good, but it's not like the ones I used to make. Close, but not quite.

However, I won't tell my son it's wrong. Such honesty is not necessary in this moment, even though I've always believed in telling him the truth no matter what. This is about so much more than a cookie.

So, I tell him the only thing I can tell him, and for the first time in my life, I lie to my son to make us both feel better and go into this meeting with whatever joy we have.

"It's perfect, honey."

And in the face of what I'm heading into in just a few moments, it is.

He is.

I've never realized how truly, truly lucky I am until just now.

And for the first time since I told Ryker I'd try again, my fear of bad news is bigger than my hope as we arrive at the place where I'm about to find out if I'll live or die.

MORE NERVE-WRACKING THAN GOING THROUGH THE TESTS, is waiting around for the damn results.

It's about an hour into our wait that Sterling realizes a certain someone is missing and asks, "Uh, isn't Dad supposed to be here?"

I don't even look up from the book I'm reading on my phone as I sigh. "Yes, but something came up and I told him to go deal with it."

"And he just went and is missing this because you said so?"

"Well, he did try to argue about it, but yes, basically."

He doesn't counter with anything, so I figure I've given him a sufficient answer and focus on my book once more. But two minutes later, he makes a sound which can only be described as hovering between disbelief and confusion.

I shift my gaze to where he sits beside me and raise a brow. "What, Sterling?"

"I just…" He waves his hand in the air and I squelch the smile itching to surface to my lips. "I don't get why he'd miss this just because you told him to."

"Well." Thinking about it for a moment, I decide complete truth is the way to go. "There was an emergency. Someone he knew got into some trouble and your dad is the only one this person can trust. I know it and he knows it, and so, they needed him more than I did. After all, I've got you here with me."

Sterling scowls, crossing his arm over his chest, and sits back in his chair. "Renee doesn't listen to me. I don't understand this shit."

A small chuckle slips through my lips, which I can't hide, and he glowers at me even more.

"Hon…what doesn't she listen to you about exactly?"

"Anything."

I swear, sometimes he's so open, and other times he isn't, usually when you need more information to give him the help he clearly wants and won't straight up ask for. "Like?"

He lowers his eyes away from mine, and focus on the mp3 player in his laps, which he's fidgeting with his hands. "Well, like…she tells her friends we have sex, even though we don't, and I told her to stop but she says it doesn't matter because it isn't true. She just wants to fit in, and I don't get it."

"Having sex at fourteen isn't something to be proud of." He lifts his eyes to mine, and I see the relief in them, making my heart lighten at knowing him talking to me is something he wants to be able to do without judgment. Something I'll happily give him. "What else?"

"I know Aunt Felicia wasn't poor, but Renee's family is rich. And she never came over to Felicia's but now she wants to come here. And I think it's because Dad has money and so it means she's dating someone her parents will approve of now."

"Ah." I reach over and grab his hand, which he lets me do without shying away. "So that's why you really don't want to invite her over for dinner."

I want to ask him why he's still dating this girl if she's like this, but I don't. I remember being a kid enough to know that any questioning of a relationship just makes them want to do it more.

"Yeah."

"Well, what do you want to do?"

"What do you think I should do, Mom?"

Don't give a 'mom advice' answer, it's a trap!

Giving his hand another squeeze, I let go before giving him the only advice I think he needs. "You should do what you think is best. A girl should like you for you, not for who your dad is, or how much money you have, or anything else like that. If you think it's over, then tell her. That's what being an adult will be all about — the ability to stand up for what is best for you."

"So is that why Dad isn't here?"

"No," I say with a shake of my head and a soft smile. "That's the other thing being an adult is about...putting others before yourself when you know they are needed somewhere else more in that moment."

He doesn't get to respond as the nurse calls out my name.

And after a short walk down a long hallway, Sterling and I sit in the doctor's office, waiting for him to come in and deliver the news.

"*H*oly fuck…"

My first glimpse of Veronica in the hospital bed, beaten so badly I had to make sure I had the right room because none of her facial features are recognizable, had me running into the bathroom to get sick.

Then, I decided I'm going to kill the motherfucker who did this.

Ex-wife or not, she doesn't deserve to get abused like that.

Nobody does.

After washing my hands and taking a few deep breaths, I approach the bed, and sit in the chair next to it.

"Veronica," I say in a low voice as I'd been instructed to by the doctors, covering her hand with mine. "It's Ryker."

I'm not sure if she heard me at first, but after a moment, she turns her head toward my voice even though her eyes remain closed. I question if she's even able to open them and the longer I look at the abuse she endured, the angrier I become.

Turning her hand over so her palms up, I clasp it in mine and squeeze a little. "If you can hear me, move your hand a little."

Nothing. But I was informed she's not in a coma, and was responding earlier, so I wonder if she's ignoring me.

And I try again.

"Veronica. Move your hand. Let me know you hear me."

Then, a flutter, the tip of her nails brushing lightly against the palm of my hand. Leaving my hand in place, I keep talking.

"Good. Now, Baron did this to you, didn't he?" She's still once more and I don't need her to answer me to know I'm right. "I don't know why you wouldn't tell me, Ver. I would've helped you."

It occurs to me I said pretty much the same thing to Angel and it's clear the women in my life have a habit of not sharing their secrets and problems with me for some stupid fucking reason. Considering I'd do anything to protect the people I care about, maybe I need to make a damn rule book titled, 'Ten ways to tell Ryker you're in trouble and need help before you piss him off by not telling him until you end up in a hospital bed.'

"You need to say something, Ver. He needs to be arrested for doing this to you."

The tiniest of sounds comes from her, her hand clutching mine a moment later as she moans. I know she's objecting, but she needs to realize he almost killed her and not let him get away with it.

"I know you don't want to." I turn her hand over and clasp it in mine, giving it a gentle squeeze as I give her the harsh truth she doesn't want to hear. "But you can't even speak for fuck's sake. He probably said he'd kill you if you told. But...if you could see yourself right now...why would you want to give him another chance to do it again? He almost killed you this time!"

She may not be able to respond, but I know she's hearing me because a tear slips from between her closed eyelids and down her cheek.

"I know you want to keep your job, Ver. You were doing such a good job. I've been so fucking proud of you and the way you seem to have started taking control of your life and taking care of yourself." And it's true, I have been. I didn't know she had it in her, and I love being pleasantly surprised. I want her to succeed. "You need to do the right thing here. The next time you might not be so lucky. Do you understand?"

As more and more tears course down her cheeks, she moves her thumb a little back and forth on my finger, letting me know she at least understands.

"I'm the only one allowed in to see you right now unless the person works here." I give her hand another little squeeze before letting go and standing up. "I'm going to go make some phone calls. You're getting a bodyguard from this moment forward until Baron is behind bars. They'll be outside your room when I'm not here. Get some rest. I'll be back later."

Stepping out of the room as the nurse comes in, I verify with the staff their agreement to let nobody in except staff and me for now. Then I head out of the intensive care unit — which they have her in until they're sure there isn't any major damage — to make some phone calls.

THE FIRST CALL I MAKE IS TO MY MOTHER.

"Ryker! Did you two get the results already?"

Her question has me wincing and cursing in my head before I answer, "No. Unfortunately I'm not with Angel. Something came up and I need your help if that's possible. If you're free, I mean."

Voice filled with instant concern, she asks, "What's wrong?" When I fill her in on what's happened, I hear her gasp in horror. "Oh my god, Ryker. What in the world…?"

"I know." Shoving a hand through my hair, I blow out a heavy, frustrated breath. "I'm fucking angry she didn't tell me. We had and still have our problems, but shit."

"Don't go beating yourself up about it. She's never been one to tell her problems to you, after all."

"True. Yet we both know this can't be the first time he's hit her. She left him and got her own place—" I groan as I realize something. "Dammit. He's been harassing her. At one point she came in wearing this long sleeve shirt which wasn't appropriate for this time of year at all, and brushed it off as having to forget to do laundry."

"You didn't have a reason to believe otherwise. He's never went this far before or I'm sure you'd have heard of it, so perhaps she didn't think he would do this to her."

"You're right. She probably didn't." Looking down at my watch, I notice Angel's appointment was an hour ago, which mean she's likely done by now, and I should call her. "Mom, I wanted to ask if you'd come sit with Veronica for a little while. I'm going to hire someone to guard her for now, but I don't want to leave her alone."

She clucks her tongue. "Of course I will, Ryker. Give me all her info and let them know I'll be there in about an hour or so. You going home?"

"After a few more calls, yes. I hate the fact I had to come down here at all to deal with this. I should've been there with her, but—"

"But you have a wife who cares more about protecting and helping others than herself," my mother inserts, the smile clear in her tone. "She's lovely, son, and so is Sterling. I hope the news is what we *all* want it to be. I'm choosing to believe it will be. I don't think either of you will accept any less."

"Me too. Thanks, Mom. I'll call you later."

"Yep. Let her know I'm coming. Bye, honey."

Hanging up the phone and letting out a sigh of relief, I dial Angel's number. Only it rings and rings with no answer. Choosing not to leave a message, I dial her again with the same results.

A call to Sterling's phone gets me nothing, so I assume they aren't done with the doctor yet.

Making another few phone calls, including one to hire a bodyguard for Veronica, takes me about an hour to get all set up. But finally, it's over and I let out a sigh of relief, glad I have the resources available to get things done.

Then I head back in to check on Veronica and give the staff all the information they need to keep her safe along with permission for my mother to enter the room, so I can go be with my wife and son as I should be.

The closing of a door wakes me up from my rest.

After getting my results, Sterling and I returned home. Although I hadn't intended to take a nap, I definitely feel much better, especially after the reality of what was happening had sunk in. The emotional impact alone had been enough to tire me out.

Sterling had cried. I've not seen him cry in a long time, so it caught me off guard. I'd taken him in my arms and cried right along with him as the doctor sat across the desk holding the results in his hands.

Just as I'm about to roll over and see who walked in, the bed dips next to me, the deliciously sweet and subtle scent of Ryker's cologne filling the air around me.

"Angel…" He rests his hand gently on my shoulder, leaning in to whisper soft words in my ear. "Are you awake?"

"Mmmm, no."

"Funny." Nipping the upper part of my ear with his teeth, he moves so he's lying next to me. "Turn over and face me. I want to hold you."

Rolling over, he doesn't even give me a chance to get comfortable before I'm wrapped in his arms and hauled against his body. With a hand on the back of my neck, he brings his lips down on mine, and I give him what he wants, and get what I need. His other hand is around my waist, and it feels like he's holding on for dear life.

It's clear this kiss is to give himself fortitude to hear what I have to say, and to give me the strength to say it, whatever the news is.

Our mouths tangle together, his tongue toying with mine in a slow, leisurely dance of love and seduction. A moan is torn from my throat as he finds the bottom of my shirt in the back and slips his hand under, sliding it over and up the side of my body, caressing the whole way.

Yes is the word I would say if I could speak and tell him what I want. *Yes, please* is how I would beg for him to continue. I would arch my body into his hand, pleading for him to never stop touching me.

But, like the knowledgable and devoted lover he is, awareness of what I need is forefront. I don't have to say a word because he knows what I want. What I need.

Ripping his mouth away, he growls, "Get naked, now."

"Don't you want to know—"

He moves fast, tugging the shirt up and over my head after he releases me from his hold, stopping my words in their tracks, and shakes his head once I can see him again.

"No. Naked, right fucking now. We'll talk after we both get what we need."

"Well, all right then," I reply, laughing as he rolls away to take off his clothing, and I remove my bottoms. Lying back on the pillows, I watch him as he finishes undressing, and then as he returns to me.

Welcoming him with open arms — and open legs, honestly, which he crawls between — he traps my body beneath his while seizing my lips once more. Slipping his hand down between my legs, he finds me already wet for him, and makes a sound of approval which is lost in the play between our mouths.

Moving into his touch, eager for more, he's quick to take away his hand and replace it with his cock. Thrusting hard and quick, whimpers and moans and groans all mix together as he maintains an unyielding and deliciously fast pace while fucking me. Before long, I find my hands above my head, held together at the wrist with one of his hands, while the other caresses and teases my breasts, and the stiff nipples beg for equal attention.

He shifts and I shift, and when he's angled just right, he's hitting the perfect spot inside me. Winding me up and up, until I feel as if I'm floating in pleasure and joy and love, not knowing where his body begins and mine ends. And when I break apart, he's right there with me.

And this. This is what I love.

The sex we have, the harmony between us even when we're so angry at each other I just haul off and bite him, and the love which only seems to grow by the day. The way we're both panting, breathing hard after he's done fucked us both silly, and he rolls over, taking me with him as I burst into tears at the overwhelming emotions coursing through me.

And mostly, the way he cradles me close, kissing the top of my head in the aftermath as he says in a rough, tortured voice, "God, Angel, tell me you're going to be okay. Or at least on your way there."

As I lift my head to look him square in the face, I see the tears leaking from my eyes reflected back in his eyes, the ones filled with his overwhelming agony at not knowing.

I stare at him, tossing the words I need to say around in my mouth, but all I can manage in the end is one simple motion: a nod.

And just like that, the torment in his eyes disappears, the light and desire and happiness rekindling in them as he grins big and wide, gathering me in his arms with a whoop. In a flash, I'm back under him, and he's kissing me all over my face and neck.

"Thank fuck," he says between kisses, over and over again. "God, I love you."

"I love you, too."

It comes out in a barely there whisper, and maybe he doesn't even hear me, but that doesn't matter.

Because right here, right now, the only important thing is being in his arms, arms I'll be spending a lot of time in thanks to the hope he'd given me all those weeks when I'd been lost.

The same hope I just handed back to him tenfold.

And the one we'll hold on to with everything we have from this moment on.

"It was the hottest sex of my life."

The water I'm drinking gets up my nose as Ness' words catch me by surprise and she bursts into laughter while I cough like crazy.

After a few deep inhales and another cough or two, I manage to get out, "What have you done with my best friend who can't discuss sex without blushing like a virgin?"

"I think my fiancé fucked her into oblivion."

"Oh my god." I'm right there with her in the laughter department now and once we've both calmed down, I say, "I'm so happy for you, Ness. You two deserve all the happiness in the world."

"And you, girl! Where the fuck was my phone call yesterday?" She doesn't give me time to answer. "Yeah, yeah, you were getting it on with your man and I'm so happy the treatment is working and you'll probably be in my wedding, but you couldn't even send me a text?"

Her words might seem mad, but she's not. The truth is, her voice is filled with joy; joy I feel all the way through the line as if she's in person and hugging me.

"Hell, I forgot my phone was on silent in general. Ryker apparently tried to call me, but I came all the way home and went to bed because I just couldn't believe it. Don't even remember the ride home. I don't think I've ever cried so hard in relief in my whole damn life."

"Shit, I've been leaking tears in relief this whole phone convo, Danita." She sniffles even though the smile is evident in her words. "You're my best friend and I don't want to lose you. I want you to live forever."

"Aw. I love you too, Ness. And I'm not going anywhere. Hell, I'm feeling so well and the results were so great, they've toned back my medication a bit."

"So now you drool a little less which means the next time I hug you, I won't have a wet patch on my shoulder?"

"Ha ha! Shut up!"

"Never." She giggles, teasing me with her follow-up statement. "Hey, what color do you look terrible in? I wanna make sure I pick that color for the bridesmaid dresses."

"I look good in *every* color baby. But at your wedding, you'll be the one to shine because you're all Freddie will be looking at."

"Well, duh. 'Course he will, especially since I'm going to look as beautiful as you did."

"Suck up."

She chuckles. "Seriously, when do you wanna go dress shopping with me?"

"After you set a date and have a day off. Unless I have a treatment, I can meet you any day, anywhere, and you know it."

"All right, I'll let you know." She lets out a heavy sigh.

"Aaaaand, I gotta go now. My hour break is almost over and I've gotta finish my lunch. I'll text ya later."

"K. Love ya 'Ness."

"Love ya, too. Bye."

Standing up, I slip the phone into my pocket and head up the stairs to Ryker's office since he's working from home today. One of the other receptionists at the office has stepped in to cover any stuff Veronica is responsible for, but other than that, I don't know anything about what's gone on beyond what he told me on the phone yesterday.

His door is open and I enter without knocking. At his desk writing, he isn't aware I'm approaching and when I slide my arms around his neck from behind, he jumps a little. He's quick to grab my hands though and give them each a kiss, his hold on me keeping me trapped.

"How's Vanessa?"

"She's good. Excited about her wedding, plotting what horrible ugly thing she can make me wear. You know, her usual behavior."

"You'd look great in anything."

"That's what I said!"

He lets go of my hands, and as I step back with a laugh, he twirls his chair around. Wrapping an arm around my waist, he guides me into his lap. I lean into him and put my head on his shoulder with a sigh.

"Talk to me," I say softly. "How is she?"

"Terrible. He beat her severely...the bruises and swelling...she looked so terrible. It made me sick." He exhales deep and long while running his hand, palm down, up and down my arm. "The police can't do anything until she tells them who it was. I told her to, but I can't make her tell them anything."

"So nobody saw him do it? Who the hell found her then?"

His other arm comes up and he hugs me close, and I feel his head rest lightly on mine. "A neighbor saw her door open and went to check on her, I guess. From the sounds of it, they didn't have much to go on, so they need her to tell them what went on."

"Wow."

"Yep. So, I hired protection for her, at least until he's arrested. And my mother sat with her yesterday. She's taking care of her for me."

"Your mom's the best."

"Of course she is. She had me."

We both laugh then before falling into a comfortable silence.

But it only lasts a few minutes until Ryker asks, "How did Sterling take the news?"

"He cried like a little boy." My heart twists as I recall his reaction yesterday, my own eyes tearing up at it. "I knew it was hard on him like it was hard on me, but god, I didn't know how much he hurt over it. I never want to make him feel that way again."

"I hated missing it. I wanted to be there with you both."

He moves as I lift my head and look him in the eyes, knowing mine are filled with the love I have for him.

"You're always with me, Ryker, even if it's not in person. How do you think I survived for so long?"

Lifting a hand, he cups my face in his hand and leans down, placing a light kiss on my lips before saying against them, "I know. I just want to be next to you all the time. With you is my favorite place to be."

"I thought being in me was your favorite place."

"Right." He chuckles and kisses my lips again. Once. Twice. "You got me. They're tied in first place."

"You keep putting those lips on me and…" I look over his shoulder at the stack of papers on the desk. "How much work you got to do?"

"A lot. But, never too much to take a break for a snack."

"Like for what? A KitKat bar? Or we talking more like a Snickers?"

Snatching my hand, he places it between his legs and grins at me. "Sex is as good as chocolate, isn't it?"

He doesn't let me answer as he moves us from the chair to the floor, where he gets us just naked enough to use his Ding Dong to treat me like a Ho Ho.

Kidding.

But he's got it wrong. Sex is better than chocolate, hands down, especially when it's with him.

And I hope it stays like this forever.

One week.

It's been one long and incredibly fucking blissful week since Angel found out the treatment is working.

Seven whole days where once I was done with my work, I spent each evening with my family. We watched TV shows together, went out to dinner, played board games, and sometimes, we simply sat around in the same room doing our own thing, content with being near one another.

I refuse to take one moment with them for granted.

And I know they feel the same.

A good example is this morning. Right now.

Angel lies beside me in bed, cuddled up close to my side and sound asleep. Her hand is flat on my chest, palm down, and I've covered it with mine. Caressing her skin with the pad of my thumb, I give the top of her bare head a kiss, something I know she wouldn't let me do while she's awake.

Aware of the fact it's her own insecurity when it comes to not wanting me to see her without her wig, I pretend I haven't, even though I tell her every day that I'd love her with or without it.

And so, each morning, I lie here next to her, appreciating her strength and recovering health. I hold her as close as fucking possible, and give her that kiss on the top of her head.

Which, as always, causes her to stir.

Closing my eyes, I pretend I'm asleep, and feel her move away from me as gently as she can. I crack an eye open as she slips out of the bed and walks to her vanity, making sure she's quick and quiet. I watch as she puts her wig in place before walking into the bathroom and shutting the door.

When she returns to the bed, she creeps back under the blankets, and gets close to me once more.

That's when I roll over, catching her by surprise as I cover her body with mine, and kiss one corner of her lips as she gasps in response.

"Good morning."

Her face flushes. "Hi."

"Your breath smells minty fresh. How do you do it?" At my teasing, the flame of her cheeks burns even brighter, and I laugh while bringing my mouth close to hers. "I want a taste. Open up."

"Uh uh." She sticks her tongue out, but before I can catch it, it's back inside her mouth and she presses her lips together tight.

"Oh, it's like that huh?" Slipping a hand under the blankets, I skim a hand down her naked body until it rests on her waist, and let it linger there. "Shall I tickle you so you'll let me in?"

"No! Don't you—"

She's so easy to distract and therefore, trick. My mouth is on hers before she can shut it, but that's okay, because her hands land on my shoulders as she gives in to me right away.

I put everything I feel right now into that kiss, knowing we'll spend most of the day apart. We'll go together for her to get her treatment, and once she's home where Sterling can watch after her, I have to go see how Veronica is doing and relieve my mother for a bit, who has been spending most of her time at the hospital.

But I don't want to think about that right now, so I shove the thought aside and drag my mouth away from Angel's with a marked reluctance.

"We should get up and get ready to go. Don't wanna be late."

She pouts, sticking out her lower lip for effect, and moves her body into mine. "Are you sure you don't want to play?"

"I always want to play and you know it." With another quick peck on her lips, I roll over and away. "But you need all your strength today."

"Yeah, yeah."

Sitting on the edge of the bed, I pick up my phone as the alarm sounds and shut it off. Angel comes up behind me, encircling my waist with her hands, and resting her cheek on my back.

"You watch me every morning when I get up and you're here, don't you?"

Snatching up one of her hands, I give it an affectionate squeeze. "Of course I do. I told you, you're beautiful to me no matter what. You've no reason to hide from me. Not now and not ever."

She sighs, and after hugging me tighter for a moment, removes her hands from around me. Then, getting off the bed, she turns to me, and holds out one hand. I take it while she uses the other to take off the wig, straightens her shoulders while looking me square in the eyes, and says, "Let's get a shower together then."

And without another word, because the moment doesn't need any, that's exactly what we do.

"Sterling, you're here."

My mother looks up from the book she's reading as I enter Veronica's room and after saying that, holds a finger up to indicate I shouldn't say anything.

Nodding toward the door, I exit and after a moment, she joins me in the hallway. Having relieved the bodyguard for the time I'm here, who stays while my mom is here to guarantee both her and Veronica's safety, we sit in the chairs outside the door.

"How's she doing?"

"She's been asleep all morning, after sleeping all night." She runs a hand through her hair, frowning. "I think they're starting to get worried about her. Her face is healing pretty quickly and she can talk now, but she won't say anything about what happened, not even to me."

"Dammit."

"I know one of her Doc's wanted to speak with you about something urgent. He said to let the nurse know you're here and he'll come by as soon as he can."

"All right, I'll let them know. And thanks for being here. I know you and her never got along—"

She cuts me off with a wave of her hand as she stands and yanks her purse strap over her shoulder. "We didn't, but I always knew she wasn't brought up right and had simply been misguided in her attempts to get your attention. It's hard to know better when nobody teaches you what you can and can't do ."

"Yeah. Well, she needs to tell the cops what her husband did to her. That's a good start."

Standing on tiptoe, my mother gives me a kiss on the cheek and gives a nod after stepping away. "It will be. Let me know how it goes and when you leave. I'll probably return this evening for a little bit."

"Will do."

Once she's walked away, I turn on my heel and find the nurse's station, letting them know I'm here if one of the doctors wish to speak with me.

Pulling out my phone as I return to the room, I send

315

Angel a text message I know she'll see when she wakes up: *I love you. Hope you slept well.*

I sit in Veronica's room a good hour as I wait on the doctor, but finally he arrives, and has me step outside. Closing her door behind him, he stands there looking quite nervous, flipping through her papers.

I don't have this issue. I want to get to the heart of whatever the fuck is going on and snap at him, "Yes?"

"Mr. Redding, we wanted to make you aware of something. We haven't told her yet, because we're not sure of her mental state right now..."

My stomach drops as he pauses in whatever he's gonna say. I can't explain it, but the look on his face is one of complete misery, and I'm not sure I want to know.

"Is she sick?"

"No." His mouth works and I'm pretty sure he's... angry? "I'm sorry to say Mrs. Larson is no longer pregnant as a result of the beating."

It takes a moment to process what the fuck he just said, and then I can't believe what I think I just heard. "I'm sorry...What?"

"She was about ten weeks, but the fetus no longer has a heartbeat as of last night, and we may have to perform surgery if her body doesn't pass the fetus on its own."

"Holy shit..." Swiping a hand down my face, a heavy sigh escapes me as I ask the most important question here. "Does she know?"

"No. We're not sure she even knew she was pregnant, as she hasn't said anything about it." He closes her file and says, "We already have any papers we need for her care, so if she needs surgery, she will receive it as soon it's deemed necessary to avoid infection."

"Absolutely. And I'll tell her. It's probably best coming from me."

He nods, saying nothing else as he walks away, leaving me to deal news I never thought I'd have to to my ex-wife.

On the inside, I'm fucking glad because I'm sure she was pregnant with her scumbag of a husband's child and she doesn't need to be tied to him in any way. And if I'm terrible for thinking such a thing, I don't give a shit. That son of a fucking bitch doesn't deserve children and I'll tell him so.

On the outside, I keep my face neutral as I enter the room and sit next to her.

When she finally opens her eyes thirty minutes later, she searches me out and turns her hand palm up as she catches sight of me.

"Ryker," she whispers, wiggling her fingers a tiny bit.

I take her hand, knowing she'll need all the comfort I'm able to give her when I tell her the news.

"Are you sad?"

Out of all the things I expect her to say, that isn't it.

I counter with, "Are you?"

"Always."

Her voice is filled with so much pain, I swear I feel it. What's sad is knowing this is probably the most honest she's ever been with me, and that hurts. I thought, without fail for our entire relationship, that it was clear she could come and tell me anything. But she hadn't, because well, here we are in a fucking hospital with her beat by the man she left me for.

"I'm sorry."

"Shh. Don't be sorry. You've been through a lot, you probably should save your energy."

"No." She grips my hand and keeps her eyes glued to mine. "I want to say something. Let me?"

Her desperation is clear, my curiosity getting the best of me, and mixed together, both reasons have me telling her, "Go ahead."

"Marrying you was the best decision I ever made. Cheating on you was the worst one. And I'm so sorry. I'm truly fucking sorry like I wasn't before, because you're a good man and I screwed up." She takes a deep breath and squeezes my hand tighter as a tear leaks from her eye. "I wanted your attention in every way and I didn't know how to get it. I thought it was you doing wrong, because my life was lacking even though I had everything, and…it wasn't you now, I know that. It was me. I had no self-esteem or sense of worth."

"Veronica—"

She interrupts my attempt to disagree, her words rushing out while a fire in her eyes I've never seen before flares in them. "No, Ryker. Look at me. This is where I've gotten myself, because he told me everything I wanted to hear and I ignored the signs. A slap here, a mean comment there once we were married, and I ignored it because by then, I thought it was too late for me. I was trapped with no job, no money, and no you. I told myself I deserved it for betraying you."

"Your actions justified our divorce, not to be beaten for it, for fuck's sake."

"I told myself that too. I tried to leave. I got a job with you, I got my own place, but he wouldn't leave me alone. He apologized and came to my house that one night and begged, and he…he said all the right things…" She takes a shuddering breath, the tears sliding down her face faster now. "The other day he came to ask me to move back in, but I didn't want to, not yet. I wasn't ready so I said no… and he hauled off and punched me—"

I rip my hand out of hers and stand up. "No more! You need to tell the police this so they can arrest him, but I don't want to hear the details. And not because I don't care—"

"I know you care." Her voice is so low I have to stop speaking to hear the rest. "You're here when you don't have to be, not after what I did."

"I told you I'm not an asshole, but…there's something you need to know."

Looking tired all of sudden, she swipes at the tears while keeping her focus on me. "What?"

I've learned the best way to get something difficult said is to spit it out, but seeing her as she is in this moment, I'm not sure I can.

And she knows what's going through my head because she glares at me. "If it's about me, I have a right to know, Ryker. What aren't you telling me?"

"Fuck." I pace for a moment, then sit down and take

her hand once more, my grip firm enough I'm sure she won't be able to pull it away. "Did…did you know you were pregnant?"

Mouth working as she brings up her other hand to cover it, her eyes going wide, and I'm sure the words are registering one by one in her brain. She confirms it by asking through the fingers covering her mouth, "Were?"

"About ten weeks. But the beating—"

Her wails of despair burst forth, drowning out my words, and it's all I can do to hold onto her hand while she sobs uncontrollably. I hate feeling like an utter bastard at having to deliver the news to her, but even if they could've told her the surgery was for something else, it was her baby and she deserved to know what the bastard had done.

She curls into a ball, her free hand cradling her stomach, and I do my best to comfort her while she cries.

I don't know how long she cries, but after a while, her anguish-filled eyes find mine once more as she grips my hand like it's all she has left.

"Stay with me," she whispers.

I squeeze her hand and respond, "I will. I'm not going anywhere right now."

She gives me a smile before closing her eyes, her breathing slowing until I know she's asleep.

Then, as I go to pull my hand from hers, she flatlines.

*H*ow the fuck did today end up with me attending a funeral instead of a wedding?

I hate death.

I hate the subtle reminder it leaves hanging around everyone, a potential consequence of anything someone does, an imminent threat around every corner that practically screams, 'You're next!'

I try not to think about it.

I try to avoid it, and cherish every day I have, knowing death may take me any time it pleases.

And Angel.

God, I don't know what I'd do without her. She's my whole life.

Fuck. She clings harder to my side, her body shaking with uncontrollable sobs, and I'm worried she'll never be the same after this.

I wish I could take away her pain even though I know she's strong enough to handle it.

I don't want her to be in pain. She's been through so much, we all deserve some uninhibited joy for a while.

But life doesn't see it that way.

And neither does death.

So I'll let Angel cling to me as much as she wants while hoping it doesn't come for her next.

Four Weeks Ago

"I'm fine, Ryker." Veronica swats at me with her hand as she takes a seat on the living room couch. "Stop fucking hovering. Don't you have a wife to bother?"

"Yes, but apparently, I'm surrounded by females who either prepare or actually attempt to die on me. And you did, in fact, even if it wasn't for long, so I'll check on you all I want." For the hell of it, I say, "And watch your fucking language."

"Screw you," she grumbles, crossing her arms like a petulant child, and looking at anything except me. "I didn't wanna come here anyway. I can't believe she agreed to it."

By here, she means my house. And, well, it's obvious whom the 'she' referred to is — apparently my ex-wife can't believe how kind Angel is. Truth is, neither can I, but I don't dare say that out loud.

"Why not? She's not an asshole either, even though

you're rude as fuck to her. Should be nicer to her. Hell, you should be nicer in general."

An exasperated sigh escapes me as her lower lip starts to wobble, and just when I think she'll start sobbing, she takes a deep breath and says, "Sorry. Old habits and all."

"No big deal." Shrugging, I hand her the remote she'd been searching for and cover her with a blanket. "You need to ring the bell if you need anything, and stay resting like the doctor said. He only let you come here because I promised him you'd do as he said, so knock it off."

She nods, her voice small when she replies. "Okay. I will."

"You weren't always like this Ver. And I know you're hurting and all from everything that's gone on, but you need to go back to being more like the woman I met all those years ago. You were funny, bright, happy, and knew you were worth loving."

"I never knew that," she mutters, glaring at me. "It was all an act. I wasn't allowed to show anything but happiness around my parents. Did it for so long it became impossible for me to be anything else."

"So what, Ver? The true you isn't a miserable bitch with no self-esteem either."

"It might be."

She makes me want to slam my head against a wall with her stubbornness. "It's not."

"Grrrr. Go away dammit."

"No."

She turns on the TV and flips through the channels

while completely ignoring me as I take a seat in the nearby chair. Pulling out my phone, I check my email and read some news while she continues to look for something to watch.

Eventually she tosses the remote down beside her with a clear sigh of frustration as there's a knock in the entryway before bellowing, "What?"

Turning to see who's coming in, Meg tosses me a smile as she walks toward us with lunch for Veronica and says, "I'm sorry, Ryker. I didn't know you would be in here. Would you like me to go bring you some as well?"

"Yes, please Meg. That would be nice. Thank you."

She nods and walks over to stand by Veronica, who takes her time sitting up straight in order for Meg to place the tray over her lap. Meg's worked with me long enough that I know even though she's got a pleasant smile on her face, she's annoyed as hell by Veronica's behavior, and always has been. I like the fact Meg is closer to my side than Angel's on having Veronica here — which is, both of us wish Baron would be caught already so she can get out of here and move the hell on with her life. Yes, I loved her once and yes, I care about her in a way nobody else does, but man, she's a pain in the fucking ass.

But he hasn't been seen and Veronica's recovering from his assault, so this is how it has to be for now. And I don't know how Angel deals with her, a real smile on her face all the time; I'm pretty sure I married a fucking saint. While I'm glad the woman I love can deal with this bullshit, I'm close to pulling my hair out and it's only been a few days.

So, when Meg leaves the room and Veronica begins eating, I decide now is as good a time as any to inform her of my plans to help her on her road to recovery. A road that will help her leave me the hell alone.

"You should know that beginning tomorrow a counselor will be coming here to the house to see you." Her fork pauses halfway to her mouth as she stares at me, wide-eyed. "You'll have a private room to talk with her, undisturbed. Twice a week, Veronica, and she will have your full cooperation, do you understand?"

"Why?"

"How is that even a question after the past few years? Hell, after your whole life? You need help, and the best place to start is with someone to talk to who can help you heal and teach you proper coping skills."

She finishes taking her bite, chewing while glaring at me the whole time, then puts down her fork. "I had a counselor when I started to 'cop an attitude' as my father put it. Know what they told me? 'Just do what your parents tell you. You have it all child, don't you know how lucky you are?' It wasn't helpful, it was bullshit."

"I assure you this lady isn't like that. Angel recommended her and assured me she's top notch."

"Oh, your wife recommended her? Wow, I'm sure gonna trust her opinion on the matter."

"Your sarcasm is unappreciated and like I've said, I don't give a fuck what you want. It's clear to everyone except you that you've got no control over your life and you need to get some, along with a damned clue."

She flinches at what I've said and I rise from my seat, unable to stay in the room with her any longer.

"Enjoy your lunch, and be nice to everyone, including my wife and my staff, or you won't like what I'll say to you if you're not."

As I go to leave the room, Meg is returning with my lunch. I walk with her to my office where she leaves me in peace, closing the door behind her, which is a clear sign for everyone to leave me alone.

And not for the last time, I wonder why the hell I let Angel talk me into bringing Veronica here.

*P*eople who start out as enemies can become friends. Sure, there might be a lost cause here and there, but most people aren't lashing out because they enjoy it. They're calling for our help in the only way they know how. And in some cases, they don't know they are asking for help. They're simply reacting to their situations, to their feelings, to their devastation, and helping them is the only way to really fix things for them and those around them.

Turning a blind eye only leads to more blindness, until the idea of 'every man for himself' becomes so real, nobody questions it. Charity and someone asking for assistance or help in anyway becomes a dirty thing; as if someone could possibly see everything coming their way and plan perfectly, let alone react properly.

I know I had no idea at age fifteen how to cope with what was happening me. How can anyone expect people who aren't taught the right skills, because the people raising them don't have the right skills either, to do any better than where they come from out of the gate? It fucking took me years to come out of the fog after leaving everything behind to save myself, and although those closest to me knew why, it was the ones looking in from the outside that judged me without knowing.

And I knew. I felt it. And it hurt even though it shouldn't, because we all want to be liked. We all want to be understood, loved for everything we are instead of desired for everything we aren't. Every scar, inside and out, displays the battles we've been through, and sometimes the answer might be to step back when someone is acting out. To take a look and try to see something beyond the obvious even if it's hard. Even if they're breaking our hearts with their every single action.

I could go through so many if only's but in the end, they don't matter.

What matters is all my hate and anger didn't solve a thing. Cutting myself off from everybody I loved because I thought I was protecting them didn't solve a thing. It made small hurts even bigger, leaving me alone when I needed people the most. I spent time away from my son I'll never get back, and now can never make up for, but I'm lucky he understood even if he didn't like it. I'm lucky I have the chance *to* make up for everything.

Some people aren't as blessed.

And so now, while Veronica sits on one end of the couch with me at the other, I'm giving her the space she desires while still being available. I'm treating her as I wish to be treated. Because she's hurting and I know what it's like to hurt so deep it starts to eat at your soul.

She doesn't speak to me though. She hasn't since the day she arrived three days ago. It's been two weeks since Baron abused her, one since she flat-lined, and she's been here since they released her to Ryker with medical supervision. She talks to everyone except me, although most of the time it's nothing more than a simple greeting, but I'm not offended. I simply told her on her second day here if she needed to talk, I'm always available to listen. I haven't spoken to her since.

One of us will give in first, and it won't be me.

Every day, I come downstairs at the same time and sit here, reading while listening to her mutter about how there is nothing interesting on, and how bored she is. An occasional glimpse will show her stabbing at the button on the remote as if it has offended her in some way, and after two days of this, I brought a book down yesterday and sat it on the table next to her side of the couch.

It hasn't moved from its spot, and I've almost given up on her touching it, until fifteen minutes after I've joined her she turns off the TV and places the remote on the table with a heavy sigh. Peeking at her from under my lashes while pretending I'm engrossed in my novel, I have to hold back a smile when she picks up the book and turns it over to read the back.

Success!

Her snort of disgust a few moments later has me

lowering my book and looking her way, waiting for her to say something. Which she does while continuing to avoid looking at me.

"I can't believe you read this shit. Knights in shining armor, my ass."

"Romance books aren't about the specifics. Nobody who reads one should actually be looking for a knight in shining armor. It's an ideal, not a reality."

With a grimace, she opens the book and stares at it for a moment, then asks, "If it's not about specific things, what's it about?"

"I'm saying it's not about finding someone who literally rides a white horse. It's not about finding a man who is perfect in every way. Those are fantasies. The lessons in romance novels are deeper. Many show women they should value themselves and others. How they shouldn't be so quick to judge because everyone has story. Also, many show how much work relationships take to succeed, and what kind of things are and aren't acceptable from a partner."

"Why did I always hear how they set unrealistic expectations then? I always felt that way when I read them, especially when I started dating."

I laugh, knowing this is a random conversation, but glad she's talking to me at all. It's a start so I'll take it. "Because they do in a way. We all want the perfect relationship, the man who will do anything for us, say exactly what we want to hear, but they don't exist. Someone can be perfect *for* us, but it doesn't mean anything will be a breeze."

She worries her lower lip with her teeth while using her

thumb to run over the corner of the book, causing the pages to separate and make noise as they smack back together. I almost want to tell her to quit caressing my book like that, smiling as I realize how absurd that is, and it's at this point she looks at me.

"What's so funny?"

"Thinking about a book."

Hey, it's kinda true.

She doesn't question what I've said though. Instead, she gets real serious, frowning. "What if they never find him?"

"Don't wanna be stuck here with me forever?"

My attempt at humor fails when she grimaces, looking down and away, eyes on the book once more. "Ryker said he'll take me to work with him when the doctor clears me, but I'm afraid to go anywhere while Baron is still out there."

"Don't be. Ryker wouldn't let anything happen to you, not while you're with him. And he's pretty much got everybody on alert for the scumbag."

"So you think the cops'll find him soon?'

"Absolutely. But until then, you've got nothing to fear. Your first counseling session is tomorrow right?"

"Yeah."

She looks so sad, staring down at the book while plucking at the blanket, and I wish I could make her feel better. But I can't. All I can do is try to be a friend even if she doesn't consider me one.

"Read the book and tell me what you think after. Try to

enjoy it without analyzing it to death. May take your mind off everything else for a while."

It's not much, but she gives me a muted smile and nods. "I doubt that, but okay."

She starts reading while I go back to my book and for the first time since she came here, I don't feel as if a knife is going to find its way into my back via her hand when I'm not looking.

"*H*ow're you feeling?"

Sitting on the edge of the bed with my hand resting on her leg, Angel gives me an exhausted smile, only visible in the predominantly dark room thanks to the soft glow of a lamp across the room.

"Tired but happy I don't have to do this again for another eight weeks now."

"Me too. Four treatments down, four to go." Leaning over to give her a light kiss on the cheek, I feel her smile before I dip into the crook of her neck to kiss her there as well. "Good thing too, since I'm running out of buckets."

"I'll buy you some new ones with your money."

When I kiss the most sensitive spot on her neck she shivers, and it's my turn to smile against her skin. "If you wanna spend our money on buckets, then you go right ahead."

"Mmkay." She lifts her arms from where they rest on

333

top of the blankets and slides them up my chest until she wraps them around my neck. "Lay down and cuddle me until I go back to sleep?"

"You want me to get under the blankets with you, hold your half naked body against mine with one hand cupping your tit, and not fuck you with what's sure to be my rock hard cock the moment it comes in contact with your ass? Sure Angel, I'd love to." She laughs softly, dropping her arms as I kick off my shoes, and strip down to my boxers before climbing under the covers. Once I'm in to the exact position I described, she wiggles her ass with a giggle, and I nip at her ear in retaliation. "Tease."

"Nah. After a few days, you'll have practically seven weeks to fuck me all you want."

"I'll fuck you? You just gonna lie there like a blow up doll or something?"

"Are you into that? I had no idea, but if me flat on my back with my legs spread and mouth hanging open floats your boat…"

She squeaks in surprise as I pinch her nipple. "Hush with this talk. I can't fuck any part of you right now so it's not fair. Besides, I like my partner to be into it."

"The blow up doll is into it. That's its job. Duh."

"Fuck, now I'm thinking about you naked, just lying there while I give it to you." I grind my arousal against her ass which makes us both moan at the same time. "Now look what you've done."

"If you're not horny, I'm not doing it right."

I tighten my arms around her and give her a gentle kiss

on her shoulder. "Aren't you supposed to be resting instead of fucking with me?"

"Yeah, yeah. I always hate the day after, sucks feeling like this." She pats the hand covering her breast. "Messing with you makes me feel at least a little normal."

"Then mess away."

She goes silent and figuring she's going to sleep, I decide to take a nap with her and close my eyes.

"Ryker?"

"Hmm?"

"Everything's going so well, makes me wonder what will happen to screw it up."

Until that point, I kept my eyes closed but the worry-filled words have them popping open. "Nothing's gonna happen, Angel, but even if something does, there's nothing you can do about it."

"I know." She sighs, cuddling closer to me until every inch of our bodies are connected, and I toss my leg around hers. "I still haven't heard from Felicia you know. It's been too long."

I hate the agony in her voice. After the last time she called her, I had Felicia checked on and the apartment complex said she moved out a week after we'd been there and taken Sterling home with us. Nobody has seen her since. At least, nobody I've contacted to look for her.

"Anyone else you can call to see where she's at?"

"Only her ex-husband, but I'm not sure he'll know. Who knows how long it's been since they spoke to one another."

"Well, it's worth a shot isn't it? Do you want me to get ahold of him if I can?"

"Yes, I guess so."

I assume she is answering yes for both. "Okay, I will. But for tonight, focus on getting rest. You have all that bridesmaid stuff to do with Vanessa in three days if you're up for it."

"Oh, I will be. Her wedding's coming up fast."

"Mmhmm. And when's her bachelorette party?"

"Three days before. We're just gonna go out to dinner, and then have a few drinks. You know, probably talk about old people stuff like marriage and babies." She pauses with a deep breath, then asks out of nowhere, "Think you'll ever want another kid?"

I blink, then blink again, stunned. And when I'm stunned, I ask stupid questions, such as the one popping out of my mouth now. "Uh, with you?"

"No, with your third wife." She lets out an exasperated laugh and squirms until I loosen my hold on her. She turns in my arms and rests her head on my chest, throwing an arm around my waist as she sighs, content. "Yes, with me. One day when I'm all better and it's safe. Would you want that?"

I've never thought about it. Not until this exact moment when she asks me, but it hits me straight in the fucking chest. Angel pregnant by me again, with our second child, and I'm with her every step of the way. Getting to be with her in a way I didn't get to with Sterling, experiencing parenthood with her love and guidance from the beginning.

The thought alone makes me hug her tight and kiss the top of her head, especially with her saying when she gets better, and not if. The fact she has such hope thrills the hell out of me.

"Want it? I'd fucking love it, Angel. You just let me know when."

"Me too, but what if I...what if I can't after this?"

With a gentle press of my hand under her chin, I make sure her teary eyes are locked on mine as I say, "If you can't, that's okay too. We have an amazing son who will grow up and maybe have a family of his own. One child or ten, whatever we end up with will be perfect." Then, after a long, slow, and deep kiss, I pull back and make sure we're both comfortable.

It's not long before she's sound asleep and I just lie there holding her, enjoying her closeness as I think about our future.

No matter what happens, I mean what I said. Our life will be perfect whether we have more children or not. As long as we have each other, nothing else will ever fucking tear us apart again.

Dinner two evenings later is a treat.

Once the meal is on the table, Meg and her son join us at my invitation. So it's Daniel, Sterling, and his girlfriend on one side of the table, with Veronica, Meg, and Angel on the other side, and me at the head of the table. Angel is to my immediate right, and Sterling my left.

Angel's face is neutral as she studies Sterling's girlfriend. Renee's done nothing but stare wide-eyed at everything since she arrived. I can't decide if I'm annoyed or amused, especially since Angel told me he's not sure whether he wants to keep dating her or not. She seems nice, if a little flaky, but with the little I know about girls her age, it's normal.

I don't think it's either of our places to tell him to dump his girlfriend and I told Angel that. Only if there's something bad going on — such as abuse — will I feel as if I should step in. Otherwise, the ability to deal with others, men or women, is something he should learn to do mainly on his own even if he makes mistakes along the way.

And then there's Veronica.

Angel told me they had a nice conversation last week, and Veronica's been super polite to everyone as far as Angel knows. I haven't heard any complaints either so I'm glad she took what I said seriously. No problems with therapy so far and she's almost completely healed physically from Baron's assault.

Baron, the asshole who still hasn't been found, and it's starting to piss me off.

Personally, I hope he's lying dead in a ditch somewhere. People would probably find it harsh, which is why I haven't said it out loud, but any man who abuses a woman doesn't deserve to breathe, in my opinion. Well, really, that goes for anyone. Because as much as I love Angel, if she truly wanted to leave, I would let her; I wouldn't beat her, because I don't fucking own her.

I don't count when she first arrived because it had been clear she needed help. I'd gone with my instincts and they'd been right, but I would've made her face the consequences of her drunk driving if she hadn't accepted my help, because she had to get better one way or another. And to this day, she doesn't drive and she no longer drinks; not that I've forbidden her from either. She seems to have made both choices on her own, and personally, I think she likes the fact she doesn't have to use what little energy she has on driving herself places because Kevin is willing to take her anywhere she wants to go.

And honestly, knowing she's in his trustworthy hands makes it easier for me to work and worry less about how she's doing, because the whole staff keeps me informed on how she is when I'm not home.

Truthfully, I want that for Veronica. I want her to find someone who loves her the way I love Angel, and would do anything for her. But of course what I want even more is for Baron to be found and locked up because she needs to go back to her life, get herself straight and healthy, and everything that comes with it.

Really, I just don't want her living with me anymore, even if she's turned into a fairly decent human being recently.

Renee's loud voice interrupts my thoughts. "Meg — I can call you Meg right? This food is amazing. You're such a great cook. Our cook isn't real good at her job but my family won't get a new cook because she's been with the family for a-a-a-a-a-ages. Like another generation or something?"

"Maybe they care more about the person's job than what you think of the food," Daniel mutters, making me try to hide a grin as everyone else gasps. "Or something."

Meg is the first to respond with a mixture of shock and an amusement only those who know her would hear in her voice because her face shows clear disapproval. "Daniel!"

"I'm just saying what we're all thinking, Mom."

"Psh," Renee shoots back with a dirty look at Daniel and a quick scowl to Sterling who is gazing down at his plate before she stands up, the legs of the chair scraping the floor as she uses one hand to flip her hair over her shoulder in the patently teenager way. "I'm done eating." She turns her gaze toward Angel and I. "Where's your bathroom?"

Daniel, who is looking daggers at Renee, pipes up with, "The servant's bathroom is down the back hallway, just before the back door, where you should exit and go back to your castle."

I groan as Renee's eyes water seconds before she whirls and stalks from the room, while Sterling's face flushes red as he stares down at his food in mortification, and Daniel busts into laughter.

Well, until Meg — whose voice is now empty of all amusement while her anger is evident — stares at him in a pointed and disapproving way. "You will go and find the girl and apologize right now, Daniel. Even if she's annoying, you've no right to be so rude."

"But—"

"No. Either go and apologize or you will be sitting in your room for the next month with nothing to do but twiddle your thumbs. Right now."

Daniel scoots back his chair and stands up, tossing a glance at Sterling before stalking from the table to head the way Renee did. And that's when I say something to Sterling.

"You need to go find your girlfriend as well, son." His gaze snaps up to mine, and when he opens his mouth, I shake my head at him. "Next time someone is saying things to a girl you're dating, you should do more than simply sit there and stare at your plate." When he nods and stands up, I add in one more thing. "Oh, and if you'll take anything away from this Sterling, it's that you should notice Renee didn't retaliate."

As his shoulders droop, he leaves the room and it's silent for a moment until Meg says softly, "Sorry about Daniel. I don't know what got into him—"

Veronica snickers, picking up her wine to take a drink, and setting down the glass with a smile while we all look at her expectantly until she finally says, "Uh, he likes her. I can't believe you guys don't see it."

Furrowing her brows, Meg looks lost in thought, while Angel and I merely stare at each other, perplexed at the whole situation.

That is, until the shouting starts; specifically, Sterling's.

"I'll see what's going on," I remark while standing up with a heavy sigh, not enjoying the thoughts about what I'm about to walk into after Veronica's comments, and head toward where the yelling is coming from.

As I approach, it's clear I'm late to the party because the only thing I see as I round the corner is Sterling's fist connect with Daniel's face. Renee screams from where she stands behind him, and as Daniel stumbles back with one hand covering his face, I walk faster and yell, "Hey!"

"He started it." Sterling's face is red with anger, and he points a finger at Daniel along with a glare. "He was leaning down and about to kiss her when I came around the corner—"

"What, dude? No, I wasn't—"

"Stop it, now." My command is loud and firm as I stop a few feet from all of them, and both look over at me with embarrassed faces while Renee cries softly with her face in her hands. "Are you five, Sterling? 'He started it?' Seriously? You don't just go around punching people. What the hell has gotten into you?"

Meg and Angel suddenly appear — I'm guessing Veronica isn't interested enough in some teenage drama to join us — and Daniel winces when Meg gasps, holding up a hand to halt her approach as he says, "I'm all right, Mom. He punches like a girl."

Predictably, Sterling's hands curl into tighter fists as he takes a step forward. "Fuck—"

"Sterling!" Angel cuts him off, stalking over and grabbing him by the arm, his face instantly burning with mortification at realizing his mother has joined us. "You are grounded, young man."

"And so are you," Meg says with a waggling finger at Daniel. "He didn't have a right to punch you, but the way you spoke to that girl is what started this." She takes a step around him and approaches Renee, putting an arm around her shoulders, which still shake with her sobs, while asking in a lower voice, "Are you all right?"

"I hate boys," she wails, giving each of them an unpleasant look before entering the bathroom behind Meg, anything else she said lost behind the door as it closes.

Both start running their mouths again at one another, and I let them for a minute, Daniel denying he tried to kiss Renee while Sterling saying he knows what he saw. Basically, they get nowhere and tired of hearing it, I point a finger in the direction we came and for the first time ever say to my son, "Go to your room, Sterling."

Angel lets her hand fall from his arm as his mouth drops open, and when she doesn't say anything in response to what I've told him, he snarls at Daniel before storming off. "Thanks a lot man."

It's not long before Meg emerges from the bathroom with Renee, who has stopped crying and when she says she needs to talk to Sterling, I send her up to his room to talk. Daniel apologizes to all three of us, continuing to swear he didn't try to kiss Renee, and Meg decides to take her leave with him after cleaning up from dinner.

About a half hour later, Veronica having retired to her bedroom while Angel and I sit on the couch with her curled into my side, Renee comes into the living room with a nervous look on her flushed face. We both focus on her at the same time, Angel sitting up to get a better view.

"My dad is almost here to get me," she says in a soft voice, hands clasped in front of her body. "But I just wanted to tell you not to be mad at Sterling. He didn't do anything wrong. I wanted him to get jealous because I was afraid he didn't like me anymore because he hasn't really been talking to me much lately, so…so I kinda asked Daniel to help me—"

"Wait a sec." Holding up a hand, I interject with a scowl. "That was planned?"

"Well, it was totally not supposed to end up that way." Her flush darkens, eyes darting away to look out the window as she continues to talk. "I didn't think Sterling would hit him. He didn't even kiss me, he just got really close and pretended once he heard someone else coming. I didn't mean for him to get hurt, I swear." Then, she looks back at us, a glowing smile on her face, and her eyes glistening with tears. "I've never seen Sterling so mad like that, it was awesome. And now I know he loves me. I just didn't think it would get him in trouble—"

Angel starts laughing softly next to me as I stare in disbelief; apparently, teenage girls are beyond my comprehension, which I'm sure is something to be thankful for and feel sorry for my son at the same time because he's right in the center of it. But before I can formulate a reply, the door opens, and Henrietta announces the arrival of Renee's father.

"Please," she begs while staring at me, her lips

wobbling. "Promise me you won't ground him for long. It was my fault."

"I will think about it," I say with a nod, and when she goes to turn away, I tell her, "How about next time if you wonder how he feels, you just ask him? Boys can't read girls' minds, just like girl's can't know what a guy is thinking, no matter what they believe, all right?"

"O-okay, I will." She gives me a shy smile and turns away, glancing back over her shoulder to say, "Thanks for dinner and having me over. It was nice to meet you both, but especially Sterling's mom."

Angel returns her smile, her voice sweet in reply. "Nice to meet you too, sweetie. We'll see you again soon, I'm sure."

Then, she's gone, leaving Angel and I to go right back to enjoying the peace and quiet for the rest of the evening together.

*N*ess smiles at me as she turns in front of the mirror while wearing the fifth dress she's tried on today.

"I love it, Ness. It suits you."

"Good," she says, turning around and looking over her shoulder to gaze at her back in the mirror. "Because I think this is the one."

"Well, it's prudish like you," I joke with a laugh. "No cleavage showing, covered from shoulder to wrist, no leg slit. You look like a princess."

"I love you too, bitch." She holds out a hand and I help her down from the step. "You know Frederick and I have gone from vanilla to semi-kinky. I think by our one year anniversary, he'll be a downright naughty man just for me."

"Yep, and you're welcome."

She winks at me. "I'll be right back after I take off this dress and we'll go get some lunch."

"Kay."

Looking down at my phone, which buzzes as she walks away, I open it up to find a text from Ryker. *"How's it going?"*

The fact he can't go a few hours without texting me makes me smile as I respond. *"Great. How's things at home?"*

"Renee just arrived. Sterling's with her and Ver's upstairs too, I guess. Entertain me."

He's like a kid sometimes. It's funny. *"You know I have to focus on Ness today. You'll be fine. Go masturbate or something."*

"...Do you want a picture?"

"Haha, no. Love you. See you later."

"Love you too."

Ness comes out then, the associate walking behind her with the dress over her arm, back in its bag. I follow them to the counter, where Ness pays for the dress, and they give her a date to come back for the first fitting. She twirls around after the associate hands her the receipt, loops her arm through mine, and smiles.

"All right. Time for food, I'm starving."

Since the bridal shop is connected to the mall, we head to the food court, which is only a few minutes walk away. After we both get our food and sit down at a table far from anyone else, Ness looks at me with an expectant look.

"Well?"

I know what she's waiting for and quickly put her out of her misery. "Most recent tests show that everything is improving much faster than they expect. I'll finish the trial no matter what now unless progress stops."

"It won't," she says with a smile and teary eyes as she

reaches across the table and covers my hand with hers. "The universe knows how much I need you in my life girl."

"As much as I need you in mine." I pull my hand away from hers with a laugh before lifting a brow at her, instantly trying to lighten the mood. "Now, stop being so sappy. You don't want me to barf up this food, do you?"

She rolls her eyes, even though she can't hide her smirk, and both of us fall into silence while we eat our lunch. She gets done about the same time as I do, both of us pushing our plate away as she says, "So tell me about what happened at dinner with Sterling and…what's her face? Renee?"

I fill her in with everything I know from start to finish, and by the end she's laughing hard.

"I suppose that's one way to get your boyfriend's attention," she remarks as her amusement subsides. "What did Sterling say? He still grounded for punching Daniel?"

"Nah. He was provoked, but Ryker did tell him that's not the way to go, obviously."

"Of course. Sterling's a good kid."

"Yeah, he is." I fold my hands on the table, lean in, and say, "Now, tell me. Have you guys chosen where you're going for your honeymoon yet?"

"We're not going on one." At my look of surprise, she shrugs and sits back. "Taking time off right now isn't a good idea. Wanna know why?" I give her a 'duh' look and she stuns me with the way her whole face lights up as she says, "Frederick and I need to save up for when I leave work since we've decided to try for a baby once we're hitched."

It takes me a second to realize I heard her correctly, but then I'm the one grinning like a fool. 'Oh my god. Ness, I'm so happy for you!"

"Me too. It's all happening so fast." Her eyes tear up as she beams with happiness. "I've wanted this for so long, hard to believe it's finally happening."

"You deserve it."

"Yeah, I do." She looks at me pointedly. "And even better is that my best friend will be here for it all."

I can't resist teasing her. "Do I know this best friend?"

"Shut up," she says, laughing while standing up and grabbing her stuff. "All right, let's get going to find you the perfect dress for being my maid of honor."

"Isn't it matron since I'm married?"

"Who cares? It's my wedding, I'll call it whatever I want."

"Okay, bridezilla."

She sticks her tongue at me while I loop my arm through hers, glad everything is finally falling together for both of us.

All I can think is, it's about fucking time.

And I've never been happier.

WHEN I FINALLY RETURN HOME, EVERYTHING IS QUIET, AND Ryker's sitting alone in the living room working on his laptop.

The moment he looks up and sees me walking toward

him, he sets his computer aside while closing the lid, and indicates I should straddle his lap by patting it.

"Hey," he says the moment we're face-to-face, staring at me with a twinkle in his eyes, and a naughty curve to his lips. "It's about time you got home. Did you two have a nice time?"

"The best." Wrapping my arms around his neck, I lower my head into the crook of his shoulders while his arms encircle my waist, and hold me close to him. "I'm so excited for Ness and Freddy. She's the happiest I've ever seen her and that makes me really happy too."

"I'm glad to hear it."

"Of course you are." I press a kiss to the soft skin of his neck, following it up with a lick, and enjoy the subsequent shiver that passes through him while his arms tighten around me. "My being happy means you're about to get laid."

"I am?" He yawns in an exaggerated fashion, laughing when I pull back to slap him on the arm as he presses on with his charade. "And here I was, about to go to bed because I'm exhausted."

"Oh really? Is there enough room in that bed of yours for me?" Lifting my arms straight in the air, I stretch and yawn just like he did, following it up with a seductive glance at him from underneath my lashes. "I mean, I'm pretty tired too, and I really need to take off these clothes and shower, but—"

He stands up while keeping me secure in his arms, causing me to squeal as I immediately wrap my legs around his waist, and one of his hands finds my ass to squeeze it as he carries me out of the room. We make it to our bedroom without running into anyone, Ryker using his foot to close the door before carrying me into the master bath, where he sets me down barefoot on the tile.

Turning on the shower, he says, "Strip."

"God, I love when you get all demanding." Lifting my shirt up and over my head at the same time he takes off his, I watch as his eyes drop to my bared breasts, giving me greater amusement as I obscure his view by bending to take off my jeans and panties.

He drags me into the shower when I straighten, backing me against the sidewall, hot water pounding down on us while he wastes no time in crushing my lips beneath his as I rewrap my legs around his waist. He doesn't seek entry into my mouth, he takes it, and it's everything I want and need all rolled into one. His passion, tenderness, and devotion are all mine with every stroke of his tongue and every moan between us.

Both of his hands are cupping my ass, but now one moves to slide down in-between my legs from behind, two fingers seeking and finding entry into my pussy. He pushes them inside, groaning into my mouth at finding me slick with arousal, ready and waiting for him, as always. He does it for me; he's all I need, want, and desire.

When he releases my mouth to kiss down my jaw and neck, I whisper, "Take me, Ryker. Now. I can't wait."

"Yes you can," he retorts with a naughty-sounding chuckle, sinking his teeth a bit into my neck, making me hiss while turning me on even more. "It's been a week; a few more minutes won't matter love."

"It will." To accentuate how needy I am, I thrust my hips, which has the added effect of my pussy riding his fingers, leaving me gasping as it sends sparks of pleasure throughout me. "Please...I need..."

His mouth returns to mine as he gives me a sweet peck on the lips before muttering, "You're never going to let me make slow, sweet love to this gorgeous body of yours, are you Angel?"

"Slow, fast, hard, soft...it's all making love with you," I tell him while gazing up into his eyes, making sure to peek at him from under my lashes and bite my lip gently as I thrust my hips a little once more. His defeated groan is everything I want and more as I say, "Now give it to me."

And he does.

Every inch of his body adores every inch of mine as he slides his cock inside me with a smooth, hard thrust that has us both shuddering with the exquisite pleasure of it. He fucks me, worships me, and loves me with each movement; in and out, his hands grasping my ass and holding on like he'll never let go.

It's impossible for me to keep silent, my mouth ripping away from his as he moves his hands to grab my hips, lifting me up and down, faster and faster as the pleasure spirals higher and higher until finally my orgasm explodes.

"Oh...oh god." The words are ripped from my throat as I stiffen in his arms, my body going limp while the pleasure rolls through me at what seems like high-speed, making me whimper and dig my nails into his shoulders. "Ryker—"

"Fuck yes," he growls out, his head inclining until his forehead's resting on mine, and he thrusts hard. Once, and then twice, pausing with a low moan deep inside my pussy as he comes right along with me.

Neither of us move; not that I'm sure we could even if we wanted to.

And right there, with our bodies connected, the realization of what I would've missed out on had I truly given up hits me like nothing else ever has.

If I hadn't driven that night here to Ryker's, I wouldn't know *this* — the feel of his arms around me, the beat of his heart against mine as we both cling to one another, the absolute deep and real love he feels for me — and in this moment, I can't even fathom it. Not having this, not having had the chance to clear up the past, my son not knowing his father while I was alive?

All of it, every single thought, is like a punch to the chest. It steals my breath, my heart swelling with love for this man and this life, and I know Ryker feels it because his hold tenses, his voice whispering in my ear not even a second later as I feel one his hands leave me and shut the water off. "You all right Angel?"

I lift my head, finding his warm gaze with my teary one as I say, "God yes. I'm fine. I…thank you, Ryker. Thank you for saving my life. Hard as it was for me, you…this…I…"

Even though tears overtake me, and the words jumble

in my throat, I know Ryker gets it. He gets me, especially as he responds in a voice hoarse with raw emotion, and a grin on his face. "No need to thank me, sweetheart, but you're welcome all the same. I never would've given up on you, not even for a second though. You just needed reminded of why living was the better option, and you have to admit, being able to fuck me on a nearly daily basis is reason enough."

It's a serious note broken up by both of us laughing — after all, he's not really wrong, fucking him *is* one of the things I enjoy the most — and that's what makes it one of the most significant moments of my life.

Because I know no matter what happens in my life, he'll always be there for me. He'll always fight for me, for us, whether I can fight along beside him or not.

That's love.

And I never want to live without it or him ever again.

*M*onday morning at work is quiet.

Veronica sits at her desk, working on all the stuff that piled up over the weekend, while I'm shut in my office.

Picking up my phone, I'm about to do the first important thing on my list, which is calling Felicia's ex-husband to see if he knows where she's at, and why she hasn't contacted Angel in all these months.

After getting his name from her, and eventually tracking down his number as of Friday, I wanted to wait the weekend before calling just in case she finally showed her face. Of course, she hasn't, and it's just pissing me off because she never struck me as the type of person who would ignore her family, even with all that happened between her and Angel.

Dialing him up, I'm afraid it's about to go to voicemail when he finally answers, sounding confused. "Hello?"

"Hello. Am I speaking with Chris Melbourne?"

"Yeah. Who are you?"

"Ryker Redding. I'm looking for your ex-wife Felicia. I'm her sister Danita's husband."

"Oh." He clears his throat, sounding more confident now as he replies, "She told me you might call, but that was months ago, after you fired her."

I decide not to clarify it's not even been two months, let alone acknowledge his statement, telling him why I'm calling in hopes this conversation won't take forever, and I can get back to work. "Her sister wanted to give her space at first, but she's been leaving Felicia messages, and she hasn't heard back from her. Do you know where she's at?"

It's silent on his end for a second before he says, "Uh, yeah. She's been here with me, but she's not here right now. She went to the store. I had no idea she's been ignoring Danita's calls though, especially since she told me she's sick and all."

All I'm thinking is, what the fuck, are they back together or something?

I don't ask though. I only have one purpose for this call and that is to get Felicia's ass to my house to speak to Angel.

"Look Chris, I've got your address. Tell Felicia she has until the end of this week to show up at my place — she knows where I live for sure — and talk to her sister, who she's obviously been ignoring. If she doesn't, I will come pick her up and bring her to the house myself, got it?"

"But—"

I interrupt him, saying something I know isn't true but

admitting will most likely work with Felicia anyway. "If she doesn't, Chris, then tell her she will owe me the money I paid her upon firing her; money I didn't have to fucking give her, yet did because she's Angel's sister and took care of our son. Am I clear?"

"Uh. Yeah. Got it. I'll tell her when she gets back."

"Thanks Chris," I say, hanging up the call without waiting for a reply, chuckling to myself. "Too easy."

Next, I dial Percy, who I promised to update with Angel's situation, and have completely pushed to the side for too long now.

"About damn time you called me," he grumbles upon answering, but his smile is obvious. "How's things?"

As always, I'm a dick to him. "You know you can call me, Prissy, don't you? My phone isn't a one-way walkie talkie."

"Hey, I've got a baby in one hand, and a patient's file in the other most of the time. Or did you forget my wife was prepping for the baby the last time we talked?"

I resist the urge to laugh at how harried he sounds. "Are you whining? Maybe your nickname should now be pussy instead of prissy."

"Shut up, asshole." He pauses, shuffling something around on the other end before continuing with a chuckle. "So tell me, how's fatherhood to a teenager treating you?"

"He's great, of course. He's my kid, after all."

Prissy snorts, and I'm sure he's rolling his eyes right now. "Right, how could I forget."

"It's all good, I'll forgive your lapse this time." We both

laugh at that, then I say, "Everything is good man. Real good. Sorry you missed the wedding. Your kid's arrival was terrible timing."

"Oh, yeah. She's great though. Wife says she's done, but I may talk her into one more in hopes of having another boy so there'll be three girls and three boys."

"You're fucking insane."

"Did I send you a picture?"

"How about you come see me in person? Bring the family, we'll have a cookout sometime this summer. Got vacation time coming up?"

"Sure, I'll check into it." I hear him scribbling himself a reminder before he asks in a softer tone, "How's married life? Are the treatments going well?"

"Great. It's working man. Anything beyond that is a fucking bonus."

The fact he's smiling is clear in his reply. "Glad to hear it. I look forward to meeting her and seeing you. It's been too long."

"Agreed." A baby wails in the background at that moment, and Percy groans while I chuckle. "Guess you better get going before the kid bursts both our eardrums."

"Yep. See you later."

I'm just about to say the same when I realize I need to tell him one more thing. "Hey Prissy?"

"Yeah?"

"Thanks, man." I clear my throat in an attempt to hold back the emotion clogging my throat. "For helping with Angel and getting her in the trial, I mean. I appreciate it."

"No problem," he says as the kid wails louder, sighing as I laugh again. "I'll call you soon. Later."

He hangs up before I can respond, leaving me to shake my head as I hang up the phone, and envy him a little. Five kids, his own practice, and he still wants more children on top of everything he's got going on. It makes me think back to the conversation I had with Angel about having more children, something I truly want more than anything, but I'm thrilled to have her and Sterling. Forever, if that's how it goes down.

Because, like I told Percy, anything else is a bonus.

I learned long ago to be happy with what I have, rather than always wishing for something more, because it meant I appreciated whatever happened when it came along in a way I might not if I just always desired something extra.

And speaking of appreciating what I have, I slide the bar across the screen on my phone, open up my messages, and send one to Angel. "*Love you.*"

Her reply a minute later has me laughing. "*Good, I love me too. <3 xoxo*"

Shaking my head even as I grin from ear-to-ear, I set my phone aside, recognizing it's time to get to work so I can get home and show Angel how much I love her with actions instead of mere words.

The day goes pretty fast and soon I'm doing just that.

Thank fuck for uneventful days.

THE WEEK FLIES BY, AND AS FRIDAY ROLLS AROUND, NOTHING too exciting has happened.

Percy, after speaking with his wife, called me back earlier today to let me know the cookout is on. I talked to Angel and we agreed on next weekend, since the one after that is Vanessa's wedding.

So, Percy and his family will arrive next Friday to stay the whole weekend, which both Angel and Sterling seem excited over. I know Angel is not only looking forward to meeting Percy and his wife, but also being surrounded by children. And I have to admit, I'm anticipating it a little myself as I'm sure it will give me a taste of what little children are like in case I need it in the future.

Which I hope I fucking do, but I'm smart enough to be pragmatic, since Angel's health comes first, always.

Angel shifts beside me on the couch, bringing me back from my thoughts, and when I look down at her it's to find her smiling brightly at me.

"Don't think too hard," she teases while snuggling closer to me and resting her hand on my chest over my heart, tilting her head until it rests on the outer part of my shoulder. "Don't want you to hurt yourself, Ry."

I lower my head until my mouth hovers next to her ear as I whisper, "The only thing that's gonna be hurting around here is your bottom if you keep teasing me like you have been."

"If you're trying to deter me from teasing you, a threat like that's hardly going to stop me."

"Sounds like a dare."

"Gag!"

I turn my head to glare at Veronica's comment as she enters the living room, only to realize she's joking around by the smile on her face, and Angel sits up straight beside me at the same time.

"You finish that book yet, Veronica?"

"Yes," she says while plopping down in the chair with a grimace. "I rolled my eyes so hard at the cheesy ending I feared they were gonna fall right out."

The disgust on her face amuses me enough to ask, "What book are you referring to?"

"Laird of my Heart, it's called." Veronica lifts a brow as she looks over at both of us, the corners of her mouth lifting up in a smirk. "Should've been called Laird of the Pussies, if you ask me."

Angel lets out a cute snort of laughter before giving her lighthearted reply. "You know you want a man like Duncan. Big, rough around the edges, but with a heart of gold and a cock so big you orgasm before it's even all the way in—"

"Shut up," Veronica says at the same time she tosses a throw pillow in our direction.

I've no doubt she meant to hit Angel, but instead it smacks me in the face, causing both of them to bust out laughing as I sputter and the pillow falls to rest on the floor.

As strange as it is to hear them giggling with each other, the fact they're getting along is better than anything else I could ask for, even if their discussion makes me want to plug my ears.

Just as I bend to pick up the pillow to retaliate, all three of us turn our heads to the door at the sound of someone running down the hall, and seconds later, Meg comes through the doorway before stopping abruptly at the sight of us.

"Turn on the news quick," she says, gasping for air as she tries to catch her breath, and then coughs before clarifying, "Channel five."

Swiping the remote from the end table at the urgency in Meg's voice, I level it at the TV and hit the power button, changing the channel the moment the screen lights up.

On the station are pictures of a red vehicle crushed underneath a garbage truck, the reporter saying, "Initial reports indicate the car, belonging to one Mister Baron Larson who was pronounced dead at the scene, came to an abrupt stop—"

Anything else the woman says is drowned out by the sound of Veronica's screaming, my eyes torn from the screen to see her hands coming up to cover her mouth as she slides off the chair and onto her knees. Before I'm even able to think or react, Angel jumps up from her seat and walks over to Veronica, kneeling and enveloping her in a hug while she continues to sob.

Returning my gaze to the TV, I hit the mute button, and right as it goes silent, the doorbell rings.

A minute later, Henrietta steps into the room as I turn toward the door, an obviously pregnant Felicia standing directly behind her, arm-in-arm with her ex-husband Chris, which leaves me with no doubt about how fucking long this evening will be as I deal with everything happening at once.

"*A*ngel," Ryker says, stepping toward me and holding out his hand for me to take. "Felicia is here."

Unable to see anything sitting on the floor as I am, Veronica holding on to me as she cries, I frown at him and hiss, "I'm a little busy right now."

"I've got Veronica." He crouches down and opens his arms. "Chris is here with her and…" His words halt, mouth firming into a thin line as he pulls Veronica away from me and into his hold instead, sighing as she clings to him as she had to me just seconds before.

"Just go. She's finally here to see you and—"

Knowing I've been waiting for nearly two months to talk to her, I nod, cutting him off as I stand and turn to face the door, only to stop cold at the sight of Felicia.

Her protruding stomach, in no way hidden by the pretty light blue summer dress she's wearing, is the first thing my eyes take notice of, but I'm quick to lift my gaze to hers even as I swallow down my surprise. Everyone says pregnant women glow, but until this moment, I had no idea what they meant. Even though she has a slight look of confusion about why Veronica is crying, her mouth's lifted in a slight smile, her hair is hanging down her back, and she's practically radiating happiness.

And I'm shocked as hell to see her — not to mention Chris — let alone able to quickly process the fact she had to've been pregnant the last time I saw her, and I hadn't had the slightest clue.

"Felicia. Chris," I say while walking toward her, stopping a foot from them, and toss a smile at Henrietta. "Thank you for showing them in. I'll take it from here."

She inclines her head and exits the room. With a final glance over my shoulder at Ryker, I refocus on Felicia and Chris, lifting a hand, palm up, in the direction of the hallway. "Let's go into the other room, shall we?"

We walk across the hall and once we're inside, I turn on the light and shut the door. While the other room is the living room, this is also a room with a couch and a chair, and is sort of a mini-library with the bookshelves lining the walls. I've only been here a couple months, but I don't think I'll ever get used to this big house and its multitude of rooms.

They both sit down on the couch, and as I take a seat across from them, Felicia starts speaking before I can even say a word. "I'm sorry I didn't return your calls."

I barely manage to tamp down my urge to ask if hell has frozen over and to pinch myself from sheer disbelief at what I'm hearing. Felicia apologizing to me? Never in the past fifteen years, since I showed up at my father's house, has she ever said sorry for anything.

Instead I drop my eyes from her, giving a pointed look at her stomach, before lifting my gaze back to hers. "How far along are you?"

"Six months." She lifts her right hand from the chair arm, using it to cradle her stomach, her body visibly relaxing as the smile on her face grows. "We're having a girl."

So many questions, but one really nags me, so it's the one that pops out. "Why the hell didn't you tell me that day?"

Her smile disappears, replaced by a grimace, sucking in an unsteady breath as Chris places his right arm across her shoulders. "I didn't know. I…thought I was sick again."

"What?" That word has me on instant alert as I scowl at her. "What do you mean by sick *again*?"

It's Chris who speaks this time, Felicia lowering her gaze to her lap, and fidgeting with her hands. "Felicia lost an ovary and a fallopian tube due to cancer two years before her parents' died."

His statement makes me feel as if I've been slapped across the face, my mouth dropping open as I continue to stare at Felicia, my own heart squeezing as I watch a tear fall onto her lap.

"I didn't know—" I stop talking as she lifts her watery gaze to mine, and it's this second her despair is clear to me, explaining why she'd always been so angry at the attention I received. My own eyes fill with tears as I whisper, "They didn't know either, did they?"

"No." Her chin lifts a little defensively, although her eyes are still warmer than I've ever seen them. "They had their own problems, and they were taking care of Sterling. I didn't want to worry them."

To apologize seems so inadequate, but I don't know what else to say. "I'm sorry. You should've told me, I would've cared. I would've been there for you."

She chuckles at that, the smile remaining even as her laughter dies away. "We've never been the best of friends, so while I think you think you would've, I also would've deserved you laughing in my face." She pauses, eyes dropping to her belly as she rubs it a bit, then she looks back up at me. "You were right that day, and I'm sorry for being so rotten to you. Nothing you ever had going on warranted my anger or dislike, nor did I have a right to insinuate you are a bad mother."

The sincerity in her words eases the leftover hurt from that day at her place, and I smile at her in return. "It's all right."

"No, it's not," she says with a shake of her head, eyes growing misty once more. "I've not even met this little girl of mine yet, but I know that I would do whatever it took to make sure she grows up happy and healthy, even if it meant doing what you did in the event of me getting sick or whatever else."

With a swipe at the unexpected tear sliding down my cheek, I give her a watery smile as I say, "Truly, I forgive you. We all have our troubles, and I should've been more aware also."

"Thank you."

"As for this—" Waving my hand wildly at them, hoping to change the subject to something happier, I lift a brow while glancing between his face and hers. "Last I knew, you two hated each other. What changed?"

"I could never hate Felicia," Chris states with a bit of fire, his arm tightening around her shoulders, and pulls her close to his side so he can kiss the top of her head. "I've always loved her, but we had our problems, and we weren't ready for each other the first time around."

Felicia laughs, her face flushed as he releases her, and she sits up straight again while tossing him a look filled with love that I recognize all too well. "Yeah, well, you're stuck with me this time."

"No argument from me."

Something makes me look down at Felicia's hand for more than a brief glance, smiling at the sight of the rings on her left hand as I state, "You two got married again."

"Congratulations." Ryker's unexpected comment from the doorway startles all three of us, and before I can even turn my head to look at him, his hand comes down to rest gently on my shoulder as he stands beside me and says, "Times two, in fact."

Their smiles are identical — bright, happy, and hopeful — as Felicia says, "Thank you. And yes, we did get married again. Just me, Chris, and the JoP."

I lift my hand to cover Ryker's as I say, "I'm happy for

you both." Titling my head back a little, I lift my gaze until Ryker is staring down at me. "How is she?"

"She'll be all right. I took her to her room; Meg and Henrietta are going to take turns making sure she's taken care of."

Both of us focus on Felicia a second later when she asks, "Who?"

"My ex-wife." When she looks confused, he clarifies what we're talking about even though his eyes are back on my face as he speaks. "Her husband assaulted her and subsequently disappeared; she's been staying with us until he could be located. Right before you arrived, we discovered he died earlier this evening."

"So she's free of the scumbag then." Chris is the one who says this, and when Ryker flicks a glance at him and nods, Chris comes back with, "Good. I can't imagine why anyone would want to hurt the person they've promised to cherish their whole lives."

"I'm sure she'll probably see it that way eventually, but right now, she's heartbroken." I rise and stand next to Ryker, who puts his arm around me. "Asshole or not, she loved him at one point."

At the sound of someone clearing their throat in the doorway, I look over my shoulder and smile at the sight of Sterling. But Felicia speaks up before anyone else has a chance.

"Sterling! It's so good to see you, honey."

I have to bite my lip to keep from laughing out loud at the obvious bafflement on Sterling's face, remembering him telling me all those weeks ago about Felicia always being grumpy, but he quickly hides it behind the grin of a kid who loves his aunt.

"Hi," he finally responds.

Second later, when his eyes round, I don't even have to look back at her to know he's surprised at her pregnancy, and can only smirk while staring at me after she walks over and envelopes him in a hug.

As she pulls back, Chris walks over and takes her by the arm, smiling down at her before saying, "We should get going. It's been a long day and I don't know about you, but I'm exhausted."

"I am, but, in a moment." Felicia looks over at me, her eyes scanning me from head to toe before asking, "Everything all right? You look…much better than the last time I saw you."

"Are you saying I'm fat?" There's no heat in my words even as I keep my face neutral, only grinning when she starts blushing, before I walk closer to her and take her hands in mine. "I'm great. I told you in my voicemails that I'm in a trial, and everything is working as they hoped. No worries."

"I'll never not worry about you. You and Sterling are my family."

She pulls *me* into a hug, and I swear if she wasn't gripping me so tightly, I'd fall to the floor in utter shock. My eyes tear up as I return her embrace, saying softly into her ear, "You're gonna be a great mom, and thank you so much for taking care of Sterling."

"You would do the same for me. And it was my pleasure."

As she releases me and steps back, Ryker speaks up, wrapping his arm around my waist as he tugs me close to his side. "You two should come next weekend, we're having a cookout and a bunch of people will be here."

Felicia nods while Chris clasps her hand in his. "We'll see how I feel, but most likely, we'll see you then."

"Call me and let me know," I tell them as they turn to go.

"Will do," Chris says with a final glance our way as they step into the hallway, and moments later, the front door shuts behind them.

Sterling speaks then. "Wow. Was aunt Felicia's body taken over by an alien, Mom?"

Both Ryker and I respond to his observation the only way we can — with laughter.

"You can stay as long as you need to, you know."

Veronica smiles at me while continuing to pack, insisting, "I'm fine. Truly."

"You should stay here through the weekend. Percy and his family will arrive tomorrow and be here as well—"

"Danita," she cuts in with a laugh, zipping her duffel bag and tossing it over her shoulder as she walks toward me. "I want to be in my place, with my things, with nothing but peace and quiet."

"Okay, but if you need anything—"

She lifts her free arm, her hand landing on my shoulder as she levels a serious look at me. "I appreciate the concern, but I can handle it from here." Then, after a quick squeeze she drops her hand, clears her throat, and gives me a nervous smile. "Thank you for being so kind to me. I didn't deserve it after the way I acted toward both of you and it's clear why Ryker loves you like he does."

Her words catch me off guard, and I have to admit, I'm worried about her. Since she found out about Baron's death six days ago, she hasn't seemed herself, at least not the woman whose spent her time here up until that point.

It's not that she's been unkind; in reality, except for right after she arrived here, she's been downright friendly. Well, as friendly as she knows how to be, which is probably a lot of effort for her when compared to how she used to behave.

No, my problem is she seems sad, almost despondent, even if she's hiding behind a strong, happy play-act.

And the fact I'm picking up on this makes me feel as if I'm missing something important. I haven't wanted to come right out and ask her for fear of upsetting her, but if I can make her feel even a little better, that's what I want to do.

So giving into the temptation to be nosy, I ask my question in a gentle tone. "Did something else happen at the hospital that wasn't shared with me?"

Her smile slips, her eyes growing guarded before she looks at the ground and mutters, "I'm not sure what you mean."

"Hey." When she lifts her unhappy gaze back to mine, I

keep my words soft and kind. "You're welcome, although as long people are nice to me, I'm generally the same in return. However, my question is due to the fact you seem sad to me, and I know it's not over that man."

She drops the bag back onto the bed and plops down beside it, placing her head in her hands as she mumbles, "I thought Ryker told you."

"Told me what?"

"I...was pregnant. You know..." Her voice chokes with emotion as she lifts her eyes to mine, her pain palpable. "Before."

I've never lost a child, but I don't need to in order to know how painful that would be, especially if she thought she'd never have any. "Oh. Oh, Veronica, I'm so sorry—"

Tears start to trickle down her cheeks as she holds up a hand to interrupt me. "Don't apologize. I...I never expected to become a mother. I thought I got over it, when the doctors told me that originally. I thought I was okay with it. Then—then to lose...to lose a pregnancy when I didn't even know..." A sob escapes as she trails off, only to grab ahold of herself with a huge intake of breath, which she lets out slowly at the same time she curls her hands into fists. "And that fucking bastard... he took so much from me...and then for him to rob me of the baby too?"

She breaks down after that, her head dropping toward her lap as her hands come back up to cradle it at the last second, and sobs wrack her whole body while I stand there feeling like an idiot. It's clear she hadn't cried about it, and all I can think to do is sit down beside her, putting my arm across her shoulder and hugging her to my side in an attempt to bring her some comfort.

We sit like that for a few minutes until her crying subsides a little, and when she pulls away while wiping at her eyes, I decide to help her feel less guilty about how she's acted toward me.

"You know, I was honestly surprised how kind Ryker was after finding out about our son. He missed out on a lot, and it was kind of my fault. After I became an adult, I could've found him; I could've told him even if Sterling stayed with my family."

Reaching over to the nightstand for a tissue, she tugs out one while nodding, tossing a glance at me before bringing it to her nose. "He would've forgiven you at any point in time. He's just that kind of man. He was always nicer to me than I deserved; not even as his wife did I deserve everything he did for me." She uses the tissue, and dropping it into the trash beside the bed, clasps her hands in her lap. "Until I messed up like I did, I think he would've done anything to make me happy."

"He cares for you even now." I place my hand over hers in a gesture of reassurance. "You take time for yourself, and grieve all you need, because I think—no, I know that when you're ready, you'll find someone who will be perfect for you, and who'll want the same things you do."

"I don't know…"

"Nobody does."

"But—"

"I got lucky." After a kind smile, I remove my hand

from hers and stand up, walking over to the window to look out as I continue saying what I think she needs to hear. "When I walked away from this place, I never expected to see him again, to have to face him. I was self-destructive; hell, the night I ended up here I was trying to die."

There is no look of shock on her face at my admission. "Ryker told me all about your life, you know. At the time, I thought too fucking bad, but I grew up so privileged, I really did. Next to you, I shouldn't have ended up this way. I mean," she says with a self-deprecating laugh, "look at me. I'm a mess. I've always been a mess. And...and look at you."

Her voice softened at the end of her statement, but I still spin around with a lifted brow and a slight frown. "Like I said, I got lucky, and that's all there is to it. I was reckless, I aimed to die, I hurt myself and others, although the latter wasn't on purpose. I was a lost girl even when I became an adult. I spent a lot of time in my life feeling sorry for myself because how I grew up was all I knew. But don't think I didn't pay for it, because I did. And you...well you messed up. You made some bad choices. But those choices don't always have to define you. None of our choices ever have to define us always. We can always do better, learn better, be better, if we only give ourselves the chance."

"See?" She lifts a hand to her face, swiping at a tear as she watches me with a watery smile. "That's why Ryker loves you."

Walking over to the bed, feeling for this woman who

LOVING MY ANGEL

reminds me so much of myself when I was younger and lost, I bend down in front of her and take her hands in mine, my words filled with the passion for life I need her to feel. "You're afraid nobody will love you like he did, but nobody can ever love you like he did. Everybody's love is different, but it doesn't mean someone won't love you and want to be with you now or ever again. You have to have faith that you'll get everything you desire, be grateful for what you *do* have, and accept that if something doesn't happen for you, it doesn't mean you're doing anything wrong at all. It may simply mean it's not meant for you in that moment, not that it'll never happen ever, because you can't know that."

"It's hard to feel that way when I feel like I've never done anything right."

"What's right?" She shrugs, but I insist because I'm sure she has something more to say. "No, tell me. What, exactly, is the 'right' way to do things?"

"Not how I did them, obviously. I loved Ryker when we got married. As idiotic as I was, he gave me more than enough attention, but it never felt like enough, and instead of realizing it was an issue with me and talking to him about my feelings, I did everything I could to get him to pay attention to me, even if it was negative." Her face is filled with absolute misery as another tear slips down her cheek. "I blamed him for everything, even my inability to get pregnant, even though I now know that makes no fucking sense. And I never meant to cheat on him, it just began as an innocent flirtation because I was trying to make Ryker jealous. Instead I lost the one person who truly had loved me."

"No, you lost him as a husband, but you didn't lose him completely." With a final slight pressure of reassurance against her hands, I release them and stand up, grabbing a tissue and handing it to her. "You're not perfect, Veronica. You've made mistakes and even now when you've learned from them, well, you'll never be perfect. Nobody is nor ever will be perfect, so just keep that in mind. As long as you're doing your best, that's all anyone can ask of you."

"Thank you," she whispers, dabbing at her eyes and sniffling.

Before either she or I can say anything else, there's a knock at the door, prompting me to call out, "Come in," at the same time Veronica turns her face away from whoever will enter.

The door opens a little, Henrietta sticking her head around the frame, and smiles upon seeing me before resting her gaze on Veronica. "The car is ready and waiting for you, Miss Veronica."

Veronica lifts her hand in acknowledgment while still looking the opposite way, keeping a happy-sounding lilt to her voice as she responds, "Thanks Hen. Tell Kevin I'll be down in five minutes, please."

"Of course."

She leaves without another word, Veronica standing up once the door closes behind Henrietta, and tosses the tissue in the trash. Turning to me, she picks up her bag once more, tossing it over her shoulder with a sigh and a final look at me.

Her voice has a bit more confidence than it did at the beginning of our conversation when she says, "I really am looking forward to being in my own place again."

"I know." She starts to walk toward the door, stopping when I tell her, "Promise me you'll call if you need anything. I know we're not really friends, but to me, that doesn't matter. If you need help, I will do whatever I can."

With a final, prolonged and contemplative look in my direction, she nods and says, "I'll hold you to that."

Then, a moment later, she's gone, and I sit down on the bed while truly appreciating my life. Because, while it hasn't been the easiest or the way I thought it would, I wouldn't want to be Veronica for anything.

And that alone is enough to make me go find Ryker to make clear how much I love and appreciate him.

*P*ercy's arrival with his family is as loud as I've expected it would be.

His wife, Marigold, is the first through the door with a toddler on her hip. Although her smile is genuine as her green eyes locate me, her curly black hair's wild and falling from her up-do, the little boy chomping on that same hair clutched in his grasp as she comes to a stop. Percy enters right behind her, one hand holding the arm of a baby carrier, the other gripping the tiny hand of what I consider a mini-me of his father.

Two sets of blond hair and blue eyes stare back at me, Percy setting down the baby seat and releasing the kid's hand before pulling me into an enthusiastic, cheerful-like-him bear hug.

"Ryker," he says before pulling back, grinning at me as he drops his arms and steps away a bit. "Four years since I saw you last; you haven't changed one damn bit."

"Neither have you." Crouching down and making eye contact with the little boy, I smile as I ask, "And who might this be?"

"This is Lane. On Mari's hip is Lonny, and the littlest one, as you know, is Poppy."

Lane runs over to his mother, hiding behind her skirt as I chuckle and stand up, addressing both Percy and Marigold. "I take it he's a bit shy."

Marigold nods, anything she's going to reply halted by the arrival of their final two children. Myra and Freya, their fraternal seven-year-old twins, are the last to come inside. Myra, with her mother's black hair and her father's blue eyes, shuts the front door while Freya, with blonde hair and blue eyes darker than Percy's, only takes a couple steps inside before leaning against the window next to the doorframe.

"Well, hello there," Percy says, causing me to turn my head to see who he's speaking to, only to find Angel standing nervously at the bottom of the steps that lead upstairs to the bedrooms. "You must be Angel."

"I am," she replies with a delightful smile, her luminous eyes dropping to the baby carrier on the floor as she takes a step forward. "It's really nice to meet you, but all I really want to do right this minute is hold that precious baby of yours."

Percy laughs, leaning down to unbuckle Poppy before standing back up and offering Angel the baby, who takes her after a quick happiness-filled glance at me.

The look on her face as she stares down at the child says

everything she's feeling and makes me look forward to the day when I might get the opportunity to see that same expression of pure delight on her face as she stares down at another child of ours.

In this moment, I'm incredibly fucking jealous of Percy, even though there is no reason to feel this way.

Angel and I have everything we could possibly need and want at this point even if it's not everything we desire.

And with her hyper-focused on the baby, Marigold walks over to stand next to me, saying in a soft voice with an equally affectionate smile on her face, "She's lovely."

"She is." With a chuckle, I tilt a little toward her in a conspiratorial manner and joke, "Think I should keep her?"

"I know for a fact you've no other option."

Angel giggles then, giving away the fact she's listening, lifting her head to stare straight at me with the softest look on her face I've ever seen before giving Marigold her attention. "She's beautiful. It reminds me of when Sterling was a baby—"

"Whoa!" Sterling's voice rings out from the doorway, and he smiles when everyone looks his way. "How cool is it that I showed up at the exact moment you said my name?"

"Holy shit—"

"Percy!"

Marigold's exclamation cuts him off as she tosses a glare his way, the twins giggling while both Angel and I try to hide a smirk, but Percy's wide eyes find mine as he clarifies his reaction. "You weren't kidding. Not even in the picture you sent me was it clear how much your son resembles you."

"According to my mother, I'm more handsome." Sterling busts into laughter along with everyone else as he steps into the room, walking to stand next to his mother and glance down at the baby and asking, "Are you all just gonna stand around here or what? Meg's got dinner ready."

The twins take off running through the door Sterling's just come through, so I extend my arm in that direction as I say, "Shall we?" I wave my hand when Percy looks down at their stuff with a pointed glance and shake my head. "Don't worry about it. Henrietta will put your stuff in your rooms. Let's eat, I'm sure you're all starving after the long flight."

Marigold begins to follow the twins with Lonny as he starts to whine, exiting the room as his whine turns into cries. Angel, still cradling the baby close, holds her hand out to Lane, her smile tender as he takes it, and her eyes watery as she takes a quick peep at me. Her whole face softens, all her feelings unmistakable on her face and in her eyes, before she turns to lead the children to the table.

Percy steps up next to me, clapping me on the back as we watch her walk away, only speaking when we're completely alone. "Congrats man. Not that I had any doubts after Veronica pulled that shit on you, but if I did, the way you look at her and your son answers every question I or anyone else could possibly have about how much they mean to you."

I'm not even able to form a coherent response to what

he's said as we walk toward the dining room because I'm well aware of how transparent my feelings are for my family.

Especially since they've become my whole world in such a short time, and even with all my positive thinking, the fact I'm not sure how long it will last scares the shit out of me.

ONCE THE KIDS ARE IN BED AND ASLEEP, MARIGOLD announces she's too tired to stay up any longer, even though it's only ten.

Surprisingly — or perhaps not, considering the pure amount of crazy energy the children let out in the three whole hours they were awake — Angel also heads to bed after telling me to have some nice alone time with Percy.

Heading into the library once she's gone, I pour us both a drink as Percy settles in one of the comfy wing-backed chairs. Then, once we're both seated with glasses in hand, he lifts his in the air, grinning with pure satisfaction when my actions mirror his.

"To our beautiful wives and children," he says with a wink. "As well as a lifetime filled with happiness."

"Cheers."

We both take a sip, after which I'm unable to resist teasing him. "Did the missus tell you to say that?"

He smirks, lifting his glass to his lips as he responds with, "Absolutely."

Chuckling, I shake my head at him, with both of us

finishing our drinks in the comfortable silence that falls between us. Percy's the first to put an end to that, sets his empty tumbler on the table, and stands up with a yawn.

"Don't tell me you're going to bed as well."

He stretches, making exaggerated noises to go along with it, before turning toward the door. "I am. Between the new baby and work, along with the long flight, I'm beat."

"Jerk."

With a snort of what I think is disbelief, he glances over his shoulder at me with one brow raised. "Jerk? What's next? You gonna stick your tongue out at me like a little kid?"

I do exactly that just because he said it, and he laughs, walking out of the room after saying, "See you in the morning."

Standing up once I've finished my drink, I make sure everything is put away before grabbing his glass, heading toward the kitchen to put both his and mine in the dishwasher after shutting off the library light.

The house is pretty quiet, everyone having gone to bed already, and when a long, hard yawn finds its way out of me, I have to finally admit I'm pretty beat as well. Heading up the steps, I use the bathroom in the hallway so I won't have to make any noise once I'm in the room in order to avoid waking Angel; she needs her sleep and the last thing I want is to disturb her when she'd been tired enough to retire early.

But it's clear I needn't have worried when I open the door and Angel is wide-awake, sitting in bed with the lamp on reading a book. She lifts her head, her gaze locking on mine as she shuts the book and sets it on the table beside her, and then pats the bed beside her.

"I thought you would chat with Percy longer, but joining me is also an excellent idea."

Tugging off my shirt and shorts, I toss them on the nearby chair and walk closer to her, not thinking about the next words to come out of my mouth. "He's an old man and went to bed after one drink."

"And you're not?"

"Oh, you're going to pay for that," I murmur while pulling back the covers and climbing into bed, pulling her into my arms before she can muster a protest and trap her beneath my body. "Better start pleading for mercy."

Her breath hitches, her lips parting just a little while her arms come up to wrap around my neck, and her eyes search mine briefly before she lowers them to stare at my mouth. Her tongue darts out to playfully lick mine, and after letting out a warning growl, I lean in to capture her mouth with mine, only for her to turn her head away and giggle when my lips land on her cheek instead.

"Laugh away, Angel. Don't forget I know how to make you squirm and beg." Kissing across her jaw and then up, I nip at the lobe of her ear when I reach it, and give a dark chuckle when her arms tighten a little at the same time she lifts her hips into mine. My whisper into her ear is triumphant, teasing as I grind back against her, causing her to moan deep in her throat. "Do you need something, sweetheart? You'll need to tell me what it is you need before I can help you."

As she turns her head back, I draw away and once our eyes are once again on each other's, she grins and wiggles against me with a naughty twinkle in her eyes. "I need the pig to quit porking around and give me a little sausage."

"Just a little?" Both my eyebrows rise along with my amusement at her charming playfulness. "Sorry to disappoint you, but I only deal in bulk."

"Then I'll take one bulk order of little sausages."

Her face was straight as she began the sentence, but by the end, she busts into laughter when I can't prevent my own grin from slipping through.

"I love you," she says when her giggling subsides, although a thread of amusement is still lingering in her words. "And your friends are great. Those children are beautiful and so adorable."

"As are you." Pressing a gentle kiss to her lips, I whisper against them. "I love you too, Angel. And the image of you holding Poppy in your arms with that loving expression on your face...I'll never fucking forget it."

"Me neither," she replies on a soft breath, then smiles gently. "It's been ages since I held a baby. I avoided them for a long time—"

The kiss from me that interrupts what she's saying is tender and affectionate, and I only pull away when I know I can say what I need to say without making her feel bad about anything. "All I thought when I saw you holding Poppy was how natural you looked, and for just a second, how sad I was that you and I never got the chance to experience that together. And I swear if we ever get that chance, I'll cherish every single moment of it."

"What if…" She bites her lip, looking nervous and a little fearful, making me give her a comforting kiss until she sighs and continues. "If I can't…would you…want to adopt?"

If I weren't already absolutely fucking crazy about this woman, I would have fallen in love with her in this moment. "Sweetheart, we can adopt either way. We can have as many kids as you want and the same goes for adoption. We can fill this house up with children to drive us both happily insane. All right?"

"Yes," she whispers with watery eyes, followed up by a beautiful smile as she pulls my mouth close to hers to say, "We'll need lots of practice for having another of our own down the road. Let's start now."

"I like the way you think."

After that, there's no more talking for the rest of the evening.

*A*lthough I had joked with Ryker all those weeks ago about what Ness and I would talk about at her bachelorette party, Ness and I are sitting in a bar discussing everything except the topics of marriage and babies.

Her two friends, Greta and Macy, are her other bridesmaids, and they're only able to come in for the wedding day. Both of them are married, have kids, and were unable to get any days off from work, but as Ness said, the only thing that matters is that they are there for her wedding.

So, that leaves me and her celebrating her upcoming nuptials, which is damn fine with both of us.

Never one to drink much if at all, she laughs over her one and only drink as I slowly work my way to tipsy and then drunk, promising me she'll keep a close eye on me so I don't do anything I shouldn't.

I haven't drank since the same night I ended up at

Ryker's house the first time, which also means the alcohol hits me harder and faster, but it feels nice to just sit here with my worries pushed to the side and have fun while bullshitting with my best friend.

It's three days until she gets married. She's been planning to have the wedding at a church near her apartment where I used to live with her, and tonight, we're at the bar we used to hang out at together years ago. It's a good twenty-five minute drive back to the hotel where Ryker, Sterling, and I are staying — I'm here to help her prepare and set up everything for the wedding — since her place isn't big enough for all of us, and thirty minutes to her place.

"I think I wanna go back to the hotel now," I tell her, my words slurring as I sit there with my head down on the counter. "I miss Ryker."

"You sure you don't wanna stay another half hour?" She laughs when I glare at her. Well, I think I glare at her; I can't be sure and don't want to move too much at this point. "Watching you like this is the highlight of my evening. You used to be able to drink anyone under the table girl!"

She's right, damn her, and I admit it. "Uh huh. Guess I've changed. You can thank Ryker for that."

"Yes, you have, and I do thank him. I thank him for a lot. And one of those is now because I doubt you'll touch another drink ever again after the hangover you're gonna have in the morning."

"Screw you, Ness." I stick my tongue out at her playfully. "Take me home, bitch."

Even as she busts out laughing, she helps me up from the bar after paying our tab, and we head out to the car. She helps me into the passenger seat, buckles my belt, and shuts the door before going over to her side. Sliding in, she starts up the car, puts on her own belt, locks the door, and turns on the radio with the volume low before driving out of the parking lot.

On the way, I mostly try to focus on not getting sick, and Ness seems lost in her own thoughts. I let my eyes drift shut, only to snap them open when the "Escape" song comes on the radio, and I smack Ness on the arm to get her attention as she slows down to a stop at a red light.

Turning to look at me with a laugh, we both burst out into song, singing at the top of our lungs about Pina Colada's and getting caught in the rain. We laugh even harder as the light turns green, we drive through it, and it starts pouring down rain all around us as if us singing the song called it forth.

It's silly, but it's the thought that sticks in my brain as we drive through another green light, and the thought becomes a moment I'll never forget at the loud blare of a horn paired with a bright set of lights appearing to my left.

I scream. I'm not sure if it's Ness' name or what, but it's too late. She never even saw the truck coming right at us, at her door, and the airbags deploy as her screams join mine for only an instant before she goes silent while the truck pushes us across the intersection even as the faint squeal I hear means the driver is slamming on his brakes.

When the car finally stops, I reach my hand across the center, unable to see much of anything because of the bright lights from the truck glaring in my face, and find Ness' hand. Clasping it in mine, I hear her moan, and a sob escapes from my throat as I struggle to hold back my tears. Sirens blare in my peripheral, and I wish I could move but I know better. I'm not in pain, but it doesn't mean I'm not hurt somewhere, so I stay where I'm at hoping for the best even though I want nothing more than to escape.

"I'm here Ness," I tell her as my own brain fogs, everything getting blurry around me. "Hang on. I hear the sirens. They're on their way. I love you, girl. I'm sorry, we should've stayed. I'm so sorry—"

I feel her hand move as she moans again, until I'm sure I hear my name. "Dani…"

I swear I also hear her say she loves me too, but I can't be sure because the sirens get closer and closer. And suddenly, there are people surrounding the car, and I black out while still tightly holding her hand in mine.

WHEN I WAKE UP IN THE HOSPITAL BED WITH RYKER clutching my hand with both of his, his eyes red and swollen as my gaze meets his, I know today — the bright sunshine telling me it's the next day following the accident, at least — is the worst day of my life instantly.

He doesn't even smile at me, misery clear in every inch of his face, and tears begin streaming down my cheeks as I ask the question every fiber of me knows the answer to already yet willfully refuse to acknowledge.

"Ness…?"

"I'm sorry, Angel," Ryker chokes out, lifting my hand to his mouth and kissing it as my chest squeezes so tight I feel as if I can't breathe. "She didn't make it."

His words break my heart, crushing what little hope I clung to in the car and now as I awakened, sobs wracking my body as I break down. I feel Ryker move, sitting on the edge of the bed before pulling me up and into his arms, which makes it worse because I know if he can move me like that I'm likely not hurt much at all.

I cry harder with my arms wrapped around his neck, at some points gasping for breath because of how much it hurts, and Ryker's hold isn't enough to ease the pain this time. He doesn't let go though. He sits there, clutching me close, and stroking my hair while his face is buried in my neck, no doubt crying once more himself.

When the torrent of tears slows enough, although the vise doesn't let go of its grip on my heart, I manage to croak out, "What…happened?"

Ryker's voice is hoarse and broken up as he lifts his mouth to my ear, speaking softly. "Guy said it started raining so hard he couldn't see, which is why he honked his horn, but he was drunk. He ran the red light doing sixty, and…and…she never had a chance, sweetheart. She died on impact."

"No." I shake my head, trying to pull away from him, which is impossible because his hold is strong. "She didn't. I heard her say my name. I told her I loved her and she told me she loved me. She…she was alive—"

He shivers as if what I've said haunts him. "Angel—"

I interrupt what I know he's going to say, unwilling and maybe even unable to handle it, and lift my arms to pound on his back as I start screaming while sobbing even harder.

The words I shout at him, they don't matter, not as he puts me down on the bed at the same time nurses rush into the room. He holds me down while they give me a shot of something, the look on his face one of pure torture as he stares down at me with tear filled eyes.

Lots of thoughts flicker through my mind as numbness slowly fills my veins and I start to fall asleep.

This can't be happening.

This isn't reality.

Why her and not me?

Why do I get to cheat death once again? What did I do to deserve to live and she to die?

And how will I live without my best friend?

Questions I'll never get the answer to as the drugs take over and I drift off once more, holding the hand of the man who refuses to let go, even when I feel like I deserve nothing more than that.

*G*od, I can't handle seeing Angel like this. She's crying on and off, and has been for weeks now, and I get it. She's in a lot of fucking pain since the accident and Vanessa's funeral, but all I want to do is fix it. And I can't because Vanessa is gone. She's not coming back, and I can't comfort Angel like she needs. It's fucking killing me that I can't do anything; there's nothing more I hate than feeling helpless when it comes to her.

"Why her? She's...she was my best friend. I need her." Her teary gaze meets mine as she says the one thing I don't want her to ever think. "It should've been me, not her."

"Oh, Angel, don't—"

"No." It's a scream, a cry, as she points an angry finger at me. "It should've been me. I've been dying on and off for years. Years! Why her? She's a good person, always has been. She took care of herself, she took care of *me*!" I take a step toward her in desperation and she retreats, making me halt in my approach while tears stream down her face, her voice dropping to a whisper I can barely hear. "And for what? So in a few more years, it can come back and try to kill me again?"

"Please don't think like that," I plead with her, feeling more helpless than I ever have since the moment Angel came back into my life, and told me she had cancer and was dying. "She wouldn't want this. You didn't do anything wrong; the drunk driver did when he chose to get behind the wheel. You were with her every moment, you held her hand until help came. You did everything you could, sweetheart."

"It's my fault. She wanted to stay a little longer. We left because of me. If we hadn't—"

"Angel," I say forcefully, raising my voice to a level that startles her, and has her wide eyes on me just as I want it. "You have to stop this. Right now. You're only torturing yourself over something you had nothing to fucking do with."

"But—"

Stalking toward her, I grab her before she can evade me again, and use one hand to hold her chin so she can't not look at me while keeping the other around her waist. I speak softer but just as firmly. "All the fucking what-if's in the world won't do you any good now. You can't change what happened. You can't what-if Vanessa back to life, sweetheart. Blaming yourself is useless. You're alive, you survived, and dammit, she wouldn't fucking want you to condemn yourself and the choices she made *with* you like this. Accepting reality is what you need to do."

When she simply stares at me, looking lost in thought, I figure what I've said is sinking in. But it's not long before she shatters that notion, the fighting light going out in her eyes as she whispers, "Let me go and leave me alone, please."

Her quiet defeat fucking murders me because I know when she gives up fighting, she's depressed to the point she needs more help than I can give her. And it's clear therapy isn't helping her either.

"Please," she says again, closing her eyes as another tear escapes and rolls down her cheek. "Leave. I'm...I'm just going to sleep."

"All right." I press a kiss to her forehead before releasing it as I say, "Get some rest. Love you."

It hurts when she simply turns around and goes to the bed without another word; without telling me she loves me like she usually does.

And when her continued silence as she climbs in and buries herself beneath the comforter is something I feel with everything in me, I turn and leave the room before I break down myself.

In my desperate attempt to keep from giving into the uncontrollable fear that Angel is going to give up, something I can't let happen after everything we've been through, I walk toward Sterling's room to check up on him, and hope he's got an idea for what we could do to help his mother.

After all, I didn't fight for her survival all these months only for her to give up — on life, on me, on our son — because she feels guilty about her best friend's death.

I want to punch something, and part of me wants to take a stick to a tree as I did once before, but I can't. I have to fucking hold it together, because I'm the only person right now who isn't breaking down, although it might not take much to get me to that point at this rate.

Which is exactly what I tell Sterling who, after giving me a comforting hug as he responds with, "Let me talk to her," exits his room with quiet determination, leaving me standing in the middle of it with nothing but my own grief and fears for company.

Today is my fifteenth birthday, but there are no presents and no cake.

As I stand just inside the closed door of my mother's bedroom, I admit I'm okay with nobody thinking about what today is, because my mother is my concern at this point.

She's laying on the bed in the almost completely dark room, buried beneath the covers with only her head visible, and facing away from the door. There's no crying anymore; simply silence while she hides from the world. She's been like this since the day Vanessa died, and nobody's known how to help her before now, not even me.

I've sat in here with her a few times since then, mostly telling her about school since it started back up a couple weeks ago, and even though she listened, I know she did it only because she loves me.

I heard her tell dad how she doesn't understand why

she's still living when her best friend is now dead, and it makes me sad, because all I want to do is scream at her that she isn't allowed to die. Because I need her and she needs to be here for me, especially now that she's in my life every day just like I wanted her to be when I was a little kid. I know her thoughts aren't rational; she loved Vanessa and I loved her too, because she took care of my mom when nobody else would.

"Mom?"

Her reply is soft, instant, and full of concern for me, which is unsurprising. She's always been concerned about me, even though I've never been the one who's needed it the most. "Honey? What's wrong?"

"Nothing." I walk across the room, rounding the bed before pulling up a chair, sitting down and facing her. "Came up to see if you wanted some dinner."

She moves her arm, offering me her hand palm up, and only responds after she's clasping my hand with hers. "No. I'm okay."

"You have to eat."

"You sound like your father," she says in what's practically a whisper. "He was just up here ten minutes ago saying the same thing."

I can barely see her in the dark, but the scratchiness of her voice gives away the fact she's been crying. I know because I've heard her before, not to mention Renee sounds the same after she's been crying too. Must be a girl thing.

Knowing it won't do any good to 'nag her,' as Dad says,

I decide to remind her of how important she is to me, how she always has been and always will be.

"Actually, I sound like you." Squeezing her hand, a sound between a chuckle and a rough cough escapes my throat, while memories make their way out. "Like the time when I was eight, terribly sick, and I refused to eat anything. You came over after getting a call about me and my stubbornness, brought soup in that little stupid bowl that kept it hot for hours, and sat by my bed singing all those stupid songs until I ate just so you would stop."

"You've always hated my singing."

Her amusement is barely there, but enough I hear the smile in her voice, and this time the sound I respond with is pure laughter. "It's not the singing, it's your song choices. You're the only person I know who can turn the 'three little pigs' chorus into a song to torture me with."

She doesn't say anything, so I keep talking, hoping something — anything — will get her out of bed and back into life.

"You remember when you came to visit when I was eleven, after I got into my first fight?"

I swear she sniffles at the same time she sighs. "Of course I remember. Your first, and last, black eye."

"Yeah. Do you remember what you said to me too?"

"I don't." She pauses, clutching my hand a bit tighter with hers, and lets out a longer sigh. "I said a lot of things to you. I always have. You're my son and I have to make sure you don't do stupid things."

"Ha." After pausing for a second, I continue with,

"Anyway, you told me that even though people were mean to me, I shouldn't be mean to them. I could be mad, but I couldn't do to them what they did to me, because that wouldn't solve my problem. You told me their aggression and need to bully others probably came from how powerless they feel in their life; that there was even a chance some of them were abused at home and didn't know what they were doing was wrong."

"And I was right, wasn't I?"

"Yep, but it was what you said after that." Releasing her hand, I stand up and walk over to the window, opening the curtains even as she makes a sound of protest while sunlight brightens up the room. "I said I was hurt and angry, and asked what I was supposed to do if I couldn't be just as mean to them as they were to me. And you told me I had to find a way to let the hurt out without hurting anyone else."

"Sterling—"

"No, Mom." As I turn back toward the bed, she rolls over onto her back, turning her head until she locates me with a frown at the aggravation in my tone. "I heard you tell dad, you know. Vanessa's dead, you're alive, and you don't know why. But it doesn't matter. You have to get up, find a way to let the hurt out, and get back to living."

I watch as her eyes water and her lower lip wobbles, almost feeling sorry for what I've said until she softly utters, "When did you get so grown up?"

"I always have been." Walking over to the empty side of the bed, I sit down beside her and smile as I admit, "I've always worked hard to make sure you could be proud of me. You did everything you could to make sure I had a stable life, I didn't want your sacrifice to be for nothing."

A tear slips down her cheek as she reaches over and covers my hand with hers. "Oh, sweetie. I am proud of you, and I always will be no matter what."

"I know, but I still worked hard anyway. You never cried in front of me, but I knew you did every time you left me because I watched you get into your car and lower your head to the steering wheel while you gripped it, your shoulders shaking the whole time."

The tears come harder as her eyes flutter shut, her hand clutching mine so tight it starts to go numb, her strength surprising me. "I hated leaving you."

"I hated you leaving me, but I always loved you. I always understood, even though I was afraid every time you walked out the door, you would get sick again and die, and I'd never see you again."

I'm not sure how it happens, but one-second she's lying down, and the next she's sat up and thrown her arms around my neck. Shocked as I am for a brief moment, she starts crying harder the instant I return her embrace, and my chest tightens with all of my own withheld emotions.

"I'm sorry," she says, crying into my shoulder. "I feared that too, and it shouldn't have been your worry, you were just a kid."

"I'm your kid, Mom. Whether you like it or not, your worries are my worries, and when you're hurt, I'm hurt too."

With a deep, shuddering breath, she whispers in my ear, "I miss her so much."

"Me too, but she wouldn't want you to be sad like this, and you know it. She'd be mad at you for saying the stuff you've been saying because it was an accident. She didn't deserve to die, but you don't either just because you're sick."

"You're right." Her confession is hoarse, and when she pulls back, she places her hands on my shoulders while looking me square in the eyes. "And rationally, I've known that. Just like I knew every time I left you that I was doing what I thought best, yet my heart didn't care. It still hurt all the same."

"Well, you have to stop. I'm here and you're here and we've got dad. She wanted you to live and be happy; you have to do that for her, for yourself, for dad." I swallow hard, blinking rapidly to keep my own tears inside until I'm alone, needing to be strong for her right now. "And for me because I need you."

"I know." She clears her throat, taking another deep breath as she closes her eyes, silence falling between us for a little bit, until she opens them again and nods at me. "I'm here and I'm not going anywhere. I promise."

"Good." Leaning in to peck her on the cheek, I back off the bed and stand, sliding my hands into my pockets while staring down at her, and speak with the intent to lighten the mood. "By the way, you stink, Mom."

Even though her first reaction is to glare at me, I'm happy to see the corners of her mouth curve up as she rolls her eyes at me, and waves her hand in the air dismissively. "Go eat your dinner and tell your father I'll be down in a few, okay?"

"Sure."

Knowing dad will be ecstatic to know Mom will be coming downstairs, I whirl around and walk to the door, only for my mother's voice to stop me.

"Sterling?"

With my hand on the knob, I look over my shoulder with a genuine smile on my face. "Yeah?"

"Happy Birthday, sweetheart." My surprise must be obvious because she laughs softly and says, "I'd never forget your birthday Sterling. It was, and remains, the most important day of my life."

There's so much I can say to that, yet it's so good to hear her laugh I don't say anything other than, "Thanks Mom," while walking out, gently shutting the door behind me before heading downstairs to tell my dad everything's okay.

All the while hoping it stays that way from now on because if anyone deserves long-term happiness in their lives, it's my parents.

And even though I know I'm young, I know one thing for sure — I want a relationship like theirs one day.

51 - RYKER

J'm sitting in the chair taking off my shoes when Angel steps into the doorway of the master bath, her arms hanging down at her sides, and just as I'm about to say something, she slowly lowers herself onto her knees.

With legs bare since her dark purple nightie only goes to mid-thigh, she leans forward to place her palms flat on the carpet, her negligee unbelted and covering her feet. As she crawls toward me, her approach on all fours is reminiscent of the day she informed me of our son's existence, and her gaze locks on mine the whole time.

Setting my shoes to the side, she halts in front of my feet not even two-seconds later, lifting her hands and placing them on my knees. Nothing is spoken between us as I stare down at her, my hands coming to cover hers, drinking every inch of her in while I have the chance.

Two days ago she walked downstairs after Sterling

spoke with her, had dinner with us, as well as cake for Sterling's birthday. He thought we'd all forgotten, but I hadn't, and I'd loved his genuine happiness at the sight of the cake with the fifteen candles arriving at the table in Meg's hands.

Both he and his mother have the same smile, and right now, a genuine smile from her is all I can possibly hope for.

With that in mind, I lift a brow while questioning her current position. "Angel?"

"The first time I did this," she starts off softly, her eyes warming a little even though the pain she's in is clear in their depths, "I had made peace with where I thought my life was going, but I was still so broken on the inside. You ended up giving me what I needed, even though I had no idea I needed it, and I certainly didn't desire for you to swoop in the way you did to take care of me. It was clear, though. The moment you saw me again, I was a goner, and I didn't even know it. Our lives were giving us a second chance and it wasn't going to let anything stop us from being happy."

As her eyes begin to water, I want nothing more than to pull her into my arms and hold her so fucking tight, but I don't because I know she has a lot more to get out of her system, and I need to let her say it.

"I let you save me, but I didn't want to. I never wanted to let anyone do that, because I wanted to rescue myself. I wanted to be my own hero, but life doesn't care what we want sometimes. Well, maybe ever." Her words are rueful, filled with enough subtle irritation that I give her hands beneath mine a bit of a squeeze, because I want her to know I care — a fact she acknowledges with the love now shining in her eyes as she regards me, continuing where she left off. "I tried when I was younger, and when I failed, I didn't know what to do. I hurt so fucking badly, the pain inside me from everything that happened had nowhere to go, so I did everything I could to let it out. You've seen the scars from the attempts I made to do that."

It's a statement, not a question. With a hard swallow, I nod and admit, "I have."

"I hurt like that now." Tears trickle down her cheeks faster, but when I lean forward and try to gather her in my arms, she shakes her head and grips my legs harder. "I sat in the bathroom just now for ten minutes with a blade to my skin, wanting so badly to do that again, even though I knew it wouldn't do any good."

Her admission makes me sad and angry all at the same time. "Angel—"

"I didn't." She cuts in to reassure me, with a lift of her chin and a straightening of her shoulders, and her eyes growing firm with a resolve I haven't seen her exhibit in a while now. "I stopped myself because it…my sadness and guilt, they're my fault. It was stupid, to think when everything started going well that it would keep going that way. Even in my darkest moments before she died, all I thought about was how everything seemed so perfect and wonderful; I told myself it was our time now. We've suffered enough, surely it wouldn't go on forever. And I was wrong."

"You were hoping for nothing but the best, Angel. Nothing wrong with that."

Her reply is pure desperation as her shoulders shake, a hard sob escaping while the trickle of tears turns into a steady stream, the words pouring from her mouth. "I need you to help me, Ry. I don't want it to be this way, but...right now, I need you to help me save myself because I'm not sure I can fix how broken I feel all over again."

Not giving her any more of a choice in the matter, I scoop her up off the ground and into my arms, walking her over to the bed after she's wrapped her arms and legs around my body while letting the sobs speak for her instead.

And when we're lying in the center of the bed, with her cradled in my arms, I make sure she knows I'm always there for her — whatever she wants and needs, she can count on me.

"I'll help you however I can, sweetheart, and you know it. Just tell me what you need me to do."

In the silence that falls between us, her slow and steady breaths almost convince me she's fallen asleep, if it weren't for her left hand resting near my left shoulder, her thumb in the dip where my neck meets my chest, caressing back and forth with the pad of it while the rest of her fingers cover my collarbone. The sweet yet sensual stroke of her fingers mixed with her scantily clad body, which is rubbing against mine all over, has me wishing for her to get in a different frame of mind.

It's been too long since we've had sex, for one, and

almost as lengthy since she's let me get this close to her, so for her to even be lying here with me is an improvement.

Her caress ends as she sits up and moves away a little, crossing her legs at the same time as she mirrors the action with her arms over her chest, and says, "I...need you to give me what I've always needed."

Since the moment she returned to my life, I've never doubted Angel until this instant. Her pain's so potent it practically rolls off her in waves, making me unsure if I can keep my promise of helping her however I'm able to, which doesn't make me happy either because I know exactly what she's saying she needs.

"You're not in a good place, Angel. The last thing you need is more pain."

In a flash of movement, she's on my lap and straddling my hips, glaring down at me with watery, determined eyes. "Please do this to get *rid* of the fucking pain, Ry. I know it will rise to the surface; I've done it before when I hurt so badly I couldn't breathe. I need you to do this for me. I need you to trust me."

Her plea is so sweet coupled with the tear slowly descending down her cheek that I groan. "Sweetheart..."

"I came to you," she whispers, placing her palms flat on my chest as she leans in until her mouth is hovering over mine. "Again. A second time...on my hands and knees. Please."

Lifting my hands, I use one to grip her hip, and cup the nape of her neck with the other so she can't escape while getting what I need from her before I give into the sweet temptation of her mouth. "Promise me — no matter how dark it gets, how deep the pain goes — promise me you'll always come to me, and give me the chance to be the one to save you. Swear you'll let me be the one to try and lessen, if not rid you, of your pain."

Her lips tremble even as she seals her vow with a nod, leaving me with only one thing to do, something we both need more than either of us will admit in the wake of everything that's happened.

"Love you," I tell her, needing her to hear it as much as she needs to feel it.

Then, not waiting for a reply, I capture her mouth with mine in a rough and lustful kiss, giving my wife everything she needs and desires while easing her pain as much as I can, knowing that as long as we have each other, nothing will ever be as fucking bad as it could be.

Because she's mine, and loving her will always be more than enough for me as long as I've got breath in my body to love her with.

52 - DANITA

APPROXIMATELY FOUR YEARS LATER

*N*ineteen years since I've given birth and it's nothing like I remember.

Or perhaps it's been so long I just don't recall the specifics.

Like feeling as if my insides are being stabbed to death. I'm gonna guess that's normal though, because I'm sure if I remembered this, I might not have agreed to having one more kid once we were told it was safe to do so.

Yeah, I'm gonna go with that.

After all, I'm starting all over with a newborn when one kid is grown.

But god, with Ryker by my side, I know it'll be worth it.

I try to remember that as another contraction has me trying not to scream. Why didn't I take the fucking epidural again? Oh right, I decided all natural was what I wanted to do.

Won't make that mistake ever again.

A few ice chips meets my lips as the contraction ends, and I let Ryker put them in my mouth as our eyes meet.

"Almost time," he says with a huge smile, lifting my hand he holds in his own and kissing the back of it. "Are you ready?"

Chewing obnoxiously on the ice before swallowing it once melted, I glare at him even though we both know I'm truly happy about this. "No. Wanna switch me places and prepare to push something out of your penis while my only job is to feed you ice chips?"

"Thanks, but I'll pass. Besides, you look gorgeous Angel, as you always do."

"Don't lie to me, fucker."

He cracks up laughing, and I'm pretty sure I hear a few of the nurses and the doctor snickering as they set up to deliver the baby, but I don't bother to look.

"Not lying." Leaning down he pecks me on the mouth, trailing his lips down my jaw, and stops with a final kiss right beneath the lobe of my ear as he speaks, his husky words clearly audible to our audience. "Love you from the inside out, sweetheart. If you were ugly on the inside, not even this pretty little gift wrapping on the outside would make me stick my dick in you."

Oh yea, they are all definitely trying not to laugh full out, and Ryker winks at me.

Another contraction hits before I can respond, whatever I'm going to say the farthest thing from my mind as I crush his hand with mine in an attempt to not scream.

A little bit later, the doctor checks me, announcing we'll

start pushing in a few minutes, and turning away to talk to the nurses.

Ryker grips my hand, pressing another kiss to my lip as he whispers, "I can't wait to meet our daughter. She'll be every inch as beautiful as you are."

"I still say it's a boy."

He shakes his head while drawing his head back until he's standing straight again. "I can't believe I let you talk me into waiting to find out, but I know I'm right. You'll see."

"Whatever." I hide my smile, but we both know I'll be happy either way as long as the baby is healthy. I just like fucking with him. "You're not."

The doctor doesn't give him a chance to argue with me as he announces it's time to bring the little bundle of joy into the world.

Let's just say, I scream and cuss Ryker out.

A lot.

He smiles the whole damn way through it like the lovesick amazing husband and father he is.

And for me, as always, he's worth every moment of the pain.

WAKING TO THE SIGHT OF RYKER CRADLING OUR TINY daughter in his hands is one of the most beautiful things I've ever seen.

Seeing our son standing behind his father and staring down at his sister with a big grin of his own is another.

They aren't paying attention to me at all, and who can blame them? It's clear she already has them wrapped around her little fingers.

"She looks just like mom," Sterling says in a hushed voice. "When will I get to hold her?"

"In a few years." Ryker's joking reply is followed up by a chuckle. "Back off, buddy."

"What? That's not fair. I'm gonna tell mom."

"I saw her first. Look, she likes me best already."

"She's sleeping. She wouldn't know if a monkey was holding her at this point. Although if she opens her eyes, she'll know for sure."

If I weren't pretending to still be asleep, I would bust out laughing at their quick-witted exchange. Like father, like son indeed.

"Quit talking. You're gonna wake your mother."

"I'll tell her it's your fault 'cuz you're greedy."

"Are you jealous? You're a little big to sit on my lap but I'm sure I can make room for you."

Taking the opportunity to speak, my words are soft and filled with amusement as I interject myself into their mock squabbling. "Looks like I've been replaced. You two never fought over me like this."

"Never." Ryker's gaze finds mine in an instant, rising while making sure not to jostle the baby, and walks over to stand next to the bed. "Nothing could ever replace you, Angel. You know you're all my number ones."

"Psh. You're a suck up, and she's gonna figure out you're a softie in no time."

"She already knows," he teases, leaning over to kiss my forehead with a chuckle. "I told her just so I could be the first, before anyone else tattled on me."

"Smart. Now give her to me."

"Hey!" Sterling scowls at both of us, crossing his arms over his chest, his lips going into an overdramatic pout like a petulant child. "It's my turn."

I manage an admonishing look even as I hold back tears at his obvious affection for his new sister. "Sweetie, go get me a chocolate bar from the vending machine. By the time you return, you can hold her all you like."

"Yes!" Sterling pumps his fist in the air before winking at me. "You'll have to pry her from my arms you know. Just saying. Be right back."

The moment he exits the room, I return my laughing gaze to Ryker's face, only to find him smiling softly at me, his eyes shining. "What're you smiling at? The fact I got him to leave the room so easily?"

"No. Just you, specifically." He snatches up my free hand as he stares into my eyes, his face lighting up with a full-on grin. "The look on your face when all your focus is on her. It's something I had always hoped to see, and everything I imagined it would be. And more."

"Well, look at her." We both switch our focus to where she lies in my arms sound asleep. "She's the perfect little mix of both of us."

"Just like Sterling."

"Ha. He's definitely more like you than like me now."

Veronica's voice, sounding as if she's about to bust out laughing at any moment, rings out from the doorway. "Ugh. You two are just as nausea inducing as always."

"Hello to you too," I say, both Ryker and I looking at her at the same time, our joyful smiles nearly identical. "Are you on your own or did you bring company?"

A flush makes it way across her face as she steps inside, Freddy walking in behind her, before wrapping his arm around her waist and grinning at us as he says, "Congratulations from both of us."

It's funny to me that Veronica still flushes when she's with him around me. Although they first met at Vanessa's wake, they'd both been single until a year ago.

She's spent the time focusing on building her independence along with her career so she would never have to rely on anyone ever again, while Freddy took a year off work to grieve and heal before returning to his job, although he hadn't started dating again until just over a year ago.

That's when they'd found each other on a dating site, leaving me to feel nothing but amusement and happiness for them when they'd come to the house together asking if them pursuing a relationship with each other was okay with me. I'd told them while I appreciated the gesture, it was unnecessary. Mainly because I wanted nothing more than for them both to be with someone who makes them happy, although I'd jokingly told Veronica if she hurt Freddy, I'd kick her ass.

We'd all had a good laugh over that, Ryker especially as he knew I was being completely serious.

Since then, as a group, we've become good friends, and I've been waiting for them to announce their engagement because I know it's coming soon. Freddy told me so, in confidence of course, when he said he wouldn't make the same mistake he had with Vanessa by waiting to start their lives together; her death had taught him how precious things were and he would never forget it.

"Thank you," I finally reply after realizing I'd become lost in thought and hadn't said anything. "It's good to see you two; you're so busy lately!"

Freddy's grin grows even wider if that's possible, moving his focus from Ryker and me to Veronica as he says, "Not to steal your thunder, Dani, but that's because we've been planning our wedding. Isn't that right, honey?"

"Yes," she says with a grin of her own, at the same time I crow, "I knew it!"

Unfortunately, that also startles the baby, who jumps from where I'm cradling her in my arms and starts wailing. Everyone laughs as my own blush of embarrassment heats my cheeks, and I lift the baby to my shoulder, patting her back while shushing her. Ryker takes over the conversation then, walking around the bed toward them, giving Freddy a slap on the back before pulling Veronica into a hug as well.

My daughter — god, I'm sure I'm gonna love saying that forever — quiets down but is still fussing a little, so I move her to my chest and once she's happily eating, calling out softly, "Hey, Freddy?"

Knowing what's coming, Ryker returns to my side, Veronica and Freddy walking to stand by the bed as he says, "Yeah?"

I watch his face closely as I say our daughter's name out loud for the first time. "I'd like you to meet our daughter, and your goddaughter, Gwendolyn Vanessa Redding."

He puts his arm around Veronica as she leans into him, and looks down at me with tear-filled eyes as he croaks out a simple, "She's adorable. Vanessa would've loved her."

"I know."

Sterling returns to the room before I can say anything else, looking quite disappointed when he catches sight of Freddy and Veronica, along with realizing the baby is in the middle of eating.

"I guess I should just come back later since holding my sister isn't going to happen any time this decade," he jokes, handing his father the chocolate bar before plopping down in the nearby chair with an exaggerated sigh that doesn't match up with the smile on his face. "Don't worry about me, I've got all day."

From there they all start chatting amongst themselves while I finish feeding Gwen, handing her over to Ryker so I can get up and go to the bathroom. When I finally walk back out, Freddy is holding Gwen, Veronica's chatting with Sterling about school, and Ryker's nowhere to be found.

Climbing back into bed, I ask Freddy, "Where'd he go?"

"Your sister called from her car, said she needed his assistance with something."

"Ah." The fact Felicia ended up being able to make it

today makes me happy; her and Chris ended up having a little girl, followed by twin boys two years later, and they've loved every second of it as have I. "That means Chris must've had to work today and couldn't come with her to help with the children."

He stands up at that, smiling as he places Gwen back in my arms, and states, "Then it's about to get crowded in here, but that's okay; we have to get going anyway. Have an appointment with the wedding coordinator in about an hour."

"Oh! Of course. Let's get together again soon, all right?"

"Absolutely."

Saying their goodbyes, they leave the room, and Sterling comes over to the bed beaming ear-to-ear while holding out his hands. "My turn?"

"You're like a little kid sometimes," I tell him with a snicker as I hand Gwen over to him, my eyes tearing up as he cradles her gently in his arms, and doesn't even bother responding as he stares down at her.

The way I feel watching my first child hold my second after everything we've been through with each other and with Ryker can only be described with one simple word...

Grateful.

As Ryker returns with Felicia and her children in tow, as we return home the next day from the hospital and begin our lives as a family of four, and when we adopt seven-year old twin boys two years after that to become a family of six, it's a feeling I hold onto with everything I have.

And it's that same feeling that makes sure I treasure every single moment I have with the love of my life, and our children, for the rest of my life.

THE END

Thanks for reading! I hope you enjoyed reading Angel & Ryker's love story as much as I enjoyed writing about them! If you have the time, please leave a rating and a review on the site you purchased this book from, as your feedback is appreciated!**

To My Readers

Does Love Conquer All?

This story ended differently than I started with.
You see, Danita wasn't supposed to live.
But that's the power of love.

Love can heal.
Save.
Transform.

It can ease our pain, make our troubles seem smaller, and sometimes, it can bring us up when we're on the floor wishing we would just die.

Ryker loved the girl, and he loved the woman, and even when his Angel wasn't likable to anyone else, even him — he loved her anyway.

Danita's childhood, young adulthood, and adult life were filled with things nobody should go through, yet it's what many people go through every day all over the world. What her family did was wrong, but in the end, we can't control what others do. We can only control ourselves and how we react to things.

Oftentimes we hear that we have to "leave the past behind" in order to move forward, but in truth, it is never that easy. Danita never got to confront her demons — she had to face them without resolution, without justice, and without recourse. As a minor she believed what she was told, and that carried into her adulthood because she had so little real guidance or people who truly cared about her well-being. Her life (and the lives of many others) is proof that a lot of the time, shitty things happen to good people (like Vanessa), while people who have done us wrong get a second chance to turn their lives around (such as both Veronica and Felicia), and others get what's coming to them — like Veronica's abusive husband.

As so many in the 'real world' experience every day, Danita only did what she thought was best, and Ryker, a man who truly understood her past and her intentions, couldn't be angry with her even though he had a child he knew nothing about. Ryker knew (and Angel learned) what everyone should — that beyond anger, fear, and even hatred, there is a need for compassion, forgiveness, and understanding for those less fortunate than others. For those whose lives never showed them the way.

They were both victims of the circumstances, and in the end, he got her and their child back.
If only everyone were so lucky, but that's why I listened to Ryker.
That's why his Angel lived.

Because they'd been through so much and deserved a happy ending.

Love doesn't necessarily conquer all…but in the end, Ryker's love and his determination to not let her give up saved his Angel's life.

So, even if your day, week, or month is dark, keep hope in your heart and in your thoughts. Because even if you think there's nothing to live for, the fact you're alive is no doubt the reason someone wakes up and smiles each day of their life. This is something I've struggled with myself, and I want you to know, you're not alone.

With love,
Violet

Visit my website (authorviolethaze.com)
or if you'd like, email me at violet@authorviolethaze.com.

I love receiving email and look forward to hearing from you no matter the reason!

ABOUT THE AUTHOR

Violet **Haze** is a big fan of romance — writing & reading. The autistic mother of one, she currently spends her days writing, reading, procrastinating, & listening to her son play video games she doesn't understand, at all.

For information on other books you can read, including links to **ALL** the vendors, visit her website: www. authorviolethaze.com!

Want to contact Violet?
Email her at: violet@authorviolethaze.com or locate her at one of the links listed below!